TARASOV SOLUTION

RICHARD TREVAE

The Tarasov Solution / Richard Trevae
First Edition Paperback
ISBN 978-0-9820946-6-2
Editor: Andrea Howe
Layout: Roger Hunt
Cover Design: Molly Courtright
Editor-in-Chief: Jonathan Womack

Printed in the United States of America

Other books by Richard Trevae:
The Fusion Breakthrough

Readers may contact the author at: www.richardtrevae.com

Published by Charles River Press, Inc.
541 Long Lane.
Casper, Wyoming 82609
www.charlesriverpress.com

10   9   8   7   6   5   4   3   2   1

AUTHOR NOTE

Creating fiction from reality is very cool. As an author one can be drawn to a piece of history but not be restrained by the *historical facts* when conceiving a plausible new story. To take a piece of history, preferably engaging history, and twist it into a credible take-off on reality is what many authors of suspense and thriller novels seek. That is why after several weeks of struggling to come up with an engaging plot for The TARASOV SOLUTION, I researched the Cuban missile crisis and asked...*What if history lied to us?*

That question led me into a concept, followed by a broad plot statement, story outline, event manifest, character creation, and story development. When one comes to embrace the plot line concept and the character personas, the dialogue and narratives come forth in gushes. The result is reality-inspired-fiction. I hope you enjoy the novel.

ACKNOWLEDGMENTS

To Jonathan Womack, whose writing advice, commitment to the story, patience and encouragement helped me get the novel to a better place for readers.

To Randy, Andrea, Roger and many others at Charles River Press who helped move the process along while educating me further on the nuances of the effort.

To Molly Courtright, for her excellent adaptation of my cryptic book cover samples.

To Gloria Jasperse, whose reviews of my earlier works were accurate, constructive, gentle, and supportive. She is a great sounding board.

To Barb Yates, whose review skills demonstrate why students love her college literature classes.

To Vicki, my wife, whose propensity to read is only out done by her support and encouragement for my writing. As my first reader, she tweaked content and style through gentle, supportive critiques.

To my extended family, friends, and business associates who have expressed their joy in my writing journey.

DEDICATION

To Megan, Tyler, and Jacque

PRELUDE

CAPTAIN Demkin poured another shot of vodka. He looked out from the bridge of his Soviet military transport vessel and wondered if he would be shot for disobeying an order from his commander, Admiral Sarkov. The ship was quiet now with only twenty-four of the 220 crew on duty. Alone on the bridge, Demkin recalled his illustrious thirty-year career in the Soviet Navy. Two years ago he received a major promotion to captain, with his own ship, and assumed the commander role for a fleet of military transport vessels. Though not as impressive as a battleship command, it was a serious accomplishment for any Soviet officer. It all seemed to be on the line now with the order from Admiral Sarkov.

If he proceeded as ordered and was discovered, the Americans might use the provocation as a prelude to nuclear war. The nearby Navy warplanes would destroy the assembled Soviet fleet near Cuba. If he ignored the order and attempted to defect, his family would be killed, and he would become a hunted man. The vodka bottle seemed his only solace.

The military transport hung heavy in the water and maneuvered like a snail even in the calm Caribbean waters. Its cargo, among standard construction equipment, contained nuclear-tipped intermediate-range ballistic missiles destined for two prepared sites: San Cristobel and Sagua la Grande in Cuba. The crew had grown anxious, waiting for orders days after the American Navy set up an embargo around the Cuban landing ports. There they were the American Navy ships, two miles away, intimidating and visible during the day. The tension was growing over the increasing likelihood that a nuclear war could ignite from the stalemate over the Cuban missile sites.

A polite throat clearing announced the first officer's arrival. "You called for me, sir?" inquired the young sailor.

"Yes, Sergey. Listen carefully to me now."

Sergey straightened and focused in on the next words from his captain.

"I want you to clear the mini sub launch chamber of all personnel except for you and the two or three men you need to load two missiles in cocoons onto the cargo platforms attached to the mini sub. Is that understood?"

"Yes, sir. I understand and I know the right men for the job." Sergey could smell the alcohol on the captain's breath and knew he had been drinking for some time.

Captain Demkin looked at Sergey and nodded as if in approval. Moments passed as the captain constructed his next command.

"At precisely 0430 I want you to deploy the mini sub

PRELUDE

with the two SS-5 IRBM, ten-kiloton warhead missiles from the subsurface hatch." Demkin looked for any hesitation from the young officer; none appeared. "You alone will navigate the mini sub from our current position to the reef wall nearer Cuba and drop the cocoons in sixty meters of water. Here are your coordinates for the drop."

The young officer looked with shock and confusion at the orders Demkin just announced.

"Then when you return, if asked, I want you to report to your crew that the missiles were offloaded to our destroyer fleet for security purposes." Drawing uncomfortably close to the first officer, Demkin said, "Is that clear?"

Without hesitation, the first officer saluted, snapped his heels together, straightened, and replied. "Clear, sir. Well, actually no, sir. Why are we unloading them before we make port?"

"Because we may never make port if the Americans discover we're carrying missiles. It's for our own protection, and the order comes directly from Admiral Sarkov." The captain was angry over the orders he had to carry out. "Now do you understand?" growled the captain, his frustration growing.

"Yes, sir, I understand."

"Dismissed," barked the captain.

RICHARD TREVAE

Sergey whirled and left the bridge.

The captain reached again for the near-empty vodka bottle and slung it to his mouth, depleting the contents before wiping his lips and forehead with a towel. Alone once more on the bridge, the distant lights of the Soviet and American ships were clear and caused Demkin to say to himself, "One way or another, I will never survive this decision."

ONE

THE panel resembled a collection of old librarians: two women and four men, all in their seventies. The men were dressed in formal, ill-fitting, three-piece suits, and long business skirts and jackets adorned the women. The room was solemn and dark except for the well-lit podium where the examiners sat and an old, oak desk with a reading lamp positioned in the far right corner. That's where Dalton waited.

Jameson Dalton Crusoe had worked hard on getting this behind him, a promise made to his mother. He had managed to cram two years of intense study and work assignments into twenty months. Driven by a mother who never let Dalton slack off on any assignment and a father whose business acumen and integrity were evident to young JD at an early age, the die was cast. He graduated from the Annapolis Naval Academy two years earlier at the top of his class. His well-connected mentor, with the Navy Secretary approval, offered him a chance to forgo active military service for five years if he agreed to participate in a new curriculum for exceptional individuals in an accelerated training program in the government arena. Dalton agreed as long as he could pursue his MBA concurrently.

When his father died suddenly during Dalton's first year at Annapolis, it hit JD hard. His sorrow turned to anger then mellowed to determination to be the best at all things he pursued. He committed himself to making his parents proud by exceeding their expectations. If his thesis work was accepted, he was done and ready to move into the quasi-private sector as a consultant to his friend and professional mentor. In reality Dalton made the first steps toward a consultant role a year ago when he investigated a senator accused of corruption charges involving a complex financial influence scheme operating out of the Cayman Islands. The senator had diverted some $7 million in illegal campaign funds to offshore accounts then provided favorable votes on military contracts to the donors. The dossier on the senator was so complete, he plea-bargained himself minimal jail time for an immediate resignation and formal expulsion from the Senate. Friends advised Dalton to next pursue a law degree, yet he felt compelled to get on with his career. If he needed legal expertise, he'd hire it. That assignment, under the oversight of Ed Kosko, matured Dalton and tempered his sometimes compulsive need to be the best toward a reasoned, thoughtful approach supported by his high intellect and cool-headed decision making. The well-documented success of his first serious assignment helped him overcome the loss of his father. Dalton had proven to himself he had not failed his father's expectations.

The review had been an exhausting five-hour question-and-answer period to accept or reject his master's essay or, more accurately, an abbreviated thesis paper. He felt his analysis and conclusions were sound and he had answered all their questions directly and completely without receiving anything more than professional critiquing. He hoped they were able to follow his analysis of how international financial policy and fiscal management could be effectively used to influence trade, economic growth, and internal stability for emerging democratic economies in the Middle East and eastern Europe.

Finally, after several minutes of whispering and sharing of notes, the department head, Dr. Robbins, announced, "Congratulations, Mr. Crusoe. Your work towards an MBA in International Finance is exemplary."

With synchronous motion, Dr. Robbins and all the panel members rose in applause and spewed chatty words of enthusiasm and congratulations. Jameson Dalton Crusoe had completed his MBA at Wharton in a record twenty months, while being kept busy by his mentor, Ed Kosko. Dalton was the entire faculty's favorite and, at twenty-five years of age, looked and acted the part of an accomplished businessman and statesman.

Dalton greeted panel members warmly and thanked them for their support. Dr. Robbins approached Dalton, pulling him by the arm away from the still-chatty group, and asked, "Has Ed made you an offer yet to join his staff full time?"

"Well, I believe that's the general expectation as of yesterday morning when he called me with a new assignment." Dalton's face shone with a broad smile.

"Where do you go this time, my young friend?" inquired Robbins.

"It begins in the Caribbean and then settles into boring research and investigations, I'm afraid," offered Dalton.

"I assume that attractive lady friend of yours may accompany you on this dreadful mission," teased Robbins as he smiled and shook Dalton's hand before walking away.

Dalton gestured with a smile and a nod, careful to not reveal anything of the high-level assignment. His bags were nearly packed, and he was taking an aircraft flying in from a special hangar at Langley in the morning. The plane was the private business aircraft of Ed Kosko, newly confirmed head of the National Security Agency and friend of President Jerome Conner.

RICHARD TREVAE

Carolyn McCabe was not aware of Dalton's new assignment and had made plans for the evening days ago. She had arranged a quiet dinner at one of Dalton's favorite restaurants, Hemingway's, a seafood place with a Cuban decor and tropical themes. This was to be the prelude to a romantic night celebrating his MBA in international finance. When Dalton and Carolyn arrived at Hemingway's around 7:15 p.m., the staff had already set aside a prime booth and decorated the space with celebration balloons and streamers announcing his achievement. The meal was excellent, as expected, and after a short time, they left for Carolyn's apartment to relax and enjoy some private time. Carolyn found herself becoming more and more connected with Dalton and began to realize she was falling in love. Having lost both parents, her mother only three years ago, Dalton was the practical and emotional equivalent of family.

Dalton would have normally spent the night; however, with his early departure the next morning, he held her in a deep embrace and told her he had to leave and finish packing. Her disappointment was immediate. Pretending to pout, Carolyn attempted to flirt and dissuade him from going, although she knew he was serious and let him leave feeling guilty.

In an effort to make it up to her, without revealing

any detail, Dalton suggested they spend the upcoming Labor Day weekend in Ocean City, Maryland, where his mother maintained a beach house. Several times over the summer, the two had stole away and enjoyed the sand and surf.

Jumping at the chance, Carolyn said, "Yes, I'll drive out there Friday afternoon and open the place up for us, OK?"

"Great, I'll rent a car from near Langley on my return and be there by evening, hopefully."

Carolyn looked flirtatiously at him and said, "Don't be late, JD. You would not want to miss anything."

Dalton smiled and winked to acknowledge the insinuation, and handed her the condo key, wondering if the new assignment from Ed would turn out to be as easy as it appeared.

8:30 A.M. THE NEXT DAY, WEDNESDAY BEFORE LABOR DAY, LANGLEY, VIRGINIA

The ten-seat Gulfstream took off from Langley at 7:00 a.m. and flew to pick up Dalton outside the Wharton campus. It was refueled and ready to depart. Two men, already on the aircraft, joined Dalton on his trip to Guantanamo, Cuba: Wilson and Cotter. Both were young Secret Service types dressed in suits, armed, and wearing the requisite aviator sunglasses. Each man had a background in Special Forces and was moved out after less than fifteen months' field time to join the NSA. Their intellect and ability to work effectively together impressed Ed Kosko. He followed their progress from the beginning of their service together, eighteen months ago. No one really expected any trouble on the investigative mission, although Ed Kosko seldom took chances he did not have to.

Dalton sat down, sipped a Starbucks coffee, and opened the classified file he received just three days prior. The folder had a photo of a sixty-seven-year-old Russian exile Sergey Kreftkova, living in Cuba and asking for asylum in the United States in exchange for providing sensitive military and missile technology information. The dossier revealed nothing of detail about the exile's information except to say it went back to the Cuban missile crisis. Most agencies in the U.S. government dismissed the communication as a feeble attempt by a former Soviet naval officer to gain accommodations in the United States. Ed felt differently and assigned Dalton to interview the man.

Ed had had his eye on Dalton as well. A maturity well beyond his twenty-five years, a strong physical presence, excellent verbal skills, a lightning-fast mind, and a black belt in karate made Dalton stand out among his contemporaries. Dalton's earlier work for Kosko was so well received that other governmental units, including the CIA and FBI, were preparing to court Dalton for employment. Dalton had no such ambitions, as Ed had become a de facto uncle of sorts, following the death of Jonathon Crusoe. Included in the file on Sergey Kreftkova was a formal confirmation of Dalton's NSA Consultant's salary, initially set at $225,000, along with a congratulatory note on his MBA achievement. Dalton read the note and reflected on how important Ed had been in his life.

Dalton felt this assignment might lead to a false end. Nevertheless, he figured that Ed was challenging him with a series of diplomatically sensitive roles to test his skill sets. He liked Ed and felt his career inevitably would intertwine with his.

Damn, thought Dalton, with more notice, Carolyn could have joined me. I'm sure this interview can be disposed of in one day. However if I am delayed through the weekend, maybe she can join me in Nassau for a couple of nights.

Carolyn Katrina McCabe had been on campus about a year and immediately caught Dalton's eye. She was also studying in the finance department at Wharton, working toward her PhD. Carolyn was a striking brunette with a firm, curvaceous shape toned from years of tennis and swimming. They had been an item for almost seven months, and both were feeling their lives

RICHARD TREVAE

would be forever linked. They were romantically involved though committed to their graduate education and starting their careers.

The Gulfstream gathered speed and quickly lifted off, penetrating the sky and revealing a brilliant sunrise, which glistened as a golden glow off the chevron clouds below. He relaxed, thought of the night before with Carolyn, and fell asleep.

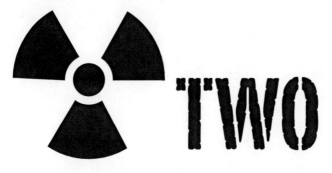

TWO

CRYSTALLIA MARINA, FIFTEEN MILES EAST OF GUANTANAMO

THE small, attractive marina had a nice outside patio restaurant and bar. The weather was a clear and warm eighty-two degrees plus the humidity effect. Sergey Kreftkova sat alone at the restaurant's far end studying a photo, now eight years old, of his beautiful niece, whom he had never met. He hoped this meeting would gain his asylum in the United States and he could connect with his only living relative. Sergey wore a large-brimmed, tan hat, sport jacket, and a blue dress shirt beneath, just as he described himself for recognition. As he tucked the photo away, the two NSA agents walked over, introduced themselves with fictitious names, and examined the Soviet exile's photo identification. After a moment, Wilson, the more serious of Dalton's men, motioned for Dalton to join them.

Dalton extended his hand, "Hello, Mr. Kreftkova. I'm Dalton Crusoe and I work for Ed Kosko."

Standing to formally greet Dalton, Sergey offered his hand. "I'm pleased to meet you, sir." His English was correct yet accented like most Russians. It was clear he was well educated, alert, and nervous.

A waitress came by and asked in Spanish if they wanted menus or just drinks. Dalton motioned, pointed to himself, and said, "Coke," then pointed to Sergey and the two companions. All accepted the drink offer, which he hoped would temper the heat and ease the building tension.

"Mr. Kreftkova, you have asked for this meeting, so we're here. What is it you have or know that may be of interest to the USA?" Dalton focused in on the Russian and looked for any evidence of deceit. Sergey pointed to the sea and said in a soft voice, "It was October of 1962. I was serving aboard the military support vessel Kladna, first officer to Captain Demkin. We were delivering four SS-5, ten-kiloton nuclear warhead missiles to Cuba." Nervous and uncomfortable, the Russian paused.

Dalton held his breath, a chill spreading through him as he waited for Sergey to continue.

"On the morning of October 31, 1962," resumed Sergey, "near the height of the confrontation, Captain Demkin received direct orders from Admiral Sarkov at the Kremlin. My captain commanded me to prepare two of our missiles in submersible cocoons, attach them to our mini sub, and off-load them through underwater hatches on the Kladna. I was instructed to drop them on the ocean floor for future retrieval after the embargo passed."

Dalton looked directly at the man and, in a firm voice, said, "We have monitored the island ever since the crisis and never found any evidence missiles landed on the Cuban shore, either before, during, or after the embargo."

"I have no doubt that is the case, sir; they are still there, in the sea."

At this point Dalton's two-man security team stiffened, looked at each other, then to Dalton. The stakes had just gotten greater, so it seemed to Dalton, although he was not about to be taken in by a wild story without confirmation and plenty of it. With no emotion or reaction, Dalton folded his hands, and asked, "Do you have proof, or am I to take this on your word alone?"

Now the Russian was exercising caution as he reached into his jacket pocket and withdrew a large manila envelope stuffed with papers. "These are copies of the ship's log and transcripts of communications between Admiral Sarkov and Captain Demkin hours before releasing two missiles. In addition, I added photos I took of the missiles and their warheads, for my own protection. I have the precise location of the warheads and missiles as was originally recorded in the log, except I removed the coordinate information. When I'm certain we have an understanding, I will give you the coordinates." Sergey held out the envelope and asked, "Do I have your assurance that I will be given asylum in the U.S. if these prove to be authentic?"

Dalton, not ready to react to the demand for asylum, asked, "Why didn't the Russian Navy come and retrieve those weapons under the guise of a fishing trawler or the like?"

"Admiral Sarkov died suddenly two days after we had deployed the mini sub with the missiles in their cocoons and told no one at the Kremlin of his orders to Demkin." Sergey studied each man at the table.

They paused while the refreshments arrived, which gave Dalton a moment to fathom the gravity of the situation. The story was brazen at the least; incredible if true.

"When Captain Demkin arrived home weeks after the embargo ended, no one at the Kremlin wanted to hear of any more issues involving the Cuban Missile Crisis. Khrushchev was embarrassed and humiliated at the Kremlin, even though the public perception was not as damning."

"The Russian leaders didn't forget about the missile inventory on your ship, did they?" demanded Dalton.

"No, sir. When Demkin realized that the Sarkov order was known to no one beyond himself and me, we changed the log to show only two missiles were loaded on board the Kladna, and it was never challenged. Since

THE TARASOV SOLUTION

Admiral Sarkov oversaw the naval nuclear weapons inventory, the information chain stopped at his office." Sitting back in his chair, appearing even more nervous, Sergey then said, "Demkin took the secret to his grave. He died thirty-three years ago in an auto accident, or so we were told by the Kremlin."

"So you think the missiles and the warheads are still intact, resting on the Caribbean bottom? Could they have survived that long?" Dalton was trying to think of any question to trap the Russian, yet the man never flinched. He was beginning to worry that perhaps all this could be true.

"Similar arrangements were made for missiles stored in cocoons along the harbors and bays dominating the Croatian Dalmatian coast, formerly Yugoslavia, where the Russian Navy was concentrated until the early 1990s. Every cocoon, dozens in fact, recovered years later preserved the missile and warhead in perfect condition."

Dalton tried a different tack. "Why don't you just stay in Cuba and enjoy the sunshine rather than seek asylum in the U.S.?" inquired Dalton.

"During the period when Russia destroyed its large nuclear arsenal, former KGB operatives discovered the manifest change on Captain Demkin's vessel. They assume I may know the details, so two years ago; I left Russia and found my way to Cuba. Unfortunately, these Russian mercenaries, lead by a Yuri Tarasov and con-

14

nected with international terrorists, have come to believe the story is true and are looking to capture me to learn what I know."

Dalton now knew this was a serious national security matter and felt Sergey was telling the truth. At least he knew the United States couldn't take a chance and let these weapons fall into terrorists' hands. Leaning in to Sergey, Dalton said, "I do believe you, and I'm willing to guarantee you asylum in the U.S. if these documents hold up against our intelligence records. I will need to inspect your documents and material in support of your story. Agreed?"

"Yes, then we are agreed. Here are the documents, although I will not provide the exact warhead coordinates until our understanding is formalized. When can I expect to be taken to the U.S.?"

"After I review the documents, I will make a few calls tonight and arrange for you to come to Guantanamo tomorrow for transport and questioning at the NSA." Dalton looked at the Russian for approval. "You must provide us the exact geographic coordinates which locate the weapons or the asylum guarantee is invalid. Understood?"

"Yes, that will be fine." Extending a small, folded paper note, Sergey said, "Here are my cell phone number and the hotel where I'm staying." Sergey stood and smiled at Dalton then extended his hand to each man.

THE TARASOV SOLUTION

Wilson acknowledged the meeting's end with a strong grasp and firm shake. "We will be in touch soon."

In choreographed fashion, Cotter placed a minute listening bug and tracking device beneath the band of Sergey's hat as he retrieved it from a vacant chair at the table. Sergey nodded, walked away, and left the restaurant.

"Did you get all that conversation on disk, as well as on camera?" Dalton asked Cotter, the younger agent.

"Yes, sir, I got it all. And I placed the tracker bug."

Outside Crystallia Marina

The vintage 1957 Chevrolet Impala two-door hardtop was in excellent shape and blended in with the numerous older cars owned by well-off Cuban citizens. Waiting in the parked vehicle's driver seat, the, Russian ex-KGB agent Taros Zolyar, watched as Dalton and his team entered the marina. The earlier wiretaps on Sergey Kreftkova paid off to a certain extent. The exiled Russian was desperately trying to get asylum in the States. Whether he'd told the story about the cocooned missiles was uncertain. The "three business types" he'd met with were most certainly Americans. Taros was convinced Sergey had been the first officer under Demkin, probably carried out the deployment order, and likely had the documentation to confirm the missiles existence and location. As Kreftkova left the marina restaurant, Taros captured a dozen facial photos of him. Within minutes, the digital photos were uploaded by satellite to the 225-foot Decadence, a yacht anchored off Cayman Brac and serving as their local command post. Fully equipped with communications, navigation, submersibles, helicopter, tenders, and small Zodiac ship-to-shore boats, the Decadence could also provide an impressive offensive attack if needed.

Yuri Tarasov saw the e-mail come in and was downloading the photos from Taros. The facial-recognition software examined inventoried early service and college photos of Sergey Kreftkova. Despite the fact that some forty-five years had passed, the software identified the face as that of Sergey with a 94.1 percent confidence level.

Speaking into his satellite phone while staring at the computer screen, Yuri said, "That's what I've been looking for, Taros. Good work. Now the security team will fly over to assist you. I want to move quickly to recover the weapons before the Americans, or anyone else, gets too interested."

After a brief pause, Taros replied, "I should be at the helicopter landing site in fifteen minutes . . . with Kreftkova."

THE TARASOV SOLUTION

Yuri Tarasov had been a section chief for the KGB five years before it was dismantled. His connections allowed him to organize a vast, successful merchant arms business, occasionally providing the mercenaries themselves. He made millions procuring and selling weapons to various splinter groups and terrorists throughout the Middle East and former Soviet states that had gained independence after perestroika. Yuri had no theology and, therefore, none of the holy jihad predispositions present in many of his customers. His interest was purely wealth, lots of it, and the power that came with it. He made a point of knowing everything he could about a proposed deal: the players, where the money was coming from, the security at the weapon's transfer point, local politicians and police to be paid off for looking the other way, and most important, how to ensure no paper trail led back to him. He was obsessed with controlling all details of his business. His reputation for performance without a hitch allowed him to charge a security deposit before negotiations began. If the buyer backed out, Yuri had compensation to complete his end of the procurement from his suppliers and keep their trust. Yuri Tarasov paid well and on time and demanded total performance from his suppliers and buyers. Messing up a deal with Yuri Tarasov was always followed quickly with consequences, usually the lethal kind. In the post-Soviet society, it was easy for an ambitious and ruthless ex-spook to develop his business relying on old KGB types still in the political arena. He had become a one-stop-shopping source for insurgent groups to arm, finance, and on occasion, recruit mercenaries for their efforts.

Never one to mix business with pleasure, Tarasov had few true friends, only well-paid stooges and mercenaries to carry out his plans and personal pursuits. He loved the water and made a point of traveling on his extravagant yacht, the Decadence, a component of his business dealings. Traveling by sea made his precise location elusive. He was careful never to overuse his satellite phones for his negotiations as they could be tracked by nosy governments and competitors. For the better part of two decades, Yuri Tarasov was a ruthless businessman to those who dealt with him and a vaguely defined entrepreneur to those who'd merely heard of him. Recent changing political winds brought his activities into the public view and spawned campaign slogans for eliminating the arms merchants operating out of Russia.

The new Russian president, Georgi Blinikov, did not come from the old Soviet system; rather he was a comparatively young reformer bent on broad democratic policies, and he was an outspoken critic of the widespread corruption in Russian politicians. Four months into office and he had already set his sights on Yuri Tarasov and his operation. Unwinding a corrupt political system and finding former Communist party members who could be trusted and willing to serve the new president's agenda was difficult. Everyone talked about the problem with dealers such as Tarasov, although few were willing to do anything about it. Tarasov had spread the money far and wide from his lucrative arms business, and his reputation for eliminating opponents was legendary. Once a partner in an arms deal with Yuri Tarasov, you were a partner for life, and if you chose to ignore or fail a request of Yuri's, you were first out the money then likely dead. Nevertheless, Blinikov made it a clear objective to eliminate arms dealers from making Russia the provider of choice for terrorists. His message was generating new hope for the average Russian on the street who was tired of nothing ever happening to help the underclass while the corrupt got wealthier.

With encouragement from American President Jerome Conner, Blinikov arranged a meeting in Washington to discuss improving relations and removing the international arms dealers operating out of Russia. Tarasov felt he could right his ship by eliminating Blinikov and discouraging the Americans from getting involved in Russian internal politics. The upcoming meeting between Conner and Blinikov was the perfect opportunity to remove all obstacles in his way.

Tarasov had heard stories about the missing nukes for years, and Kreftkova's disappearance from Russia gave the rumors new life. The first officer and Demkin were suspected of altering the ship's log to cover the weapon's release although no inquiries were begun until long after Demkin died. Kreftkova covered his role well, and never revealed the missile deployments even to his family. Sergey had lost his wife many years ago to cancer, and his only other living relative was a niece born in America after his sister had left Russia while he was at sea. His niece married an American educator and gave birth to a daughter. Tarasov could find no contact between Kreftkova and the niece, though he suspected she may know something.

Ironically, Sarkov's family, supposing murder rather than a heart attack, ultimately convinced the Russian Navy to investigate the admiral's death. In the course of their research, it was discovered Admiral Sarkov had left a written copy of his order to Demkin sealed in an unmarked envelope and hidden in his office. Only when Sarkov's old desk was being replaced did a clerical worker notice it taped to the back of the center drawer. Once she had opened the orders and told a few friends, Yuri Tarasov quickly found her and, posing as a naval investigator, offered her a handsome reward. With the letter as proof Sarkov's order was given, whether Kreftkova carried out the order remained an open question. Yuri's intense search for him could yield the answer.

Finding and securing two ten-kiloton nuclear bombs overlooked for decades by Russian and UN authorities was a dream come true for a merchant arms dealer such as Tarasov. Kidnapping Kreftkova, extracting the details of Sarkov's order to Demkin, and learning the sunken treasure's location were Tarasov's top priorities. The trail led his agents to Cuba hours before Sergey Kreftkova was scheduled to meet with Dalton Crusoe. Assuming Kreftkova had struck a deal with the Americans and told them of the missiles, the stakes had risen dramatically. Yuri knew he could command anywhere from fifteen to twenty million U.S. dollars for a usable nuclear warhead. Without an ongoing public search for missing warheads, Yuri could maximize the price and attract the largest, most sophisticated, and well-financed terrorist groups on Earth. The thought of such a windfall engulfed Yuri's mind. In any event, he wanted—no needed—the warheads to resolve his own issues concerning Blinikov and President Conner. Ever since

RICHARD TREVAE

Blinikov took office with a mandate to clean up the Russian political system, Yuri had formed a plan to have both the money and a solution to stop the new Russian president. The money gained by selling the warheads was tempting, though secondary to stopping the forces threatening to topple his thriving business.

He would use all means at his disposal, including betraying a past client and kidnapping the last remaining member of Sergey Kreftkova's extended family, a niece, living in the US.

THREE

Two Miles from Crystallia Marina

SERGEY Kreftkova shifted through the Volvo's gears as he headed back to his hotel room, pleased with the outcome of his meeting with Dalton Crusoe. He liked Dalton right from the start. The young American agent was sincere and credible, and Sergey felt he could trust Dalton to carry out his end of the agreement. Once Dalton verified Sergey's story, Sergey's asylum in the United States was essentially guaranteed. Sergey hoped tomorrow would be his last day in Cuba and that he would be looking to establish himself in America. He could not help think of his sister, now deceased, and his beautiful, young niece he had never met. If only his sister could have survived her breast cancer, she may have been able to help in his efforts to come to America. However, she wasn't alive, and it would have been a great risk to involve her in his plans to leave Russia. The fewer people who knew what Sergey knew, the better. It seemed a huge burden of fear was beginning to leave his mind.

The classic 1957 Chevrolet maintained a safe distance four hundred yards behind Sergey right up to the point where he turned into his hotel parking lot. A block farther down the road, the Chevy turned and pulled to the roadside. Once parked, the driver opened his cell phone, entered a number, and said, "He's in a silver Volvo heading to his room. Sedate him and bring him to the yacht."

A reply came forth. "We're on it."

Sergey noticed an attractive woman approaching his car on foot as he pulled into the parking space near his room. Upon opening the driver's door, the passenger door jerked open and a large hand pulled Sergey back across the front seat, knocking his brimmed hat to the floor a moment before a foul smelling cloth covered his face. Sensing time had stopped, Sergey latched on to a few vague impressions: feeling helpless; seeing a beautiful, dark-haired woman who smelled like jasmine over him, and a final strong, pungent chemical smell. Mere seconds later, Sergey was unconscious, lying in the backseat as the two assailants drove the Volvo to the helicopter pad for the return flight to the *Decadence*.

THE TARASOV SOLUTION

Wilson and Cotter scrutinized the documents supplied by Sergey at the lunch meeting. The records were deemed authentic based on corroborating information Dalton's team was able to recover from NSA and military archives relating to the period. As a bonus, thought Dalton, the yellowed pages listed the *Kladna*'s coordinates for the six days it sat dormant in the Caribbean waters while diplomatic negotiations ensued. Dalton reasoned the drop point for the cocooned missiles must be nearby.

"The *Kladna* never moved more than one hundred meters based on our aircraft reconnaissance data from the period," Cotter announced to the group. "Sergey may have removed the data from the ship's log as to the drop point; however, the missiles came off *Kladna,* and we know where it was positioned during late October and early November 1962."

Dalton listened to the message and mentally questioned why Sergey failed to assume the United States had data on the drop zone's exact location based on the *Kladna*'s position. Something was not right in the assumption, he thought. *Why withhold information Sergey must assume we already have?*

Isla Playa Bay, aboard the *Decadence*

RICHARD TREVAE

The cool, evening air relieved the day's heat. It was seven o'clock, and the luxury yacht sat in the water six hundred yards off shore. The onboard helicopter arrived with its unwilling passenger, the Russian defector semiconscious from the drugs he had been forced to inhale during his capture. Sergey was taken to the yacht's engine hold and strapped into a wooden armchair, his legs and hands taped down. Though groggy, Sergey could hear voices near him speaking English with Russian accents. He faked his unconsciousness, trying to get an understanding of what was happening to him. His mind replayed his last conscious thoughts: the powerful tug at his neck, a man forcing a rag over his mouth, the beautiful woman bending over him. Everything from that point forward was lost.

The smell of diesel fuel and gentle sway of his quarters tipped him off that he was on a boat. He eased one eye open, spying the gearboxes leading to twin propeller shafts, the sight confirming his shipboard location. He noticed his jacket draped over a nearby chair and wondered if his cell phone was in answer mode, muted, or powered off. Nearby, a woman's voice said, "Give him another fifteen minutes before we force him to consciousness. I'll let Yuri know he's coming around."

Sergey shuddered from two disturbing images slogging his mind. One of Ivana Yenko, a legendary young assassin, an expert with knives, endowed with great looks and a complete lack of fear. The second image was of a man: Yuri Tarasov. Yuri and Ivana had become an item after she took an assignment to uncover and eliminate a saboteur within Yuri's organization. Her decisive and deadly solutions pleased Yuri, as did her attractiveness and calculating mind. Sergey shivered, for he knew he was in for a long, unpleasant night, if he survived it at all.

Cotter booted his laptop, establishing a link to the NSA secure satellite in order to check up on Sergey's whereabouts. Nearby, Dalton held his cell phone to his ear, speaking with his boss, Ed Kosko.

"Yes, this material definitely appears to be copies of the ship's log," Dalton said. "Detailed assembly drawings of the missiles and warheads are also here, together with photos, dated October 31, 1962, showing the missiles being deployed into the cocoons for release to the sea from the mini sub. I need to arrange for a transport to move Sergey out of Gitmo to Langley. Can you set that up for tomorrow evening?"

"My plane will return with two extra marines to assist you and your men. Plan on a six o'clock departure, putting you in Virginia at approximately 8:30 p.m."

"Thanks, Ed. I'll talk to you early tomorrow, after I get a few more answers from Kreftkova."

"I fear the devastating outcomes that could arise if we fail to locate and retrieve the dormant warheads soon. I'm glad you're on the problem Dalton."

Cotter studied the data stored in the satellite files and couldn't believe his eyes. The tracker had Sergey, or at least the bug, located some twelve miles from the hotel location Sergey gave them. Furthermore, the audio files had only traffic noise, without any speech for eight minutes. Next came sounds of a struggle, suggesting Sergey had been kidnapped. Over the next fifteen minutes, faint voices spoke of meeting a helicopter, spending the night on a yacht, and preparing a dive crew in a couple of days.

Cotter motioned to Dalton. "You need to see this uploaded data, sir."

Dalton listened to the voices and looked over the route, confused by the tracking bug's current location. It was transmitting from a spot near the shore, some fifteen miles away to the northeast.

"Do we have his cell phone location?" inquired Dalton.

"Yes, sir. It's powered on but shut down to calls." Cotter rechecked his information. "It's within a few hundred yards of the tracker."

THE TARASOV SOLUTION

"So the cell phone and tracker are not in the same place?" Dalton checked his watch; it was 7:40 p.m. local time. "Load the Escalade with the satellite phone and side arms for each of us. We're going to find Sergey now."

THE SOUTHERN CUBAN SHORE OF THE CARIBBEAN

FROM a quarter of a mile away, Wilson peered at the Volvo through his night-vision binoculars. The car appeared empty and was parked off the road where daytime sunbathers left their vehicles. Dalton took the binoculars from Wilson and scanned the beach until the distant lights of the *Decadence* appeared in his sight. "That's our boat mentioned on the recordings," declared Dalton. "And I'll wager our Russian friend is onboard." Dalton turned to his two NSA agents. "Get me Major General Rusk at Gitmo on the SatLink phone."

Meanwhile, Wilson approached the Volvo, ducking and hiding behind cover as he neared the vehicle. With his Glock 9 mm aimed and set to fire, he stood up behind the rear windshield and surveyed the car. It was empty, as expected, except for Sergey's rumpled hat, which lay on the backseat floor. Wilson motioned an all-clear to Dalton and Cotter.

Cotter jumped to the task and within a minute had the major general on the phone.

THE TARASOV SOLUTION

Dalton called Ed Kosko on his secure satellite cell phone and briefed him on the latest events. Once Dalton introduced Rusk to his team, Ed was conferenced in, and Dalton explained the situation and his plan to rescue Sergey Kreftkova. Rusk knew Kosko and had been alerted to Dalton's investigative mission prior to his landing at the base. After Dalton explained information's importance he had collected, Rusk approved a four-man Seal team be dispatched immediately to join Dalton and assist in the rescue. Dalton would direct the overall effort; however the Seal team leader would lead the assault on the yacht.

Sergey was alert when Yuri Tarasov descended the narrow staircase to the engine room. Pulling a chair close to his guest, Yuri said, "You are Sergey Kreftkova, first officer under Captain Demkin during the October 1962 Cuban embargo?"

Sergey knew it was pointless to deny Yuri's question. "Yes, I am."

Continuing his interrogation, Yuri followed with, "And you released two ten-kiloton nuclear warheads and their missiles from a mini sub in protective cocoons to the sea upon orders from Captain Demkin?"

Ivana stood nearby, leaning against a column support,

toying with a five-inch long serrated knife while smiling at Sergey.

At this point Sergey froze, not knowing what he could say to help his situation. If he readily acknowledged the missiles' deployment, he would have to provide the exact location where they lay. If he denied carrying out the order, he ran the risk that Yuri knew more and would use more persuasive means to get to the truth. Sergey reasoned that Yuri had probably not been able to reconstruct the exact drop location since they did not record the drop coordinates in the logbook. Only Sergey and the late Captain Demkin knew the coordinates. Sergey had memorized and removed them from the documents he provided to Dalton after being assured U.S. asylum. Now with Yuri growing visibly impatient, Sergey said, "It is true I followed Captain Demkin's orders and released the two cocoons to the sea."

Yuri relaxed a bit and strolled around in front of his prisoner. "I understand you desire to live in America, yes?"

This caught Sergey off guard; he perked up and said, "Why yes, that's true. That's what I want. I don't care about the warheads or missiles at all."

"Good, very good, my friend. I think then we can come to an accord. I want the warheads from those missiles. Where exactly are they located?" Yuri waited for a response, yet Sergey sat in silence, considering his next words.

In a sudden burst, Yuri lunged toward Sergey and pushed a 9 mm Beretta underneath his jaw, forcing his head back. "Tell me where they are before I waste any more time with you when I could be searching for them on my own. The area involved is not that great."

Sergey knew that was a lie, however he'd already decided what he would do.

Ivana moved closer. Yuri stood back, coiled his left arm, and sent a stunning backhand blow to Sergey's right cheek, knocking Sergey to the metal deck flooring. Two men built like wrestlers grabbed Sergey and threw him back in the chair.

Without any better options at the time, Sergey caught his breath then stated, "The cocoons are located in sixty-four meters of water at coordinates 21°, 11', 54" north by 76°, 12', 13" west."

The words worked. Yuri relaxed, lowered his handgun, and smiled at Sergey, who then felt he may live another day. Ivana smiled at Sergey as though he were a disobedient puppy.

"Fine. See how much easier that was than the other way?" Circling Sergey with the Beretta pointed at his head, Yuri demanded, "Have you told anyone else about the missiles' location ?"

"No, I haven't. I swear. I just want to go to America

and start a new life. That's all."

"Who were the men you met at Crystallia Marina today?"

"They were officials from the Immigration Department." Sergey's mouth went dry as he told the lie.

"What are their names?" Yuri demanded.

"Two were aides, I guess, and the one in charge was . . . Dalton Crusoe, I think."

"Don't lie to me, Sergey." Yuri motioned to one of his men. "Get online and find out everything on a . . . Dalton Crusoe." Yuri walked behind Sergey, stopped, and withdrew the photo Sergey had in his coat vest pocket. "A beautiful young woman; I'd say seventeen or eighteen years old. Who is she?" Turning the photo over, he saw in faded pencil it read, *Carolyn Katrina McCabe.*

Sergey's face flushed and his pulse quickened. The thought of a beast such as Yuri Tarasov even holding his niece's photo pushed him into a rage. Delaying his emotional response, he focused and said, "She is my sister's daughter, married, I believe, and living in Europe. I haven't heard from my sister or her daughter in over six years. They are lost to me. I carry the photo as a memento." Sergey stared at Yuri and tried to look sincere.

Yuri slipped the photo back in Sergey's shirt pocket,

patting the Russian on the shoulder.

Yuri studied his captive for a moment, which felt like a jury writing a verdict for Sergey, and concluded he was telling the truth. Ivana walked next to Yuri and whispered something in his ear. The wrestlers looked for a command from Yuri.

"Untie our friend, clothe him, and lock him in a lower stateroom during our voyage," Yuri called out to his men. He jumped up the staircase and ordered the yacht steering master to set a course for the coordinates Sergey gave up. Ivana followed close behind.

The lie worked, for while the Americans knew the facts of the missile cocoons, Sergey had not supplied the location. A powerful asset for Sergey was appearing convincing in his answer to Yuri, for he had if fact not yet revealed the exact coordinates to *anyone.*

It was just after 9:00 p.m., and the sea was calm. Resting in his cabin, Sergey tried to relax and wondered how he would survive the sudden change of events. He thought of America and living a quiet life, free from pain and stress. He felt in his jacket for the photo of his niece and realized Yuri had removed it. Frantic, he felt all his pockets and found the small photo in his shirt pocket where Yuri left it after the questioning. He feared Yuri would somehow locate and harm her, assuming she knew something about Sergey's story or

RICHARD TREVAE

his plans to meet with U.S. officials. Then he noticed the powerful naval flashlight affixed to the wall near his bed. He checked the sky then his watch, thinking, *It's going to be a clear night.*

He began to conceive an escape plan.

CUBA'S NORTHEAST SHORE

THE four-man Seal team had worked for thirty minutes setting up their military-style Zodiac with ComSat gear and weapons when Dalton noticed the *Decadence* lift anchor and head out to sea. Dalton saw the yacht through night-vision binoculars pulling away and turning to the port side.

"They have lifted anchor and are moving out. Let's check with NSA and see if we can position a satellite to follow their route."

Cotter called NSA on the SatLink phone to make Dalton's request.

Dalton was worried perhaps Yuri had what he needed from Sergey and was preparing to eliminate him. With the yacht moving out to sea, the logical explanation was they were going to the missiles' resting site supplied by Sergey.

Dalton asked the Seal team to hold their readiness status until he decided what action was next needed. Wilson identified the yacht's precise location and overlaid it on a satellite image covering the general area. The real-time data flowing into Wilson's computer was able to zoom in and locate the *Decadence* on a north-north-east heading at a modest seven knots. The darkening sky and intermittent cloud cover frustrated Wilson's attempts to focus down over the yacht and examine it.

By 10:30 p.m., the Seal team, Dalton, and his NSA agents were back at Guantanamo and set up in a conference call with Ed Kosko and the president's Homeland Security Advisor, Randolph Pickler. Dalton relayed the day's events following the encounter with Sergey Kreftkova and his apparent capture by persons aboard the *Decadence*. The intelligence gained from Sergey appeared to be genuine, and if so, the United States had a dangerous situation, which if not contained and controlled, could involve terrorists obtaining nuclear warheads from the Cold War.

Pickler was a thoughtful career diplomat including extensive experience in Islamic fundamentalism with little if any background that would provide insight to the current problem. Pickler's respect for Ed Kosko, a lifelong friend and confidant of President Jerome Conner, together with the impressive actions of Dalton, caused Pickler to respectfully say, "Mr. Crusoe, what exactly do you suggest we tell the president is your recommendation? It seems to me we need more evidence before we take hostage a foreign national, and his vessel, in international waters. The press will make a joke of us if we're wrong."

Pausing to take a deep breath, Dalton began, "Sir, I believe we cannot take the risk of assuming this information is not authentic and accurate. I also feel we need to assemble a fast-response team of Seals to rendezvous near the suspected resting place if Kreftkova has already been broken and provided data to Tarasov. They must be prepared to take offensive action against the crew and possible mercenaries aboard the *Decadence* should they resist our efforts to board their vessel. And we need a special Seals unit with nuclear demolition skills to retrieve and disable the warheads."

Dalton paused to take any questions. Hearing only, "Continue, Mr. Crusoe," from Pickler, Dalton started again.

"Based on the apparent head start Yuri has on us, I assume we cannot assign a submarine in time to intercept the *Decadence* by surprise?" asked Dalton.

The Seal team commander said, "That's correct. We'd be better off approaching faster with a surface vessel and attacking at night."

"Then I suggest we use an ocean-capable Coast Guard vessel to transport our team and equipment to the area. A more imposing military vessel would draw more attention to our actions." Dalton waited for further ideas from the group.

Ed Kosko offered, "I will arrange for the Coast Guard ship. I believe we can get what we need from the Miami naval station."

Dalton responded, "Based on the position and *Decadence* speed, it should take another seventeen hours or so for it to arrive at the drop zone. Can we have our ship in the area by then?"

Ed spoke up and stated, "We should arrive within an hour or two of the expected ETA of Tarasov's yacht, assuming good seas and no mechanical or equipment holdups."

Dalton nodded his agreement to the Seal team.

The group came to a common understanding regarding the mission. It would be covert as long as possible in case the Kreftkova story was a myth. Pickler and Kosko would inform and advise the president, despite Pickler's many legal concerns, which Dalton felt were overblown. Dalton trusted Kosko to dampen Pickler's political concerns when briefing the president. General Rusk would handle overall military control, and Dalton would manage the mission strategy depending on the variable nature of real-time events. They would try to arrive at the drop zone in advance of Tarasov. If not, they were to detain or disable the *Decadence* so the release of Kreftkova and the yacht inspection could take place. The president chose to keep the mission secret from congressional oversight committees until he had information that was more definitive. Trusting this mission phase to Dalton was a huge leap of faith, made possible because Ed knew the capabilities and sharp decision making of his young protégé, and the president trusted Ed.

Dalton felt nervous and wondered if he had all the facts needed to ensure success.

Yuri Tarasov was reviewing his nautical charts and plotting a course to the drop zone coordinates offered up by Sergey. Earlier he radioed his rented salvage vessel, the *Mullet,* under the command of Captain Augustus, an Albanian seaman and sometime mercenary who had worked with Tarasov on other occasions. The conversation was brief, and Yuri indicated he had secured the needed coordinates from his guest, Sergey Kreftkova.

Augustus was accompanied by twelve others: eight crew and salvage team members and four mercenary types with dark pasts and no loyalty. Were it not for the impressive money Tarasov paid out along with the promise of a sizable bonus for a successful mission, none of the men could be trusted. Tarasov could control them based on his reputation and the knowledge that any betrayal would be answered with death. The state-of-the-art satellite phone flashed to signify an incoming call to the *Decadence* bridge: it was from Augustus.

"What is your status, Augustus?" demanded Tarasov without much protocol.

"I'm just leaving port in Providenciales, entering the Caicos strait."

"Did you receive all the underwater salvage equipment I was promised, along with the arms shipments? Is all of it there, including the ground-to-air Stinger missiles?"

"Yes, yes, relax. My men and I have all we need to conduct the salvage and defend it from any interested spectators," declared Augustus.

"Good. We may need all that stuff if my guest spilled his guts in order make a deal with the Americans." Checking his watch, Yuri said, "When can I expect you at the sunken treasure?"

"At this speed and in these seas, it should take around fifteen hours. I'll start immediately to locate the cocoons once we're at the coordinates Kreftkova gave you."

"Excellent. I'll be there shortly after you arrive."

Augustus concluded with, "And let me know if you think I'll have visitors."

The communications technician overseeing Yuri's operation came onto the bridge holding several pieces of paper. Before Yuri could acknowledge him, he bellowed out, "This Dalton Crusoe is a bigger problem than just an immigration bureaucrat. He's connected with the NSA?"

Ivana came up from below at the commotion and listened in.

"What the hell are you talking about?" barked Yuri.

"The guy who met with Sergey . . . he's not officially anything except that he consults with the head man at the NSA and his name appears in dozens of recent court and Treasury filings."

Yuri threw the nautical maps at his steering master and pushed him aside to confront the technician. "Are you saying the guy is a spook?" Yuri was irritated now.

"Yes. He's a very smooth, covert NSA agent, or a 'fixer' for the U.S. government, or at least the NSA. He gets into the shit and gets it done . . . big-time."

Yuri began to study the paperwork. Pages of Google name search results revealed the background, history, family, and college work. Many favorable quotes from various folks in the IRS, NSA and SEC were abundant. Showing concern for the first time that others in the United States could be on to his plans, Yuri's face flushed and he said, "I want to know every detail about this guy ... what he does, who he works with, and where is he now. Get on it. Damn it! I don't need this clown messing up my plans."

 **SIX**

DALTON was finishing updating Ed Kosko at NSA headquarters in Ft. Meade, Maryland, while Wilson and Cotter were talking with their counterparts at NSA about any information, history, or conversations recorded concerning Yuri Tarasov. A break came up during their search for Yuri Tarasov.

Cotter heard the entire recording from the listening bug hidden under Sergey's hatband. Motioning to Dalton as he hung up the phone, Cotter said, "Listen to this. During the call from the Cuban shore to the *Decadence* as Sergey was being loaded onto the ship's helicopter for transport to the yacht, the Chevy driver had his speakerphone on and Yuri was recorded saying this." Cotter replayed the recording.

"Is he unconscious?" asked Yuri.

The male driver said, "Yeah, he's still out. Shall we try to wake him for the flight to the yacht or just carry him?"

Yuri answered with, "No, you fool. I'd rather he not

know how he got on board. Carry him." The recording ended there.

Cotter said, "Sir, we have Yuri Tarasov's voice on record, and I believe we have enough voice material to map his voice and search for it on the communication networks." Cotter smiled at his own resourcefulness.

"Excellent. Get on it and let me know immediately if you find him speaking again over his phone."

Dalton had a delicate call to make. Sergey may be alive however in danger of being killed the moment Yuri knew he found the sunken missiles. By now, Yuri must have extracted the precise location and was heading there. Assuming it was near where 1962 aircraft video showed the armada of Russian ships heading toward Cuba, the true location was within a two-mile radius about 510 miles off Cuba. If the Seal team attacked by surprise, Sergey and others might be lost in the battle. Without the precise drop location and no one alive who knew it, the missiles could be lost again waiting for the next motivated terrorist or arms merchant to recover. If, however, he waited until it was certain Yuri had located the missiles and begun the retrieval, then a fight to the end might involve the use of one or more nuclear warheads against the Americans. Then a flash of enlightenment hit Dalton; the *Kladna* location, presumably the drop zone, was in more than four thousand feet of water, very deep for a later recovery. He reasoned, *Sergey did not move the Kladna, so the mini sub moved to shallower water for the drop.*

The big Coast Guard cutter *Ravenwood* had more than the usual complement of weapons, including SAMs, underwater depth charges, 50-millimeter rotating guns, and grenade launchers. Ed Kosko had seen to it that twelve combat-ready Seal packs were added to the cargo for Dalton, his two agents, and a handful of marines based at Guantanamo assigned by General Rusk under Dalton's control. The cutter left Miami at 1:00 a.m. the day after Kreftkova was kidnapped. Dalton and his team were to be flown by helicopter and dropped onto the *Ravenwood*.

Dalton and his team were loading the last supplies and combat gear onto the heavy cargo chopper at Guantanamo when the XO for General Rusk came running to the helipad.

"Mr. Crusoe, Dalton Crusoe! Wait! I have an urgent message for you."

Dalton turned to address the officer, now breathless from running at top speed for two hundred yards to catch them. "What do you have, Lieutenant?"

"Sir, this communication came from a pleasure yacht cruising not far from Gitmo within the last hour. We believe it may be a signal from your Mr. Kreftkova." The officer handed Dalton a typed internal communications memo that read:

DELIVER D. CRUSOE (BREAK) GITMO (BREAK) *DECADENCE* BOUND FOR 21°, 11', 54" NORTH BY 76°, 12', 13" WEST.

"We received this by radio communications at Gitmo from a private passenger yacht, which observed the message in Morse code coming from a large yacht heading out to sea. They were located near Cayman Brac, sir."

Dalton boarded the helicopter and radioed the captain of the *Ravenwood*. Based on the new Gitmo communication, the drop zone was much closer to Cuba, in shallower water, as he suspected. Once connected to Captain Thomson aboard the *Ravenwood*, he gave him the coordinates and concluded by saying, "We'll intercept you on this course to rendezvous. Keep us advised on your progress."

Dalton now believed Sergey was alive and somehow able to get the missile coordinates to him . . . or maybe not. It occurred to him that if Sergey were compromised and revealed his earlier discussions about the missiles, then his captors might have provided a bogus message with coordinates to send Dalton off on the wrong course. The growing profile on Yuri Tarasov suggested this was the kind of maneuver he might use to throw off his pursuers. It was a chance they had to take for now.

FORTY-FIVE MILES NORTHWEST OF HAVANA, ABOARD THE *DECADENCE*

The *Decadence* moved through the water with a hint of gentle sea movement. The powerful engines hummed a deep, audible rhythm. The sky was clear and filled with stars. Sergey estimated they were doing ten knots. Sergey Kreftkova was a good sailor, even at sixty-seven years of age. Moreover, he could still click out a Morse code message with a flashlight from the small glass porthole five feet above the waterline. He repeated the message four times in a fifteen-minute period and saw two boats close enough to see it, if they were even looking his way. Nevertheless, Sergey was not about to pass up a chance to get a message to Dalton, who by now must have tried to call him about the schedule for his trip to Gitmo, which he had hoped would be his last day before arriving in America.

RICHARD TREVAE

Yuri was impatiently walking the bridge and wondered if Sergey had told him everything. Ivana took note of his mood and asked, "What are you so jittery about?"

"The old Russian seaman...I can't help but feeling he's not told us everything. Maybe he did alert the American to the missile location."

Ivana checked her reflection in a mirrored door connected to the bridge. Yuri gazed at her and asked, "Are you ready to test your charms on Sergey?"

"Yes, I told you earlier that my approach to gain his trust is better than yours, and I might find out more that he knows. So I'll go down now to talk with him." She smiled with confidence.

Sergey had been alone in his room for almost three hours when the door opened. It was Ivana Yenko, dressed in the same tight jeans; cotton, boat-neck top; and a light, leather jacket. Her long, black hair was pulled into a loose ponytail. Her sculpted physique was complemented by her face, which was symmetrical and striking, with large, blue eyes; a full smile; and an intensity that left no doubt about her reputation for being ruthless.   "Would you like something to eat before turning in for the evening?"

Her voice was pleasing, almost comforting, although the vision of her earlier display with the deadly knife caused Sergey to pause. "Actually, if I could just get a cup of hot tea, I'd appreciate it," replied Sergey.

Ivana strolled to within three feet of Sergey; the cabin door, still open, was filled by a menacing-looking man armed with an H&K assault rifle. "Why didn't you tell the Americans about the missiles and warheads?"

Sergey feared that now they did not believe him about his denial of informing the Americans. The request for tea vanished from the discussion. Thinking fast, Sergey said, "I had no need to, as my purpose was to get to America and be near my best friend from the Soviet Navy, a ship's mechanic, about my age." The heat began to build under Sergey's skin with his bold lie.

"And what did they say to your request?" Ivana studied him hard.

"They felt it was possible, considering my age and that I had not been active in the Russian Navy for over twenty years."

"So the Americans wanted nothing for granting you entry to the U.S.?"

"Well, actually, I also have a sponsor for my request to come to the U.S. A naval historical organization is compiling a compendium on Soviet naval strategies during the empire's breakup." He threw another huge lie into the discussion; Sergey felt very nervous. "They have offered me a stipend to consult on their work." He could feel his rapid breathing and pulse increasing.

Ivana showed him the start of a smile. She continued to study her prisoner. Leaning in as if to kiss him, she smiled and said, "Well then, congratulations. It appears we are both entrepreneurs, using different routes to our goals." She looked about the cabin and said as she walked out, "I'll have the crew see to that tea."

As the door shut, Sergey collapsed in a trembling heap. Rubbing his neck to relieve the tension, he thought, *I think she did not believe me!*

Yuri's communications chief's investigative work on Dalton Crusoe had revealed a lot of material. Ivana Yenko was going over the material every half hour to see what else had been learned. The campus newspaper, *The Patriot,* had an article on Dalton's work uncovering a U.S. senator's Ponzi scheme. In one photo taken during a live interview outside on the business school steps, Dalton was shown responding to a question. Behind him, in the background, studying Dalton with affection as he spoke was a woman. Magnifying the photo, Ivana recognized the woman as having a striking resemblance to Kreftkova's niece. Pawing through the pile of material that kept spewing from the Google hits on Dalton's name, she found the list of graduate students enrolled in the business school. Among the 452 names, one stood out: Carolyn Katrina McCabe, PhD candidate. Ivana's face lit up with a mixture of fear and determination.

Rushing to locate Yuri, she stood before him, holding the photo, and said, "You are not going to believe the good fortune I've uncovered. Dalton Crusoe apparently has a girlfriend."

"Yeah, so what? So do I," Yuri offered, revealing a smug grin.

"But her name is Carolyn Katrina McCabe, Sergey's lost niece."

"Get Taros on the satellite phone now." Yuri snatched the photo from Ivana and studied the young woman's face. Looking to Ivana with a smirk, he said, "Damn, woman! You may have just handed me an angle on this Crusoe character."

SEVEN

ABOARD THE *RAVENWOOD*

DALTON'S team landed on the *Ravenwood* and was escorted up to the command center. A weathered man in his late fifties stood in front of Dalton and extended his hand. "Mr. Crusoe, I'm Captain Jeffery Thomson. Welcome aboard."

Knowing that civilians need not salute military, Dalton stood erect, extended his hand, shook the captain's, and said, "Thank you, Captain. I appreciate your being able to commission yourself on such short notice. Please call me JD."

"Not a problem, JD. We have been tracking that fancy yacht of yours by satellite and believe we have a fix on her course. It's going to end up where we're headed. Is that what you expected?"

"In reality it was what we were hoping for, Captain."

Dalton's team settled in and began to check out their onboard gear for the inevitable encounter with Tarasov.

THE TARASOV SOLUTION

Dalton figured that they would arrive near 9:00 p.m. the next day. They would remain more than a mile off, drifting slowly away as though not interested in the yacht. Dalton's team could use the cover of darkness to approach the *Decadence* using two powered inflatables, each carrying six men with full Seal combat gear. Satcom links would broadcast voice and image to the *Ravenwood* control room and a situation room in NSA headquarters. Meanwhile, the satellite surveillance was providing detailed images of the yacht; it had some unusual provisions and features intended more for confrontation than comfort. The radar and communication assemblies were far more extensive than a typical pleasure yacht, and the helicopter was a small, fast, armed, and fully instrumented miniature version of an Apache. Deck activity suggested a twelve- to sixteen-man crew aboard. Side panels, just above the waterline near the stern, appeared to operate, allowing surface-level launching of smaller watercraft, possibly speedboats. All this information confirmed Dalton's fear that taking control of the *Decadence* would not be easy.

The *Mullet* made good time and was able to arrive at the sunken treasure site by 4:00 p.m., several hours ahead of Tarasov. It took less than an hour for Augustus to deploy a dive team and locate the missiles exactly where Kreftkova had said they would be. They were all lying as desired, flat on the sandy bottom, with the lifting hooks readily accessible. Each cocoon, about eighteen feet long and forty-two inches in diameter, was intact and easily lifted onto the old transport vessel's deck storage area. By 7:30 p.m., Augustus radioed Tarasov to say that he had found and recovered the cargo.

Yuri was ecstatic that the nukes had been found and recovered so easily. He sent his technical team over to verify the warhead's condition. Each appeared to be intact and fitted with detonators designed to trigger an explosion at impact. He radioed Augustus and said, "Have the men remove the warhead nose cones, separate the bomb and detonators from the heads, and then replace the nose cones on the missiles."

Augustus listened then ordered his technicians to complete the warhead removal from the missile bodies.

By 8:30 p.m., the *Decadence* arrived alongside the *Mullet*. Standing beside the two cocoons, Yuri examined the empty nose cones as they lay waiting to be reattached to the missiles. Next to them were the warheads. Each of the two stainless steel cylinders with large connecting flanges on each end had several blank flanges on the circumference covering side ports for arming and powering the weapons. They appeared new and unharmed by their long rest in the sea. "Do you detect any leaking or nuclear material degradation?" asked Yuri of Ian, his lead scientist.

"No, none at all. They appear to be in perfect shape." Ian seemed confident.

"Good. I want them moved to the starboard side water-level hatch on the *Decadence* and secured in their cradles." Yuri motioned to several of his men, who grabbed the sixty-pound devices and attached them to a loading arm that swung out and lowered them to the *Decadence*. Others were instructed to start attaching the nose cones to the missile bodies.

It was approaching 10:20 p.m., and Yuri was making great time against his schedule. He approached Captain Augustus and said, "We have completed another profitable mission, my friend; here is the balance of your payment, half in diamonds and half in Euros, as requested."

Augustus took the silver briefcase and lifted it a few times, testing its weight. "It feels about like four million Euros."

"That is exactly what it should feel like." Yuri smiled. Pausing a moment to refocus Augustus, he said, "Now remember, I want you to take a slow, easterly route back to Providenciales. Keep the missiles under tarps until you arrive in deep water near Puerto Plata, at the four-thousand-foot shelf, and drop them overboard at night." Recalling every detail of his plan as he walked toward the ship's ladder Yuri surveyed the missile bodies once more. He stormed back to Augustus and pointed to the nose cones. "Damn it! Don't forget to attach those nose cones back on the missile bodies. Do it now."

Augustus nodded and waved his arms, thinking, *I'll get to it when my money is safely stowed below.*

Still fondling the briefcase, Augustus looked up, smiled, and said, "Of course, I know the plan, and I will not let you down."

Yuri glared at Augustus to emphasize his frustration at the retort.

Just before 11:00 p.m., the *Decadence* set a course for Nassau and the *Mullet* headed east. Sergey Kreftkova watched from his darkened cabin through the porthole as the warheads were loaded onto the *Decadence* and the *Mullet* motored away with the impotent missiles. He felt his usefulness to Yuri Tarasov had ended. It was time to test his escape plan.

ABOARD THE *RAVENWOOD*, 9:45 P.M.

Dalton's Seal team was mobilized and outfitted with

all the typical combat paraphernalia as they came up from the west on the *Decadence*'s location. A radar antenna rotated in silence through the cool, night air as the heavy Coast Guard vessel cut across a northeasterly chop that had developed as clouds formed from a descending cool front over the southeastern United States. Yuri Tarasov's yacht was nowhere to be seen on the radar. Satellite coverage was spotty at best with the cloud cover hovering over the region. Three hours earlier, they had a good fix on its location, although now it seemed to have disappeared. Cotter was leaning over a console monitor of satellite coverage and looking for any ship movement.

"Can we get any clear imaging from the satellite?" asked Dalton.

"Really nothing to our south and west, however patches are opening up to the east. I'll keep checking," Cotter responded.

"How far are we from the coordinate location we received from the couple that picked up Sergey's Morse code signal?"

"About twenty-two miles east-southeast, say about fifty minutes away at this speed," answered Captain Thomson.

Three spots flashed on Cotter's screen. All indicated moving vessels on the sea about eighty miles to the east.

RICHARD TREVAE

Each flashing spot displayed a message: *Identity Unknown.* Cotter looked at them and guessed two were pleasure craft based on their speed and proximity to shore, although one was headed more or less along shipping lanes toward San Juan. He tapped the screen, and it zoomed in over the third boat's location. Another tap and the image of a salvage vessel appeared. Suspicious, Cotter called Dalton to his side and said, "I have something interesting here."

Dalton looked at the screen and could see the unmistakable view of a medium-sized salvage vessel, steaming east. "Yeah, what is it you are looking at?"

Cotter entered a few commands with his keyboard and a track was drawn on the screen from the stern of the salvage vessel to the west, displaying its prior route. Then by overlaying the *Ravenwood*'s course heading on the same screen the two tracks intersected. At that point coordinates flashed, 21°, 11', 54" north by 76°, 12', 13" west. "Those coordinates are . . . let me check again." Cotter played with the keyboard again. Dalton watched as the screen refreshed.

"That is exactly the location Sergey said the *Decadence* was headed . . . to the nukes," proclaimed Dalton. "That should be the *Decadence,* but it isn't." Dalton studied the screen again for a moment. "Can we zoom closer to the ship and focus in on the deck area?"

THE TARASOV SOLUTION

Cotter said, "Yes, I believe we can. Wait a moment while I task the satellite."

Seconds passed. Dalton paced the deck and waited for the screen to change. Then in sharp images, the ship and its deck came into view, showing two cylindrical tubes covered with canvas. Reference measurements confirmed these were approximately the size of Russian SS-5 IRBMs, each carrying ten-kiloton warheads. An angled stern view revealed the name *Mullet* and a Libyan flag and registry number.

The bridge was dead quiet for a full twenty seconds, all eyes staring at the enhanced screen image of the *Mullet*'s deck, when Dalton spoke.

"He's already located and retrieved the missiles! They must have arranged for the salvage vessel to make the recovery and are now taking them to a safe harbor for warhead removal." Dalton's pulse quickened. The mission had now taken a new turn. The missiles did exist, as Sergey had stated, and the arms merchant Tarasov now had them in his possession. Dalton decided to alter his mission plan fast. Grabbing the bridge satellite phone, Dalton located General Rusk at Guantanamo and briefed him on the latest developments. Moments later General Rusk said, "We'll have an Apache helicopter armed and over the *Mullet* in forty-two minutes, as you requested. I'll have video reconnaissance also beamed to the *Ravenwood* for us to assess the next step."

"Let's proceed with caution here, General. We don't yet know the warhead's stability," warned Dalton.

"Agreed."

EIGHT

ABOARD THE *DECADENCE*, EAST OF DEADMAN'S CAY, ENTERING THE EXUMA SOUND

THE small shoals and barrier islands gave visual and radar protection to Tarasov as he maneuvered his yacht through the archipelago. Entering the open water unseen was easier in daylight when many other vessels left port and continued their journeys. Therefore, Tarasov drifted, without engine power, for several hours, following the Caribbean currents, awaiting the break of day.

Yuri's plan was coming together with precision, and he would soon come into the biggest score in his career as an international arms merchant. Completing the sale, verifying the transfer of funds, and disposing of Sergey Kreftkova remained on his list. The bridge lit up with an incoming radio message. It was the *Mullet* calling.

"Yuri, this is Augustus. We have just been flown over by a U.S. chopper, looks like an Apache, and he's trying to communicate with us."

Yuri heard a loud explosion over the radio. "Augustus,

what the hell is going on?" The speaker continued to produce disturbing sounds.

"They just fired a rocket over our bow! Hold a minute."

Yuri clicked the radio to receive and held it open. After several seconds he heard the unmistakable sound of a missile launch and a second after that, a huge, rumbling explosion came over the radio speakers. Yuri waited until he could not stand the suspense any longer. "Augustus, come in. What is going on? Are you being boarded?"

The silence returned. Then finally Augustus said, "My men just shot down the Apache; it exploded and hit the sea, just off my bow."

Yuri's mind was spinning in confusion. How could the Americans have picked up on his plans so fast? Maybe it was a random fly-by from the Coast Guard, although they don't fly Apaches, and why did they fire a rocket over the *Mullet's* bow? He was forced to believe the Americans knew more than Sergey had admitted he told him. They perhaps even knew the nukes' location to have tracked the *Mullet* some nine hours after the recovery. Yuri's thoughts returned to the *Mullet*. "Augustus, how close are you to the deep-water drop point for the missiles?"

"About twelve miles to the northeast from my current position," said Augustus.

THE TARASOV SOLUTION

"Set a fast course for the shortest route to deep water, and dump the missiles."

"It won't be under the cover of night, you realize," warned Augustus.

"Damn it, man! You've shot down a U.S. military helicopter. Get rid of the evidence they think you have. Do it soon."

"Yeah, I get it. I'll radio back when done. Out."

Dalton and his Seal team leader were on the *Ravenwood* bridge monitoring the *Mullet*. The satellite images had been combined with the real-time video from the Apache as it made its first pass over the *Mullet*. Several attempts to contact the ship over the radio were either ignored or not received. Rusk ordered the rocket shot over *Mullet*'s bow, hoping to force a radio contact. The surface-to-air handheld Stinger came from the ship's port side, flew no more than 150 yards, and struck the Apache in the engine exhaust, causing it to explode into a violent fireball. It hit the sea and sank in eighteen seconds, no crew appearing to have survived. Rusk went ballistic and began organizing a "seek and kill" response. Dalton, however, was able to calm the general and suggest a new plan.

RICHARD TREVAE

The door to Sergey's cabin was locked from the inside, yet Ivana's master key refused to turn the lock. She stepped back as a large man kicked the door in with three swift and powerful thrusts of his left leg. A shattered arm chair fell to the floor in the doorway from where it had jammed the door handle. Knife in hand, Ivana went looking for Sergey, although he was nowhere to be found. "Check the ship!" demanded Ivana. "Check everywhere right now. He's got to be hiding." She checked the small room and found no clue as to Sergey's whereabouts. Then she glanced into the bath. The small porthole was broken, smashed by a nearby fire extinguisher. Blood streaked the circular brass frame, only twenty inches in diameter.

"Clever old Russian," Ivana murmured. She looked at the blood. "Sergey must have cut himself on the broken glass during his escape."

Ivana caught up with Yuri on the bridge and said, "Sergey decided he didn't care for our company and jumped ship during the night."

"What? How? He was locked in his room."

"He managed to break the bathroom porthole window and escape. It appears he was bleeding."

Yuri looked away from Ivana then out to sea and

said, "Bleeding in these shark-laden waters, he probably saved me the chore of killing him."

Ivana watched Yuri, who began pacing the width of the bridge. He stopped, looked at her, and said, "Find out where we are on the details of Crusoe's whereabouts, and check out that niece of Kreftkova's, Carolyn McCabe. If he does somehow survive, he'll try to contact one of those two for sure, and I want to get there first. Now move."

Floating since hours before dawn Sergey looked in every direction; he saw no boats. He was swimming with one arm as the other, still bleeding from a long, shallow cut, clutched a life vest hastily grabbed as he left the *Decadence*.

NINE

THE big yacht moved along at fourteen knots with a leeward wind and less than a two-foot sea. The *Decadence* was in the main route between the Bimini Islands and Andros Island to the west. Yuri had turned the bridge over to his first officer and head of his security group while he and Ivana enjoyed the weather on the aft deck. Overnight the yacht underwent dramatic changes to look much different. A full-length blue stripe some eighteen inches in depth appeared a few feet below the deck line after a white shrink-wrap cover was removed. The name was changed to *Lady Cadence* by masking a several original letters, and the flag colors were changed from Spanish to American. Deck canvas of a rich, dark blue replaced the former white materials. Comparing the two photographs, one would not suggest it was the same ship. Boats were everywhere with at least a dozen or so always in sight. Many were headed for the Labor Day celebrations along the U.S. eastern coastline planned during the Blinikov trip to the States.

The bombs were fitted with new detonation controllers, which could be set by a remote through a variety of signals. In three days, the American president would be meeting with Russian president Blinikov at the White House and spending time visiting certain sites in the area. Both men viewed the meeting as a new turn in U.S.-Russian relations, and as a result, expectations were high in both countries. Blinikov had been a competitive racing sailor during his college years and held a love for the water and wind, as did Conner, who was an avid summer sailor. The trip was broadcast as a four-day event comprising an initial meeting to lay some groundwork for their staffs, two days of quality time for the men, followed by a day of final meetings and announcements on common accords. Yuri planned to have his bomb placed at the Chesapeake Bay shore close enough to take them both out and damaging the Washington, D.C., area. One of his two twenty-seven foot ship-to-shore shuttle boats had one bomb positioned just ahead of the engine beneath the floor-deck. If forthcoming information was accurate, both Conner and Blinikov would be traveling together within a quarter mile of the blast center, assuring a kill, claimed Yuri's nuclear expert.

RICHARD TREVAE

The *Mullet* set a new course to the north and increased speed to average fourteen knots. The crew of sailors and mercenaries were pumped up following the encounter with the Apache. All knew that unless they could dump their cargo, they would be charged as criminals in support of terrorism. Without the missiles on board, there was nothing to connect them directly to Tarasov's plans. Shooting down an Apache, however, was a different matter. Without question, the U.S. military, at a minimum, was going to intercept the ship and demand an explanation. The worst scenario carried images of the *Mullet* being torpedoed any second and vanishing beneath the sea. Only a feeble attempt declaring self-defense from an unknown intruder could explain the helicopter loss. Augustus was not at all optimistic he could get out clean on this problem. Depending on what the military sent in response to the Apache loss, the *Mullet* might just be able to fight their way to deep water considering all the armaments they had stowed. Augustus didn't have to wait long.

A voice came over the speaker system in the bridge. "Incoming aircraft from the west at a high rate of speed." It was Augustus's watch commander, Tully, and he was pointing to faint objects near the horizon leading smoke trails. Another message erupted from Tully. "Two miles out and closing fast."

"Get the SAMs on deck and armed," yelled Augustus. Several men grabbed at hatches, lifted green, metal boxes containing the surface-to-air missiles.

Seconds later an F-22 Raptor streaked by at two hundred feet over the *Mullet* and created a deafening roar as it cut hard skyward and looped back to the two AH-64 Apache attack helicopters following close behind the ship. A radio signal came in. "This is the U.S. Navy. *Mullet* you are ordered to stop engines. We intend to board you. Stop engines immediately."

Any thoughts of defeating the arsenal of weapons now settling in on the *Mullet* vanished as Augustus surveyed the surroundings: an F-22 Raptor buzzing the ship and a couple of heavily armed Apache helicopters hovering on port and starboard sides with side gunners aiming 50-caliber cannons at him. A roar came from below and behind him as Augustus turned to see the familiar streak of smoke left by a SAM in flight. One of his deck men fired his shoulder-mounted missile, however it missed at the short range and plunged into the sea. Three seconds later the starboard-side Apache fired rockets and guns on the *Mullet*. An explosion started on deck from a diesel tank, which spread to the canvas covering the missiles. The gunfire continued and a huge, secondary explosion erupted from the SS-5 closest to the Apache. The blast ripped a huge hole in the *Mullet's* deck and sidewall. She listed hard to the starboard and began to take on water. The crew were scattering for the few lifeboats when a third explosion from the remaining SS-5 engulfed the deck and blew the bridge apart. Augustus was knocked to the staircase, his arm black with burns and a broken leg, and he fell to the deck level. The ship was going down fast abandoning many of the crew to the water, which was ablaze from a diesel oil slick.

The *Mullet* went down ninety-three seconds after the first explosion. All of the crew were either drowned or killed in the explosions. Augustus, being somewhat protected in the metal staircase, survived. The Apache Seal team rescued him from the sea as the massive *Mullet* stern began to roll and sink.

Dalton and his Seal team leader watched the satellite coverage and the real-time cameras aboard the Apaches display the sudden and fiery end to the *Mullet* and crew. General Rusk had given the approval to the chopper pilots to fire if fired upon. Considering the arms at the *Mullet's* disposal, the assault had been expected. The destruction of the missiles aboard the *Mullet* was not anticipated and left several troubling questions for Dalton.

THE TARASOV SOLUTION

He saw the two Apaches hovering over the burning water, looking for survivors, when a Seal loaded a man into the lifting cradle and rode with it up to the helicopter's open side bay. Dalton grabbed the radio and said, "Lieutenant Crane, this is Dalton Crusoe. Can you identify the survivor you just lifted from the sea?"

After a pause the Apache pilot said, "Hold for one." A few moments later, the speaker broke with, "Sir, it appears to be the captain, named Augustus, but he's unconscious and injured."

"Lieutenant, can you treat him? It is very important he remain alive for interrogation. Can you fly him to the *Ravenwood* for medical care?"

"Yes, if you maintain a steady course towards my position, I can drop him off in about twenty-two minutes, although my fuel will be low."

"Understood. We'll increase speed to shorten the time to meet."

Dalton had to learn exact details of what, if anything, Augustus recovered and had stored on his deck.

ABOARD THE RAVENWOOD

The Apache made it to the *Ravenwood* at the expected time and landed long enough to unload Augustus, refuel, and take off for Guantanamo. The *Mullet* captain was still unconscious and was being treated by onboard medical staff below decks. Captain Thomson had taken the ship to the coordinates Sergey transmitted while still on the *Decadence*. The shallow water allowed for easy examination by divers, once they knew the precise location. No cocoons were found, as Dalton expected, although the seafloor showed signs of where two large, cylindrical objects had been lying. Recent satellite photographs and camera images from the *Mullet*'s last location showed no signs of missiles floating on the surface. Only an oil slick covering the explosion site was visible from the air. Any cargo, along with the ship itself, was destroyed and resting some four thousand feet below the surface.

Dalton was set up in the ship's command and communications center, waiting for the videoconferencing to begin. The extensive defensive action taken by the navy was best described as overkill, although Dalton knew he couldn't make that case. Besides, it didn't help the real problem of finding out where the warheads were and what was planned for them. He had arranged for Ed Kosko, President Conner, General Rusk, and Randolph Pickler to join in and get updated. Wilson and Cotter were present, tending to the electronics and supporting Dalton with data. A nervous tension was evident in the communications center. As the wall-sized LCD display came to life, the four men were shown, one following the other, as separate split-screen views.

Ed Kosko began with, "Dalton, it appears you and General Rusk have had quite a day so far." Ed's light-hearted tone was a welcome change from the somber mood Dalton and his team were experiencing.

"Yes, that's true, Ed, and I want to make certain we all understand the issues we now face."

Jumping in without fanfare, Pickler stated, "Is it true we lost an Apache helicopter based out of Gitmo when it was fired upon?"

"Yes, that's correct, and the three crew aboard were all killed," reminded General Rusk with a clear tone of annoyance.

"Let me take you all through this from the beginning," announced Dalton. The group seemed to appreciate the take-charge style Dalton used. The president confirmed the feeling by saying, "Yes, Mr. Crusoe, please proceed."

"We have strong evidence the Kreftkova information is true and that a Russian arms merchant, Yuri Tarasov, is pursuing the information for the purpose of recovering the missiles and warheads. Following our interview with Kreftkova, two days ago in Cuba he was abducted, we believe by agents of Tarasov, and taken to his yacht, the *Decadence*."

Pickler barged in again. "Were we not trying to provide safety and asylum to Kreftkova while you confirmed his story?"

"That is also true, and we were in the process of arranging his passage to the U.S. through Gitmo hours after his disappearance."

The president again took control of the meeting, saying, "Continue, Mr. Crusoe, with your presentation."

Pickler received a look from the president and backed off of his probing of Dalton.

"Yesterday, while aboard the *Ravenwood* en route to intercept the *Decadence*, we received a third-party communication in a Morse code message believed sent from Sergey Kreftkova." Dalton reached for a piece of paper and read, "'Deliver D. Crusoe (break) Gitmo, (break) *Decadence* bound for 21°, 11', 54" north by 76°, 12', 13" west.' Currently we're at those coordinates and have seen depressions on the shallow seafloor representing, we believe, the resting spots of two SS-5 IRBMs."

"Where are the missiles now, JD?" asked Ed.

"We monitored a salvage vessel, the *Mullet;* coming through the Caicos strait to the same location the *Decadence* was headed. We believe it was being used by Tarasov to find and recover the missiles and their warheads. We tracked the ship by satellite surveillance, and it showed two cylindrical objects on its deck covered in canvas just sixteen hours ago."

THE TARASOV SOLUTION

"So you believe the missiles do exist and were recovered by this *Mullet* vessel for Tarasov?" inquired President Conner.

"Yes, that appears to be the case. When we intercepted the *Mullet* with General Rusk's Seal team, they attacked and during the return fire, the ship exploded. However, the captain survived after treatment on the *Ravenwood.* If he regains consciousness, we will interrogate him."

"If he dies, can we otherwise confirm the missiles were destroyed and the nukes rendered neutral from the debris field?" asked Ed Kosko.

The general answered that question. "Very doubtful as the water there is over four thousand feet deep. Over the next several months, we may be able to send diving bells down with cameras to survey the floor, although finding anything definitive on the warheads is doubtful," offered the general.

Cotter and Wilson confirmed the point when Dalton looked in their direction for input.

"So what is our current confidence level that the threat of these warheads getting into terrorist hands is nil?" The president waited for an answer.

Even Pickler was content to let someone else handle this one. Dalton collected his thoughts and began, "We must assume based on the earlier positions of the *Decadence* and the *Mullet* that Tarasov has inspected the missiles. He may have even removed the warheads and either left them on the *Mullet* or moved them to the *Decadence*."

Pickler could not control himself. "Is that possible in the time they had, knowing the task of dismantling a nuclear warhead from its missile?"

"Sir, I'm certain based on our own experiments that a three- or four-man nuclear team could have removed both warheads," supplied Cotter.

"That is why we're seeking naval and Coast Guard help to locate and sequester the *Decadence* as soon as possible," declared Dalton.

Sensing the intellect and skill of Dalton Crusoe, the president directed his next remark, in a personal manner, to Dalton. "DJ, I want you, through Ed Kosko, to lead this effort from here on out, with support from General Rusk and this office. Is that clear?"

Pickler looked liked a scorned schoolgirl as Dalton confidently said, "Yes, sir, it is."

"That's all for now, I want an updated briefing in twelve hours."

The entire group acknowledged him. The air hung heavy with a sense of immense danger if the warheads could not be found or proven to be destroyed.

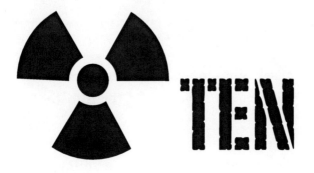

TEN

ABOARD THE *RAVENWOOD*, 10:10 A.M.

AS the sea rolled in rhythm, the big Coast Guard cutter carved a straight line on an east-southeast heading at twelve knots. The wake trailing the vessel was frothy white for at least a quarter mile behind the stern and looked more and more fluorescent as the morning sun grew stronger. The weather was pleasant, and the sea temperature averaged seventy-two degrees. Dalton was going over the satellite intel, trying to locate the *Decadence,* when the ship's speaker system came alive. "Mr. Crusoe, we have sighted a man floating in the water approximately three hundred yards just off our starboard bow. Could you please report to the bridge?"

Without any prompting, Cotter and Wilson grabbed their satellite phones and followed Dalton to the bridge. Captain Thomson stood outside the bridge in the starboard-side navigator's perch, scanning the sea. Dalton raised a pair of binoculars and looked into the calm sea, which was reflecting the sunlight as a steady stream of flashes. "That is Sergey Kreftkova out there."

Dalton studied the man to detect any signs of movement, however there were none.

"Full stop," ordered the captain. Several junior officers repeated the command, and the powerful diesel engines fell silent.

"Lower an inflatable rescue boat, starboard side, in twenty seconds." The captain's orders were acted on without hesitation.

Dalton went down below to the water-level embarkation platform. The Zodiac rescue craft was just leaving the *Ravenwood* hull when Dalton heard Cotter say, "There he is at one o'clock."

Sergey Kreftkova bobbed like a cork with his life jacket strapped to only his left arm and waist. Moments later, he was hauled aboard the Zodiac and brought to the loading platform.

"He's gone into shock. Take him to the sick bay now and notify the ship's surgeon." Dalton suddenly realized he was issuing orders on a ship he had no real authority to command. Nevertheless, the seaman assisting the rescue carried Sergey to sick bay as instructed.

Sergey was in rough shape. His right arm was cut about seven inches from the shoulder to the elbow although not too deep, so the blood flow had slowed. His body was struggling to maintain proper temperature during the cool, dark, early morning, despite the warm water. The doctor hooked up a saline drip to rehydrate him and dressed the wound. It would be some time, the doctor felt, before we would return to consciousness, if at all.

Dalton returned to the communications center and checked on the satellite search for the *Decadence*. No sightings, communications, or information of any kind had been found. Dalton thought, *I'm waiting on the recovery of two men both near death to learn where two nuclear bombs are located. No time for this.*

TWELVE MILES EAST OF ANDROS ISLAND, ABOARD THE *LADY CADENCE*

The new look for the *Decadence* was remarkable. Not only had it changed its colors and flag scheme, the name, back deck canvas, and crew attire were also altered. The small helicopter had its blades folded together and was lowered below decks for storage. Yuri had maintained complete radio and satellite phone silence since leaving the *Mullet*. A shuttle boat had been fitted with one of the bombs and was ready to launch when they arrived near the marina in Chesapeake Bay. The *Lady Cadence* moved along in harmony with four other boats of similar size toward the United States eastern coast. In two days, the Friday before Labor Day, the yacht would enter the populated bay waters and close in on the location marked as "ground zero" by Yuri and his nuclear team.

The press was all over the news of new Russian president Blinikov accepting an invitation to visit the United States as guest of the charismatic President Jerome Conner. The fact that it came only months after Blinikov had taken power in an election that survived corruption and still carried the mandate of democratic change by a five-to-four margin captured the world's attention. Most pundits were speculating that an era of open cooperation between the United States, other Western democracies, and Russia was at hand. The political potential meant improved trade for Russia, with its massive oil reserves, and another strong partner to help in the war on terrorism. China even saw the new Russian president as a man of real change and not an adversary. The schedule for Blinikov's visit was well publicized, and it blended serious diplomatic sessions with true leisure time for both men to enjoy and get to know each other.

Yuri Tarasov had followed the sailing trip news coverage for weeks and knew this was the best time for him to settle all concerns about pressure the new Russian leader was putting on operators such as he. Including President Conner as collateral damage was just an unexpected bonus. The idea of achieving a seismic shift

THE TARASOV SOLUTION

in world political power and covering his involvement through the use of weapons missing from any documented inventories gave Yuri a strong sense of security.

The twenty-seven-foot tender was really a high-powered pleasure craft meant for water skiing, casual boating close to shore, and of course, a shuttle from the yacht to ports. Its current cargo, a ten-kiloton nuclear warhead adapted for use off its missile, was well hidden and controlled by several mechanisms to assure detonation at precisely the right moment. As the *Lady Cadence* rounded Cape Fear on the barrier island off North Carolina, the tender, *Flipper I,* with a driver and a nuclear scientist would arrive at the Chesapeake Bay area in eighteen hours on the Saturday evening before Labor Day. Yuri had reserved a slip a quarter mile from the docking location for the presidential sailboat *Windancer,* an older, forty-four foot C&C fully equipped with all the communications and defense equipment a presidential ship might require. The president got about four weekends a year to enjoy it, and that was always with the accompaniment of six Secret Service men, made to look like sailors, and a presidential helicopter always within a mile and up one thousand feet in the air. Nevertheless, President Conner accepted the security impediments if it allowed his sailing time. Blinikov was also an avid sailor and missed his younger days sailing off Estonia, where his father's family had lived. The Monday sail planned for Conner and Blinikov was perfect and fell into place for Yuri Tarasov's plan.

Yuri's men were fueling the *Flipper I* and making last-minute checks on the condition of the ten-kiloton nuke that had been mounted beneath the floor boards just in beyond the engine. It was fitted with a controller that allowed it to be remotely detonated either at a predetermined time or by a satellite phone signal. A radio command could accelerate the detonation wait period to only two minutes. As a safeguard to being discovered, it was also designed with a default destruct command which would explode the device however not initiate a nuclear reaction, if tampering were attempted without entering the proper commands in the remote. After a final manual arming of the device, Yuri or his men could select the detonation sequence desired from a cell or satellite phone call. Yuri's experts were instructed to assure that either the device would detonate the nuclear bomb as planned or it would be destroyed in conventional fashion and look as if the fuel tank exploded. With the command controls set in the remote detonator, Yuri felt comfortable he could mask his involvement in an aborted assassination attempt by having the default explosion appear as a typical boating accident. There would be radiation traces, for sure, although not enough to raise fears that a ten-kiloton device was involved.

Looking down at the sleek Scarab tender as it hit the water, Yuri said, "You have eighteen hours to make the Chesapeake marina and settle into your slip, so don't waste any time on the sea. You'll have to average about fifteen knots to arrive on schedule. Do you understand?"

The two men in the boat looked up. Taros said, "We'll call you for the helicopter pickup after we hit the marina slip."

Yuri checked his watch and waved as the Scarab growled, making wake froth, and started its run to the north-northwest.

ELEVEN

DALTON was struggling to organize his next move. He prepared to share some startling news with Ed Kosko ahead of the conference call with the president. Augustus had been hit by a shock wave that resulted from the last missile hit on the *Mullet*. It knocked him unconscious with little more than minor flesh wounds from the explosions. Over the past thirty minutes, he had regained consciousness for brief periods and did not know where he was or his medical condition. Among the babble that came from Augustus were "... call Tarasov ... confirm missiles were dumped ... the missiles were dumped ... protect warheads." Based on the infirmary reports, Augustus said this or something very similar to it several times. Finally the ship's doctor called Captain Thomson and Dalton to the infirmary. Dalton arrived first. Augustus was muttering and thrashing about for a several moments then settled down to a sleep state for a couple of minutes. Without warning, he tried to sit up and spoke again. "Get me a phone . . . must call Tarasov now . . . missiles are dumped . . . you must protect the warheads . . . protect the warheads."

Dalton looked over the bed and saw Captain Thomson also staring at the semiconscious man. "Did he just say, 'protect the warheads'?" Dalton needed confirmation for what he thought he heard.

"Yes, that is exactly what I heard."

"Captain, we need to locate the *Decadence* as fast as possible. I believe Augustus was able to remove the warheads and move them off his ship before we arrived."

Back up on the control room deck, Dalton had organized the *Ravenwood*'s communications group along with Cotter and Wilson to participate in the call to Kosko.

The attentive, young communications officer took charge and announced, "The satellite link to Mr. Kosko at NSA is coming on-screen, sir."

Dalton looked up and Ed appeared bigger than life on the mammoth wall video. He was in his office, and Pickler was sitting near him in a visitor's chair scribbling violently on a notepad.

"From your voice mail, it sounds like you've had an eventful day so far, Dalton."

"Yes, I'd say that is the way we would describe it." He

looked to Cotter and Wilson, who were nodding their heads in sober agreement.

"Ed, you know we have Sergey Kreftkova and Augustus, the *Mullet* captain, onboard in sick bay."

"Yes, of course. Any change in their conditions as yet?"

"No, not enough to say they are conversant or even stable enough to assure their survival, but Augustus was heard muttering some strange . . . sentence fragments, while moving in and out of consciousness."

Pickler scribbled even faster, not even looking up at the screen showing Dalton and his group. Ed waited for the next words.

"Augustus said, 'protect the warheads' or 'protect warheads' as well as asking for a phone to tell Tarasov, 'the missiles were dumped.'" Dalton reached for several satellite photos. "I can't imagine why his mind would disassociate the warheads and missiles, even in a semi-conscious state, unless in reality they were disassociated." Holding up the satellite photos, Dalton pointed out the clear image of cylindrical objects on the *Mullet* deck too similar to not be the missiles. "We have scaled the cylinders using known dimensions from staircases, engine, and exhaust stacks for this particular type vessel and have found the length to be about 1.25 meters shorter than the expected length of the Soviet SS-5 IRBMs." Reaching for another document, Dalton held up the assembly drawing for the missiles and pointed to the nose. "The nose cone shroud is exactly 1.5 meters, flange to tip. When removed from the missile body and not connected to the cone, the overlapping inner flange extends 0.25 meters beyond the missile body itself."

Pickler and Kosko both squirmed in their chairs and focused in on Dalton.

"I believe this essentially confirms the warheads were not lost when the *Mullet* went down, although were removed earlier and transferred to Tarasov's yacht before we arrived at the drop coordinates." Dalton paused then said, "The nose cones were never reattached to the missiles. Probably they ran out of time."

Ed Kosko released a hint of a smile, looked to Pickler, and said, "Damn good work, JD, and I believe you've made your point to all of us."

Pickler stopped his scribbling and glanced at Kosko then resumed his note taking.

Ed looked into the video camera lens and said, "I'll handle the conference call with the president along with Mr. Pickler and report the findings. What is your next move?"

"I need your permission to retask several satellites to cover the possible range the *Decadence* may have traveled since her last sighting so we can find her as soon as possible."

"You've got that. Anything else you need now?"

"Just luck. Tarasov's reputation suggests he's capable of any act of self-preservation."

"You seem to be saying he may not be trying to sell these bombs to terrorist networks," Ed inquired.

"Well, let's just say that if he has two nuclear bombs on his yacht, is heading to the east U.S. coast and President Blinikov is also headed to the U.S. to meet with President Conner, we might want to consider other outcomes than him selling the warheads."

Pickler could not contain himself any longer. "Are you saying the president is in danger from this madman arms merchant?"

"I'm saying Blinikov appears to represent the kind of change in Russia which could find Tarasov in his sights." Dalton stared into the video camera at Ed. "The financial gain to Tarasov through selling is certainly attractive, however eliminating a new, powerful adversary must also be very tempting."

Ed motioned with his hand to silence Pickler before he could speak again. "Dalton, find this yacht. If you are right—and I now fear that you are—we have only days before Tarasov would make his move."

Pickler scribbled another note on his pad, stood up, and excused himself abruptly.

THE TARASOV SOLUTION

ENTERING CHESAPEAKE BAY, 5:00 A.M., SATURDAY

Taros and nuclear scientist Ian arrived at the marina slip at 11:52 p.m. on Saturday, just ahead of schedule. The harbor areas were still busy and full of sounds from the clanging of lines on masts, sails rippling in the five-knot onshore wind, and laughter from the nearby vessels whose passengers were all enjoying the mild, seventy-one degree air and the full moon. Taros was the point man on the assignment for Yuri to position the boat and its lethal cargo near the anchor point for the president's sailboat, *Windancer.* Ian, Yuri's well-paid technical support, was there to ensure the bomb and its complex detonation controls worked properly. Since Taros had cultivated a very normal American accent, he handled all the ship-to-shore communications with the marina manager.

"*Flipper I* arriving for slip assignment. Please come in. Over."

A few crackles on the open mike and Taros heard, "*Flipper I* your berth is C-21. Turn left, then right at the third row of slips. Check in when docked."

"Roger that. Thanks," Taros replied.

Many boaters were still up, drinking and soaking up the mild weather dominating the Labor Day weekend. A few waved and tipped a glass to the sleek, twenty-seven-foot Bayliner as it moved slowly to slip C-21, emitting a low, powerful rumble from its engine. Taros maneuvered the craft with skill and looked every bit the typical weekend sailor as he tied off the boat to the mooring posts. Ian stayed onboard and attempted to look like the less-experienced first mate. His clumsiness and general appearance suggested an accountant or research scientist rather than an avid boater.

"Weather sure is great, isn't it?" asked Taros as he greeted the marina manager.

Without a clue to Taros's actual background or nationality, the overweight old salt looked up and said, "Yeah, and it should continue for several more days. When do you leave again?"

"Next Tuesday, after Labor Day, say about, 3 p.m. Is that all right?"

"That will be fine. Enjoy the area during your stay."

Taros smiled, paid the slip fees, and left the marina office. *So far so good,* he thought.

Yuri was entering the south end of Chesapeake Bay along with a score of other boats, some sailing, some under power. He was well disguised from his appearance less than twenty-four hours ago. To the casual boater, he looked like another wealthy, weekend boater out on the water. Patrolling the waters was a midsized Boston Whaler Coast Guard boat, and it approached on the port side about four hundred yards out. It was exiting the Potomac and turning east to enter the bay near Cove Point. Yuri, relaxing on the foredeck, took the nearby microphone and told his shipmaster to slow the yacht to ten knots and maintain a straight course for Cove Point, Maryland. After ten minutes the Whaler was moving parallel with the *Lady Cadence* about 150 yards off the port side.

Ivana was dressed in a yellow bikini, floppy straw hat, and large sunglasses. Yuri was in a bathing suit and open silk shirt. They looked like the *nouveau riche* offering a respectful wave to the Coast Guard crew. Using binoculars to check out Ivana, the apparent captain waved back in response. The Whaler then increased speed, pulling ahead of the *Lady Cadence,* and was lost in boat traffic.

Yuri surveyed the surroundings and thought how well his plan was coming together.

TWELVE

ABOARD THE *RAVENWOOD*

A total of four advanced spy satellites were retasked to search for the *Decadence*. Dalton had Cotter and Wilson talking with NSA headquarters as vessel after vessel was found, indentified, and checked out. The NSA images were downloaded to Dalton in real time; however, the *Ravenwood* lacked the full sophistication to cross-reference the size, make, or look of the targets with other data sources for information on ownership or registry. At least fourteen boats fit the general description of the *Decadence,* with another seven almost fitting the yacht's profile and characteristics. Dalton had to narrow the options down fast, and he couldn't do it from the communications room sequestered in the *Ravenwood.*

Cotter interrupted Dalton's thoughts. "Sir, we have arranged through NSA to have a long-range navy helicopter located near Miami fly out, pick us up, and head towards the Chesapeake Bay area. It can be here in twenty-six minutes if we continue on the current course."

"Great. We'll need to take that option. We must get over these suspect vessels ahead of when the *Ravenwood* could get there. Set it up." Dalton looked again to the NSA screen of boating activity on his five-hundred-mile scan and shook his head. *Where is Tarasov going?*

The sleek chopper's thundering engines announced the on-time arrival of the helicopter as it hovered over the *Ravenwood's* fore-deck. It was a navy combat model stripped down and loaded with communications gear—not very lethal anymore although fast and with impressive range. Dalton, Wilson, and Cotter jumped onboard and settled in for the three-hundred-mile-plus trip before the suspect ships could be observed. Cotter got the computers fired up and connected to NSA satellites, which showed a split screen from four satellites, each monitoring various parts of Chesapeake Bay.

Ed Kosko called back and informed Dalton about the meeting he and Pickler had had with President Conner. The security was increased around the president, yet his schedule was firm, and he would not allow it to be revised unless a verifiable threat was confirmed.

At this point all Dalton knew was a madman arms merchant discovered and recovered two nuclear warheads. Whether the weapons were usable or not remained an open question. Tarasov's plans for the warheads were also not known. Dalton had postulated a possibility that, while contrary to Tarasov's prior behavior, made startling sense when considering the Russian president's threatening rhetoric. Pickler was right, even if irritating, that some measure of additional precautions needed to be taken for the president's safety.

The *Lady Cadence* drifted into the center channel serving the Chesapeake Bay inlet just before noon the Sunday preceding Labor Day. Yuri held off all communication between his yacht and the two men he dispatched on *Flipper I*. Instead, he sent a text message to Taros over new cell phones:

Pick up for crew scheduled for 2100 hours today at Cove Point helipad. Confirm fishing trip a success.

Several minutes later Yuri's cell phone buzzed, and a text message appeared:

Very successful fishing trip. Catch in storage now and ready for processing.

P.S. Close to retrieving the other parcel you called about.

THE TARASOV SOLUTION

These were the hidden word clues that the tender made it to its slip and the bomb was ready for detonation programming. Yuri looked again at his cell phone, snapped the cover shut, and thought, *Two more days and my life can go back to the way it was without the fear of Blinikov interfering.*

THIRTEEN

THE rich, Caribbean blue waters gave way to the deeper, darker water leading to Chesapeake Bay. The temperature had risen over the past two hours from a mild sixty-one degrees as they left the *Ravenwood* to a sunny, balmy seventy-seven degrees at noon. Wilson was busy taking detailed, high-speed photographs of the vessels beneath them as they flew over each ship selected for a closer look. Dalton was analyzing the photos for features that would confirm the presence of the *Decadence*. A cluster of power boats were moving near a pack of a dozen sailboats, keeping pace with them and observing their crafty maneuvers tacking in and out to maintain a course. At first inspection, Dalton rejected the *Lady Cadence* photos, although as he waited for more photos, he again reviewed the eleven boats they had already flown over. Something caught his eye about the *Lady Cadence*, although he wasn't certain what. He retrieved the earlier photos taken more than twenty-four hours ago from NSA satellite data on the *Decadence* and used a magnifying glass to look at the radar equipment on the communications arch high above the command bridge. Two radar arms were visible. The high-speed camera caught the port side rotating arm as though it were still. Lettering was not visible on the radar arm except from above, and it read, *Maintain One Meter Clear.* Dalton looked through the magnifying lens again and strained his eyes to see more detail. The letter *e* in *One* was half eroded away from sun and weather. The flashback came in a burst as Dalton was certain he'd seen the feature in recent photos. Dalton sorted through the collection of photos and placed his hands on the shot he was looking for among the two dozen taken from the chopper. The yacht was about the size of the *Decadence* although not marked the same at all. Dalton's mind played with the two names for a moment then realized the letter similarity between *Decadence* and *Lady Cadence.* The fonts were also the same style and size. Looking carefully at the *Lady Cadence* recent photo Dalton could see lettering on the port side radar arm yet could not read it, even with the magnifying glass. The name similarities had to be more than coincidence.

"Cotter!" yelled Dalton, trying to overcome the engine roar inside the chopper.

"Yes, what is it? Have you found something?" Cotter approached the table area where Dalton had the photographs displayed.

"This photo is marked with a time stamp of 11:15 a.m. today, so we flew over this ship about thirty minutes ago. We need to go back, fly over again from a high altitude although with maximum resolution to check out the radar antenna markings."

"I'll instruct the pilot to turn around." Cotter jumped to the cockpit.

The big aircraft pulled hard to the starboard and increased speed to the south. The pilot climbed from fifteen hundred feet to almost twenty-five hundred feet as they approached the cluster of yachts seen earlier among the sailboats. Wilson and Cotter were both using binoculars to catch sight of the *Lady Cadence*. In the distance, the armada of sporting watercraft appeared.

Cotter spoke first, "I think I have her; three o'clock on the starboard side, a mile out."

Dalton ordered the pilot to take a wide path around and behind the yacht to avoid any possible detection. Twenty seconds later, the chopper turned hard, reversing course, and was behind the *Lady Cadence*. Dalton looked down through binoculars, and the same image came into view: *Maintain One Meter Clear* with the same wear on the *e* in *One*. "We have her!" Dalton exclaimed. "Follow behind her route and record her movements with the high-speed cameras."

Dalton retrieved his cell phone which had been

turned off when he was far out to sea on the *Ravenwood*. A quick update to Ed was in order. Dalton's cell phone powered up and vibrated. A text message came in: *Missed you last night. Please call. Carolyn.* The time stamp was 9:48 a.m. EST.

Carolyn was concerned although not overly so. Dalton had never failed to keep a date before, however many times he was late. She had arrived the evening before at 4:38 p.m. and opened up the twelve-hundred-square-foot, open-air beach house. The weather was just as she had hoped: low humidity, mid-sixties at night then warming to the high seventies during the day. By 9:30 p.m., she was getting anxious waiting for JD. She grabbed the novel she had been reading, which was about a sixteenth-century English queen's maid who overheard some scandalous conversation about her queen and set out to discover the truth. An easy read for Carolyn and a nice diversion from advanced financial analysis of credit swaps. She slipped off to sleep, imagining her next few days with Dalton walking the firm, Atlantic beach sand under the warm sun.

At 9:45 a.m. the sky was already a brilliant blue with only a faint residue of white clouds near the sunrise horizon. Surprisingly she slept very well alone at the beach house, expecting at anytime a call would announce Dalton's imminent arrival. However the phone never rang, and she had fallen into a deep, restful sleep with her novel still open on the bed. Now, however, her mind was imagining all sorts of nasty explanations. She sent a text message to his phone. Suddenly the house phone rang and Carolyn ran to it and said, "This had better be you. I was getting worried."

The phone remained quiet; only the sound of an open line was detectable.

"Dalton, is that you?" Still no voice on the other end came forth.

A moment later a male voice said, "Sorry, wrong number."

Taros hung up the public phone located less than a mile away from the beach house, felt for his Walther PPK 9 mm, and lit another cigarette. He looked down the quiet beach road serving the ocean for miles, checked his watch, and thought, *Would you like a little company, honey?*

FOURTEEN

OCEAN CITY, MARYLAND, AT THE BEACH HOUSE

THE one-mile walk on the beach took less than thirty minutes, although time seemed to stall without any word from Dalton. As she entered the beach house, shut the screen door behind herself, and removed her sweatshirt, she looked again to the phone: no messages. Remembering she had texted Dalton from her cell phone, she opened her purse, still lying on the kitchen table, and began digging for it. For a moment she felt strangely distracted however attributed it to the absence of Dalton.

The blow came from behind and caught her just above the right ear. Carolyn screamed in pain and fell to the floor. Lying there, she felt faint, and through blurred vision, she saw a man standing over her, preparing to tie her feet. Instincts leaping into action, she kicked at the man, hitting him in the groin and sending him back, cringing in pain. Still dizzy, Carolyn tried to get up and run for the door, however the man grabbed her foot, tripping her, and was on top of her in seconds, covering her mouth to muffle her screams and pressing the cold, steel barrel of his gun against her temple. He wore a ski mask and said in slightly accented English, "Move again and you're dead. Remain very, very still, and I will not hurt you." His hot breath smelled of cigarette smoke and booze.

Blood ran into Carolyn's eyes, and she could not see what her attacker was doing. She feared a rape, although at this point, the man seemed focused on restraining her. She offered little resistance as she tried to clear her eyes and focus her thoughts. The man was methodical and cold. Without a single word, he tied her hands and feet, taped her mouth, and stepped aside, out of listening range, to make a call.

Carolyn could only hear muffled words spoken however no information. Her head was pounding now with the shocking attack riveting her body with pain. Tears rolled down her cheeks. She felt hopeless, destined to a horrible death. Her mind created images of terrifying ordeals to come. The fear she felt dominated her thoughts. She struggled with the fear and worried that something had happened to Dalton. *Why didn't he call?* she asked herself. *He was the one who suggested the weekend at the beach house, and he always calls me when he's going to be late. Perhaps he was also attacked and bound . . . or dead.* Her life felt as if it were crumbling fast.

The masked man appeared again and with frightening efficiency held a small towel over her face forcing her to breathe irritating vapors. She struggled for a second, yet unable to escape the man's hand covering her mouth. Seconds later she was unconscious.

Taros loaded the limp woman into the backseat of his SUV. After retrieving Carolyn's phone and rummaging through her purse, Taros found a snapshot of Dalton and her taken at dinner on her last birthday, as noted on the back of the photo. He looked down at the motionless, attractive women lying in his SUV and for a moment thought about the pleasure he could enjoy if they went back inside. The money he was to receive and Yuri's temperament burst forth in his consciousness and brought him back to reality. He thought, *Get the job done as planned, and satisfy your desires at another time.* Taros jumped into the driver's seat, lit another cigarette, and drove slowly and directly to the helicopter pickup location.

Dalton managed to take time to address the message on his cell phone. His first glance at the text message caused him to feel horrible. He had let her down again. He had suggested the weekend at the beach house with

Carolyn after she had made his celebration so special just before he had to leave. He promised himself again he would be more attentive to her and not worry her about his late arrival. He dialed up Carolyn's cell phone, and it rang several times before jumping to voice mail. "I'm sorry, darling. I completely forgot about our plans. This assignment has become a matter of critical national security, and I must follow this through. Call me as soon as you can."

Dalton felt like a cad for leaving such a pathetic message and on her voice mail at that. He knew Carolyn would understand although also be hurt and cry over the way he had moved her aside for business issues. Yet this was different, and he wished he'd been able to say more to her in person. However, it was not to be. He tried to convince himself that she would understand when she heard the entire story. For now, Dalton had to get his mind back into the pursuit of Yuri Tarasov and his nukes. Time was running out. Still, his mind lingered over why Carolyn didn't answer her cell phone.

Taros heard Carolyn's cell phone ring, let it forward to voice mail, then played back Dalton's message. He turned the phone off, smiled to himself, and thought, *Yuri should pay me a bonus for this information.*

FIFTEEN

THE *Lady Cadence* was moving at seven knots north-northwest into Chesapeake Bay with several sailing ships and powerboats in tow in what looked like a long procession of wealthy party-goers getting ready for the weekend. Dalton and his team were keeping pace at one-half mile off her stern in the navy chopper. Dalton, in the air, and the NSA team, on the ground near Langley, analyzed the camera footage, which was coming in fast now. Dalton had alerted Ed that they had uncovered the *Decadence,* now under a new name *Lady Cadence,* and were tracking her.

The photo reconnaissance revealed nothing unusual about the *Lady Cadence;* the yacht was not trying to evade or hide its presence nor did it look like anything other than an expensive pleasure yacht. Even the crew activity that was visible seemed normal for a vessel of its size and equipment. The only clue to the vessel's true nature and its owner were the radar lettering matched through satellite photos to Yuri Tarasov's boat and the similarities between the boat names. The case to stop and board the *Lady Cadence* was weak, and Dalton had NSA lawyers checking precedent to find a way to allow the Coast Guard to halt, board, and inspect the yacht. Nothing Dalton's team came across confirmed the nuclear warheads were on the vessel, even though Dalton was sure in his gut Tarasov somehow managed through Augustus to retrieve the missiles from the sea, based on Sergey's coordinates, and had removed the warheads. Proving it, however, involved either an expensive, time-consuming dive program to search the *Mullet* wreckage or finding a way to legally board the *Lady Cadence* and inspect it. Ed suggested a bogus Coast Guard safety inspection and scan for a radiation leakage to locate the warheads. However, if Tarasov had the warheads, they were likely in a container to shield radiation exposure for the protection of him and his crew. Even with a specific safety reason for a search, the time allowed and the area inspected would be a very small portion of the entire ship.

Dalton thought hard about the ramifications for the U.S. and Russian presidents if his hypothetical scenario were to play out. Time was too short to use some Byzantine legal approach to justify an inspection, and a simple vessel takeover under the claim of national security hadn't yet passed the smell test for NSA lawyers. The case for delaying or altering the presidential plans for the Labor Day weekend meetings and activities

with the Russian president was not strong enough for
Pickler to convince the president. The secret service
were concerned although prepared to protect the president regardless of a decision to proceed with the sail.
Extra caution was the action step for now, and the pressure increased on Dalton to confirm or dispel his suspicions.

Dalton felt that comprehensive satellite surveillance
could now detail any and all moves the yacht made.
However, as the meeting for the two presidents neared,
and if the yacht made no moves to distance itself from
a detonation, then the warhead bombs were perhaps not
on the *Lady Cadence*. The NSA was running simula-
tions on one and both ten-kiloton bombs detonating
aboard the yacht and assessing the kill radius. The farther the yacht moved up into Chesapeake Bay, the more
the kill radius engulfed Washington, D.C., and other
large population centers. If Yuri was planning to position the yacht for maximum potential impact then he
was closing the distance quickly, assuring his own
death. Yuri Tarasov never portrayed himself as a martyr;
rather he was a criminal capitalist. Dalton reasoned the
bombs were not on the yacht and likely positioned
elsewhere, perhaps near shore. Both Augustus and
Sergey were still unconscious and in critical condition,
so they provided no intelligence as to Yuri's plans. The
real possibility remained that Yuri simply planned to

sell the bombs to the highest bidder, as his history suggested, although Dalton still felt the darker scenario involving a plan to kill Blinikov and President Conner was a serious possibility.

Cotter moved over to Dalton's bench seat midway down the chopper length and said, "What do we do if we let this ship deep into the bay and still don't have a legal reason to board her?"

Dalton looked up and said, "I'm not going to let that happen. I *know* he's got a bomb or two on that yacht, or nearby, and we're going to find them. If I'm wrong, it's my decision alone."

"No we're all in this with you." Cotter glanced at Wilson, who nodded his agreement.

NEAR COVE POINT, MARYLAND, 9 P.M.

The evening sky had darkened in two hours earlier. Taros had arrived a short time before that, at sunset. He stopped at the marina and picked up Ian, the nuclear technician, before arriving at the helicopter pickup site. He was hungry and tired from the four-hour drive around the bay to return to Cove Point. "Go get some food at that diner and bring it back here." Taros pointed to the small greasy spoon two hundred yards away with the lit sign that read *EAT* in pink letters above the roof.

"I'm not hungry and besides, the helicopter will be here in twenty minutes. Get something on the yacht," Ian replied.

"Damn it, man! I told you to get some food . . . a hot-dog, anything. Now go." Taros stared at Ian, who looked to the backseat and saw Carolyn wake, tugging at the rope restraining her feet and arms. Tape covered her mouth.

Ian glared, disgusted, put on a ball cap, opened the passenger door, and stepped out.

Taros looked to Carolyn and smiled, "You want anything, honey?"

Carolyn froze in her efforts. She was fully conscious now however with a pounding pain in her head. In the moments before fully waking from Taros' rage she had picked up pieces of the drama she had been dragged into as Ian and Taros rambled over the past few minutes. She knew she was headed to a yacht somewhere nearby after the helicopter arrived and that a boat, *Flipper I*, was secure in a slip, and the package was signal ready. Everything else seemed to be a hazy memory. The two men were not common criminals looking to kidnap a beautiful young woman and use her. At least, that was what her senses told her. These men were rather well educated, the quiet one, Ian, in particular, and they were working for someone named Yuri. She couldn't imagine what she knew or had that they might risk a kidnapping for. Perhaps she was caught up with the same group Dalton was pursuing and they were going to use her to compromise him. She worried he, too, was in trouble.

Ian cursed under his breath as he walked to the dingy diner. He never understood Taros, for he appeared as nothing more than a strong-armed gofer for Yuri. It had been a mere seven months since Yuri recruited Ian for the technical role to verify the warheads were usable, if, in fact, he recovered them, and fit them with very sophisticated detonators. Crime, including kidnapping, was not Ian's career choice, although as the Soviet system collapsed and the disarmament programs took hold, Ian was out of work. With a PhD in nuclear physics and eighteen years' experience building two Ukrainian cobalt-based nuclear reactors, he had felt his job was secure, however it wasn't and 70 percent of the Russian nuclear scientists were let go. Most left the country for Pakistan or Iran, and Ian was considering it when Yuri approached him about a special assignment. The pay was good, and the end bonus was at least ten times the annual salary he had ever earned. He rationalized away the certain immoral and illegal issues in dealing with Yuri Tarasov, held his nose, and agreed to join his team.

THE TARASOV SOLUTION

After about ten minutes, Ian returned to the SUV carrying two disgusting chili dogs and a couple of soft drinks. Despite the fact Carolyn hadn't eaten since morning, the thought and smell of this food sickened her.

A dull rumble became louder and louder. Then the landing lights of the small, fast helicopter shone as it circled and landed about fifty yards away from the SUV. It was now very dark, and Carolyn feared the next day would never come.

The helicopter ride was uneventful and only about twelve minutes long. Landing on the small helipad of the *Lady Cadence,* Carolyn noticed the entire yacht was dark and motionless in the water. No other vessels were near that she could see; the shoreline was visible perhaps five to seven miles away and active with car lights sending random flashes toward the sea. Her sense of isolation grew stronger, and her hopes for an escape slipped away as she looked at the distant shoreline with very little boat activity anywhere. Once aboard, Carolyn was taken down below to a small cabin and told by a stump of a man carrying an automatic weapon that she could freshen up. He also said he would have some food brought to her. His demeanor was cold and matter-of-fact. He left and she heard the unmistakable click of the cabin door bolt lock engaging. Nervous although relaxing a bit, Carolyn tried to sort out the crazy turn of events. She had been attacked and bound, held in an SUV for hours traveling somewhere, and now she rested on a pleasure yacht awaiting food. None of it made any sense. Her phone had been taken, and she still had no clue about Dalton's whereabouts. She was scared.

The sound of the key turning the dead bolt startled Carolyn, as there had been no knock first. The cabin door opened slowly, and a short, pleasant-looking man speaking very broken English said, "Good soup, ma'am, and I fix turkey sandwich with greens and mustard. Bottled water, OK? Yes? OK for you?"

He was charming and polite, clearly part of the kitchen crew. He was accompanied by the same stumpy-looking man carrying the nasty assault rifle. He stared without emotion and said nothing as the kitchen worker left and the door's dead bolt slid into place again. The small meal was welcome as Carolyn was becoming weak from lack of food and water coupled with the stress of the day. Without a thought as to the origin of the food, she devoured it a near feeding frenzy.

Twenty minutes had passed when she was startled by a knock on the cabin door and a female voice saying, "May I come in?"

Shocked at the request, Carolyn said, "Yes," and the bolt turned.

Again the stumpy man was standing in the opening, when an attractive, intense-looking woman in her early thirties pushed around him and came in. "How was the food?"

"It was wonderful. Thank you. May I ask who you are and what this is all about and why was I forcibly taken to this yacht?"

"All your questions will be answered in good time. However for now I need you to tell me what you know of Dalton Crusoe." The woman folded her arms and looked straight at Carolyn.

"What? Why do you want to know about Dalton? Is he the reason you grabbed me, hoping to learn something about his work?" She began to tremble and imagined the worst for her lover and friend. "Is he here on the boat? Is he alive?" Her eyes teared up.

"Oh, he's very much alive, although for how long depends on what you can tell me and what he's willing to do to get you back." The woman smiled and paced the floor in a stealthy manner. She removed her knife from her back pants pocket and released the switchblade, displaying the lethal cutting edge. She then looked to Carolyn, who revealed genuine discomfort at the knife exhibition in front of her. Careful to hold

Carolyn's attention, the woman picked up a heavy paper napkin still folded on the serving tray, which carried the food to the cabin. She opened it and pulled the blade across the diagonal corners, slicing it in two pieces before letting it fall to the floor.

Carolyn gasped.

"Do you know where Dalton Crusoe is now?" The woman looked distracted, waiting for an answer. After an uncomfortable pause, she looked at Carolyn and said, "I'm waiting for an answer."

Still trying to sort out the unexplainable events of the past ten hours, Carolyn composed herself and said, "No. I have no idea where he is. He was supposed to meet me at his mother's beach house last night when he returned."

"Returned from where?"

"That I do not know. He never told me."

"You are lovers, yes?"

"Yes, I love him, although he never reveals much information about his consulting assignments."

"He's a consultant, you say? For whom?"

"Mostly financial matters, sometimes involving corruption among government officials or businessmen, I guess." Carolyn began to worry about the trouble Dalton and she were now in. The questions were too focused on Dalton and his activities. She now knew she had been taken hostage to exert leverage on Dalton. Her mind kept imagining horrible outcomes for him ... and for herself.

The woman pressed harder. "No, I asked for whom he consults."

The move was swift and accurate. Ivana delivered a punch to Carolyn's right cheek, sending her to the floor. Before she could even grasp what had happened, the woman had her by the hair and jerked her back to her knees. The knife was positioned close to Carolyn's left eye. "Whom does he consult for?"

The stinging pain just compounded the blow she took earlier in the day from Taros, however she was able to speak. "He works for a friend who is with the government, Ed Kosko."

"And what does Ed Kosko do, my dear?"

"Ed heads the National Security Agency for President Conner," whispered Carolyn, struggling to speak.

The grip on Carolyn's hair loosened, and she noticed that the woman's face changed to a show a slight amount of fear for the first time since she entered the small cabin. She released Carolyn, backed away, folded her knife, and said, "We will talk again soon."

She burst out the door and yelled to the stumpy guard, "Where is Yuri?"

SIXTEEN

SPECIAL OPERATIONS HANGAR AT LANGLEY

THE Seal team provided by General Rusk at Ed Kosko's request remained with the Coast Guard chopper as it refueled and set out again to maintain a safe visual surveillance distance from the *Lady Cadence*. The satellites tasked with capturing photographs of yachts were reduced to two since the yacht had been located and identified beyond a doubt as Yuri Tarasov's boat. The yacht remained dead stationary in the water at the south end of Chesapeake Bay. The small helicopter carrying Carolyn and her captors to the yacht ran very quiet and low to the water. Carolyn felt the chopper land softly on the dimly lit yacht. The dark sky, distant shore and intermittent cloud cover gave no clue as to her exact location.

Yuri was busy with the second phase of his plan to use the captured warheads as a backup plan for the elimination of President Blinikov. Harith Zahid had just sent Yuri an encrypted e-mail agreeing to the terms of a transaction that would net Yuri a fast €15 million plus a guarantee to assassinate President Blinikov at a later date, if needed. The timing of the transaction was ideal. In ten hours Zahid would have a "fishing trawler–looking" boat meet the *Lady Cadence* and take possession of the second warhead. From there the trawler would head up the eastern coast of the United States and meet a freight hauler destined for Lebanon, where a subsect of Hezbollah would retrieve the bomb.

Harith Zahid was a dedicated enemy of Israel who would cooperate with anyone to get the necessary equipment, weapons, and personnel to carry out his agenda. He had been a fighter at age seventeen against the Israelis, just before they ended a partial occupation of Gaza. He had seen combat, was well trained, and knew how to fight a guerrilla war in an urban setting. Injured at twenty by grenade shrapnel, Zahid lost most of the vision in his left eye and was scarred. His skill and determination drew many supporters within Hezbollah, some of whom became his hardened core group of ultra-radical fighters who were content with only the complete destruction of Israel.

The past three days had been a windfall for Zahid as well; he had been searching all his dark connections in and out of the former Soviet Union to locate weapons-grade plutonium to construct his own weapon with

Iranian help. He and his extreme Jihadists believed the time to attack Israel was now as the Islamic world was beginning to create a chorus of resentment for the Israeli policy toward the Palestinians. When Yuri notified him that a complete ten-kiloton warhead was on the market and it had been fitted for detonation via several remote means, Harith Zahid was overjoyed and jumped at the offer. He was quick to move and, with Iranian support for his subgroup of Hezbollah, he had the cash to close the deal. Within hours of Yuri's confirming the warheads were in his control, the Iranians wired cash, denominated in Euros, to an escrow account at the Swiss Basil Bank. Once the warhead was received and checked to confirm its viability, the cash would be moved to Yuri's numbered account.

The other consideration Yuri insisted on was a successful assassination by Zahid's team of skilled contract killers of a high Russian politician to be named at a later time. Harith Zahid had no problem with a contract killing. He had agreed to them in the past to support his own agendas. Yuri was used to this kind of complex quid pro quo among merchant arms dealers and the users of such weapons. Since the merchant arms dealer–terrorist community was small and generally under the public's radar, any broken agreements that were not mutually satisfied in other ways meant a backlash attack at the offending party. Yuri had rigorously adhered to this rule over the years, and he had exacted his revenge on more than a few offenders. Yuri, however, wrote the rules, or so he figured, when it came to dealing in arms for terrorists; his version of justice would not be challenged. As a major player with connections on both sides of the deal, Yuri knew who to and who not to trust. Trusting Zahid was easy for Yuri now that he knew he was an *emotional* buyer and the Iranians were a financial partner in the purchase. Yuri's deception of Zahid played out like a classic con game. In short order Yuri would set up the terrorist Harith Zahid to make a terrible mistake and have no one to blame except himself.

SEVENTEEN

Monitoring the *Lady Cadence*, Sunday Morning

THE *Sammie,* a fishing trawler, came from the east and motored at a crawl into the bay. Its nets were all spread out from the foredeck to the stern, drying out in the morning sun. The throaty diesel engines gave away the trawler's presence minutes before its course seemed to target the *Lady Cadence.* Crusty-looking crewmen were tending to the nets and scampering about. Everything looked about as normal as it should on a trawler. Cotter took the call from the Coast Guard helicopter as it continued to fly out and around the *Lady Cadence* in a random pattern to avoid being too conspicuous.

"Calling Dalton Crusoe, over." The helicopter pilot waited for a reply.

"Cotter here for Crusoe. What do you have? Over."

"We have an old fishing trawler approaching the yacht. It appears to be docking off its starboard side." The chopper pilot checked his binoculars again. "It is taking off what looks like garbage from the yacht and delivering iced tubs of fish."

THE TARASOV SOLUTION

Dalton was going over fresh kill radius predictions as he heard Cotter communicating with the chopper pilot. He stopped and looked at the satellite coverage, and sure enough there was the *Sammie* tied up next to the *Lady Cadence* and off-loading several tubs of iced fish. Quite a few large garbage containers were lifted by a movable arm at the stern of the yacht to the trawler and were laid on the open deck. Several similar bags were piled in the same area about the *Sammie*. Dalton thought, *Makes perfect sense. Avoid a dock setting, making boarding for inspection easy, and get some fresh fish in the process.* With his doubt still stirring, Dalton instructed Cotter to alert the chopper to not interfere with the meeting at sea, just continue to follow the yacht by satellite. At that moment Dalton was more concerned about taking over the *Lady Cadence* without a commotion and inspecting her rather than digging through its garbage for clues to Yuri's plan.

It was nearly 9:30 a.m., and Dalton was beginning to worry that he had not heard from Carolyn. He feared she was so upset that she had returned to campus and blown him off for the weekend. Struggling between the task at hand and the whereabouts of Carolyn, he called the beach house line, thinking Carolyn's cell phone may have been turned off. The phone rang four times and forwarded to voice mail. Dalton punched in the PIN code his mother had used for all such purposes, his birthday in month and day: 1025. This brought him to a menu that included playing back prior calls. Two calls played: one for his mother weeks earlier and one yesterday in the morning. Curious for reasons he could not explain, he selected the last call. Carolyn's voice said, "This had better be you. I was getting worried." A long pause followed then, "Dalton, is that you?" There was another pause. "Sorry, wrong number." Dalton's face tightened with fear and anger. Motioning to Wilson, Dalton said, "Run this through the computer right away for voice recognition."

Wilson took the phone, hit the replay command, and captured the voices on the computer software. The computer flashed a voice pattern over Carolyn's words and displayed, *Woman, American, educated, twenty to thirty-five, no identity on file.* Moments later the computer flashed a voice pattern over the callers words: *Male, possible eastern European, thirty-five to forty-five, possible identity match to existing file, no name.*

Dalton's head dropped in concern at what he read, for he was certain he had heard the male voice a few days earlier. Almost breathless, Dalton ordered Wilson, "Compare it to the tape of the attackers who grabbed Sergey."

THE TARASOV SOLUTION

Wilson looked at Dalton, his hands tightened into fists now, staring with fear in his eyes at the computer screen. Seconds passed and the display read: *Confirmed at 98.1% confidence level to match earlier male voice recording.*

Dalton slammed his fist into his thigh and ran his fingers through his hair before rubbing his neck.

Wilson saw the reaction and concern on Dalton's face, "What does this mean, Dalton?"

"It means Yuri has Carolyn McCabe, a very special lady to me."

At Langley Special Operations Hangar

Dalton moved to a new level of heightened awareness. Not only did he have the possible safety of the president on his mind, although now this rogue arms merchant had almost certainly taken Carolyn. It was getting very personal now, and Dalton was ready to take whatever steps necessary to board the *Lady Cadence.*

Dalton collected his team, conferenced in Ed Kosko, and told them about the phone call to the beach house and the computer's findings. His tone was controlled although intense, and the entire team began to feel that

RICHARD TREVAE

Dalton's earlier prediction for Yuri's plans might just be unfolding exactly as feared.

Dalton made the update brief yet professional, and when Ed heard the news about Carolyn, he sensed Dalton's deep sorrow. Yet Dalton never deviated from the primary concern: stop Tarasov from using his bombs if he still had them. Ed listened to the entire update without uttering a word then asked, "Dalton, what do you now recommend? We have less than forty-eight hours before both presidents will be out sailing in the Chesapeake. If you feel we must cancel the sail, then we must also think about an evacuation of the D.C. area, unless we can locate the bomb or bombs Tarasov may have recovered." Ed's heart pained for the struggle his young friend was going through about the possible fate of Carolyn.

Dalton analyzed all the ramifications of the decisions before him. This crisis had unfolded so fast after the interview of a Russian exile three days ago. It had developed into a major security matter that caught all the protective agencies ill prepared to deal with it in the time remaining. Dalton knew he was the only one, aided by Ed Kosko's support at the cabinet level, who could react to the intelligence fast enough to avoid a misstep and trigger a nuclear attack on the United States and its president. Ed said he would update the president and they would wait until further information was gathered before taking action to cancel the Sunday sail for the Russian and U.S. presidents.

Twenty minutes later the secure satellite phone rang and the female receptionist voice asked for Dalton Crusoe. Taking the phone from Wilson, Dalton answered, "Yes, this is Crusoe." A man's voice followed a click and said, "Dalton, this is Jerome Conner. I just wanted to call and express my deep concern for Carolyn McCabe and tell you that the full support of the president's office is with you on this dangerous effort. Ed has briefed me with up-to-date intel so I won't hold you long, just to say how sorry I am Carolyn was drawn into this mess. We all await your recommendation for our next move."

When he heard it was the president, Dalton straightened to his full height and, without thinking, tightened his tie. "Thank you, Mr. President. I appreciate your concerns, and I'm hopeful we get some information soon which will lead us to the warheads and their dismantling." Dalton paused to allow the president to respond.

"I have great confidence in your leadership through this crisis, Dalton, as does Ed. Keep us informed."

"Thank you, sir. I'll be back in touch as soon as possible."

Meanwhile, Wilson had been checking the satellite

images of the *Lady Cadence* when he noticed the *Sammie* had not gone into the commercial section of the bay, where most fishing trawlers were docked, rather it turned around and headed out of the bay. Now it was lost or out of range of the tasked satellites scanning the area. Wilson alerted Dalton of this unexpected change in route for a fishing trawler coming in from a night's work. Wilson posed the obvious question. "Why would a fishing trawler, now loaded with trash, head out to sea? He can't dump out there legally."

Dalton studied the screens for a moment, smiled a half smile, and said, "I'll bet if we can locate the *Sammie* again, we'll find it has the nukes. Yuri may have off-loaded them as garbage when the *Sammie* docked starboard to the yacht." Pointing to the satellite image of the shoreline covered with trawlers unloading their catch, Dalton said, "A real trawler full of fresh catch would be unloading to iced storage as all the others are right now." Looking to Cotter, Dalton said, "Get me that warrant. We're going to board the *Lady Cadence*. Keep looking for the *Sammie*."

The helicopter flying a circular route, surveying the actions of the *Lady Cadence*, returned to pick up Dalton, Wilson, and Cotter along with the four-man Seal team

THE TARASOV SOLUTION

from Gitmo. A federal judge issued the warrant for search and seizure based on reasonable suspicion the inspection would reveal something indicating a national security threat. The case was still pretty slim and based in large part on speculation by Dalton as to the various courses of action Yuri might take. Nevertheless, with the help of Pickler and Kosko, the warrant was issued.

The *Lady Cadence* remained motionless in the water and had not moved more than a few hundred yards from her position the night before. From the port side, the chopper pilot radioed the steering master of the yacht, Aaron, ordering him to stop all engines and allow the Coast Guard to board. Yuri's steering master followed the instructions Yuri had given him to the letter and played his role with extreme calm. Aaron looked out from the bridge and saw the helicopter positioning to drop men down a twenty-foot cable ladder dangling from the helicopter. Using his radio to respond to the chopper pilot Aaron said, "We are anchored and all engines are off. You may proceed to board." The calm winds and smooth seas made it an easy drop.

"May I see the warrant, please?" asked Aaron.

Cotter handed him the warrant and said, "We also would like to speak to the yacht owner, Yuri Tarasov. We believe he is aboard."

"No he is not on board; he left early this morning for a business meeting on shore," replied Aaron.

Dalton looked aft and saw the small helicopter was gone. He grew frustrated and ordered the Seal team to assemble all the crew on board and inspect every part of the ship. The men spread out, and Dalton approached the steering master.

"What is your course over the next three days?"

"The plan was to enjoy the Labor Day weekend on the Chesapeake and then motor to the Bahamas for a week near Nassau." Aaron was a polite, competent seaman, or so it seemed. He spoke perfect English and dressed in a white short-sleeved shirt with banded epaulets indicating a senior status among the crew. Yuri had left with Taros and Ian well before dawn and put Aaron in charge of the yacht until he returned.

Dalton went with the Seal team and examined every inch of the yacht. Cotter and Wilson went to the bridge and checked computer, phone, and paper files and found nothing to indicate the *Lady Cadence* was anything more than a rich man's cruising yacht. Dalton kept asking the Seals if they had seen anything suggesting the presence of Carolyn or Sergey from days before.

Finally the Seal leader confided in Dalton and said, "I'm sorry, Mr. Crusoe. It all looks normal. Our indicators reveal no radiation, and we have found no evidence the ship ever carried the warheads. Also nothing indicating the presence of either Carolyn or Sergey. I'm sorry."

Dalton stood in the entrance to the last small stateroom below the main deck; he looked around and felt restless, confused, and concerned.

"Damn, something is not right here; I just know it." Dalton rubbed his neck in frustration.

The Seal leader accompanying Dalton stopped the video recording of the yacht inspection and shrugged his shoulders at the shared frustration.

Not thirty feet away, stowed in a secret passageway meant for escape from the main cabin, Ivana held her knife pressed against Carolyn's throat. Dalton's girlfriend was bound at the wrists, and her mouth was taped. They both listened to the conversation Dalton had with the Seal team. She knew now that he was pursuing the same group that had abducted her the day before. Ivana kept the flat of the knife tightly pressed against Carolyn's throat. Any movement to escape would require only the slightest adjustment by Ivana to cut a six-inch-long by one-inch-deep gash in her throat, killing her in seconds. Hearing Dalton's voice brought tears to her eyes. Not only was she facing instant death if she could scream, although Dalton may also be hurt or killed if the crew attacked. The voices grew weaker, and the sound of footsteps climbing the ladder soon faded. In their place, silence returned.

Back up on the main deck, Dalton was trying to find some shred of evidence, some clue that would explain the strong suspicions he had about Yuri's involvement in retrieving the warheads and the abduction of Carolyn. It all just seemed too contrived to be believable with the intelligence that Dalton had already collected. He was left with few options following the futile inspection.

"We notice you seem to have an awful lot of firepower on board, assault rifles, handguns, shotguns. Why all the armament?" Dalton waited for an answer from Aaron.

"Sir, a ship this size can easily become a target for pirates, and we have the right and commitment to protect the vessel, owner, and passengers. All the weapons are legal and standard for a ship which travels much of the world's seas."

"Yes, I understand that," offered Dalton.

"Is your inspection complete, sir?" Aaron asked of Dalton.

Dalton looked to Cotter, who nodded and said, "We found nothing to hold the yacht. We cannot remain on board if asked to leave."

Aaron was a master at playing it very cool under the pressure of a federal search warrant served on his boss's yacht. He displayed a brief smile at hearing Cotter's words.

Feeling frustrated and outmaneuvered, Dalton looked back at the empty helipad near the stern and thought, *He just may have taken Carolyn away with him.*

EIGHTEEN

DALTON was not one to sit around and lament over failures. However, the lack of warheads found on the yacht shook him. He was now certain Yuri retrieved the nukes and had somehow moved them off the *Lady Cadence* before the inspection. The encounter with the Sammie might explain his suspicions. The question remained, Where were the warheads now, and what was the plan for them? Carolyn's fate concerned Dalton as well, although he couldn't take his focus, or that of his team, away from the possibility that Yuri or some radical terrorist group planned a nuclear attack, so that he could rescue his girlfriend. He hoped that in solving the national security issue, he would also rescue Carolyn. He had to force down his feelings of anger, fear, and responsibility for the woman who meant so much in his life.

Ed Kosko called Dalton. He said he realized how devastating the kidnapping of Carolyn must be to Dalton, so he began his own parallel search for her through every reconnaissance means available to the

NSA. Ed had called Cherney, one of the top NSA intelligence agents, to personally manage the parallel effort to locate Carolyn. Dalton had enough to worry about, he said. Ed didn't want his focus diminished, feeling Carolyn had been abandoned. Dalton, for the first time, realized the depth of friendship and concern Ed felt for him and Carolyn.

The next step was locating the *Sammie* and searching it. Cotter had already retasked two satellites to scan the eastern seaboard of the United States.

Forty-two miles east of the North Carolina coast, the *Sammie* floated aimlessly with the current and very near the stern of the cargo carrier *Amersythe*, registered out of Venezuela. Harith Zahid was on board, along with his special detachment of killers and bodyguards, watching as the winch strained at the pull line to drag the warhead over the ten meters of open water separating the two boats. The captain and crew were well paid to slow the *Amersythe* to a crawl and allow the *Sammie* to off-load cargo that would never appear on the manifest of the cargo carrier. Once aboard the *Amersythe*, Zahid's men opened the wooden cargo frame covering a canvas wrapping around the cylindrical weapon. Zahid motioned for his scientist to go through the efficacy tests to determine the viability of the warhead.

"Yes, it is a Russian SS-5 warhead, and the indicators show it is viable and preprogrammed for detonation, just as Tarasov promised," announced a bald, stocky Pakistani scientist with thick glasses dangling from a neck cord. The clumsy scientist packed away his mobile testing devices and tried not to fall over as the *Sammie* heaved and rolled in the ocean waves. He displayed a nervous smile and gave a thumbs-up to Zahid, who shouted out, "Load the weapon in the hold."

Zahid retrieved his satellite phone, called his Swiss banker, and ordered the release of the escrowed €15 million to the numbered account Yuri had given him. Then he called Yuri's cell phone. It went to voice mail. He said, "Yuri, it is Harith. I have the weapon, and all is fine, as you said. The funds have been released to your account. When we meet in Cyprus, we can discuss the timing of the consideration I yet owe you." Harith Zahid was beaming inside. He knew his Iranian financiers would be very pleased with his resourcefulness. His smug sense of accomplishment would be short lived.

Yuri did not want to take the call from Zahid, even on his satellite phone, although he knew it was important. Preparing to text a message rather than make a voice call back to Zahid, a smirk spread over Yuri's face. He entered a simple response: *Yes, thank you for the call. I'll connect with you as you suggest in Cyprus.*

He sent the message with an abrupt punch to the send button, snapped his phone shut, and smiled at Taros. Both men knew the ruse had worked well and toasted their con on Zahid. The shoreside restaurant had a nice water view, however the food was average. That didn't matter, for it was the isolated, public, hard-line phone that Yuri wanted to use to confirm the money transfer had been made.

Taros watched the sunbathers gathering to walk the beach as the sun increased its warming effect on the sand. It was almost noon, and he and Ian ordered burgers as Yuri made his confirmation call to his Swiss bank.

Ignoring the desire for food, Yuri sipped his dark rum over ice and ran the next steps of his plan over again in his head. Yuri was feeling very smug as it appeared everything was going his way.

Yuri's research on Dalton Crusoe was quite extensive. Sources, some traditional and some clandestine, had helped Yuri always gain a knowledge advantage on his adversaries so he could better anticipate their next moves. Dalton Crusoe, he felt, was as formidable a foe as he had ever faced, and he was not about to be out-smarted or outmaneuvered with all that he had falling into place. Yuri was amazed how a young man had gained such impressive diplomatic credentials while operating without a formal role in the government he served. The well-documented association with Ed Kosko explained much of his success, however without question, Jameson Dalton Crusoe was not to be underestimated. Yuri figured Dalton must have reasoned by now Carolyn McCabe's absence was related to the search for the missiles off Cuba. Given that, then the chopper surveillance he noticed over the past day or so must have been Crusoe recognizing the yacht and would next be preparing to board her. He put a contingency plan together with Ivana and his steering master. His timing for leaving with Ian and Taros before dawn the morning Dalton's team boarded the *Lady Cadence* was pure serendipity. He knew Dalton must have been close to engaging the yacht. Ivana knew the secret place to hide with Carolyn and stole away minutes before Dalton and his team set foot on the deck of the *Lady Cadence.* Yuri believed Dalton had not connected the meeting between Presidents Blinikov and Conner to his locating and retrieving the warheads. Less than twenty hours remained for Yuri to stay ahead of Dalton, and so far his plan was on track. Once the plan played out, Yuri's business problems would be a closed chapter in his life. And adding Conner's death to Blinikov's had Yuri now wanting to include Dalton Crusoe in his tally—a perfect trilogy of death.

NINETEEN

WILSON was checking every pass of the two new satellites positioned over the scan zone. The sky was clear of clouds, and the sun angle improved by 11:00 a.m. to allow very sharp images over the blue Atlantic Ocean. Earlier work, which showed the *Sammie* heading toward a large cargo freighter, had gone unnoticed. The earlier information was insufficient to establish clear identification, although it was tagged as a "watch target" as the scans continued. By 12:30 p.m., the watch target had been located alongside the freighter *Amersythe* and was involved in an apparent cargo transfer of some sort. The activity, while somewhat unusual, was not unexpected along the known trade routes from South America and Mexico to southern European ports. The trawler was clearly identifiable under strong magnification of a still shot, as the front tire bumpers on either side read *Sammie*.

Wilson shouted to the team, who were all deep into their own assignments of looking for e-mail communications, employing voice recognition to thousands of cell and satellite calls, and examining the probable detonation locations to assess human casualties.

Dalton stood up and said, "What do you have, Wilson?"

"Sir, I believe I've found the *Sammie*, moving alongside a freighter, the *Amersythe*, bound for Casablanca, then on to Lisbon, Portugal."

"What are they doing together?" asked Dalton.

"Well, nothing at this instant, although a drag line connects them, suggesting they have moved something, probably from the trawler to the freighter." Wilson positioned the satellite imagery to a large screen visible to the entire eight-man team in the situation center. As the screen focused in on the two boats, the trawler pulled away then powered forward in a large arc and set a course for the entrance to Chesapeake Bay.

Dalton ran a dozen responses through his mind in thirty seconds then announced, "Cotter, get me Ed Kosko on the satellite phone and find out where our Atlantic submarine fleet is now located. I want to check out the *Amersythe* for nuclear bombs."

The Seal team leader, a communications expert as well, was a real help on the satellite phone searches. He had captured a brief call from a man with an Arab dialect to another referred to as "Yuri." The Arab's voice print had a 58.9 percent match to Harith Zahid. After he washed it a few times for random background noise and strengthened the signal, he was able to confirm at a 90.7 percent confidence level that it was, in fact, Zahid's voice. After calling Dalton over to his station, he played the recording for him. *"Yuri, it is Harith. I have the weapon, and all is fine, as you said. The funds have been released to your account. When we meet in Cyprus, we can discuss the timing of the consideration I yet owe you."*

"Now read Yuri's text response," offered the Seal leader . . . *Yes, thank you for the call. I'll connect with you as you suggest in Cyprus.*

Dalton replayed the conversation several times, trying to see if the wording revealed anything about Yuri's plans.

Cotter said, "I've got Ed Kosko on the satellite video phone."

Dalton moved over to the communications console with Cotter at his side. "Ed, we just learned a few more critical bits of intelligence. First of all, Yuri did have the warheads on his yacht. He apparently made a deal to sell one of them to a Harith Zahid, a radical terrorist connected to Hezbollah and financed by the Iranian government. He just off-loaded the warhead to a freighter, the *Amersythe,* in the Atlantic about fifty miles off the North Carolina coast."

"Dalton, back up a minute. How do you know he only sold one warhead?"

"Listen to the opening words of Harith; he refers to a weapon, not weapons."

After hearing the recording, Ed agreed one weapon was sold, and Dalton convinced him the other was not on the *Lady Cadence,* for the inspection would have revealed some weak radioactivity even if it were well shielded. Ed asked Dalton if he learned any more of Carolyn's whereabouts, and he replied, "No new information on Carolyn, Ed. Thanks for asking." Silence gripped the room as they all looked at Dalton and imagined his pain. "We do know she is not on the *Lady Cadence.* We looked everywhere. We'll just have to keep searching."

Ed Kosko surveyed the team members assembled at his location, looked into the video camera, and said, "OK, Dalton. Thanks to your team for the good work. What do you need now?"

"I want a U.S. submarine to intercept the *Amersythe,* board her, and verify the bomb exists on that freighter. Retrieve the bomb and arrest Zahid as a terrorist. If we can rule out the possibility that two nukes are in the Washington area, it helps our efforts."

"OK, I'll start the process and let you know the timing as soon as possible. I'll check with our legal guys but based on the phone intercept, we have a strong case for whatever we need to do, even on the open sea."

RICHARD TREVAE

"Good. We don't need to be bogged down with red tape at this point."

Dalton reflected on the conversation with Ed then recalled the search of the yacht and thought, *Maybe Carolyn is on the* Lady Cadence. *Is it possible we didn't search* everywhere?

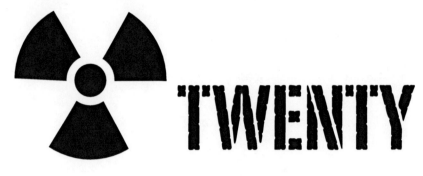

TWENTY

Sick Bay of the *Ravenwood*

CAPTAIN Thomson received word that Sergey Kreftkova had regained consciousness and was talking. He gave the bridge command to his first officer and headed down the steep ladder to the decks below and entered the infirmary.

Sergey was sitting up in bed and sipping soup from a cup. He looked very tired and had lost some weight and muscle tone during his ordeal in the water and from confinement by Yuri Tarasov. As the captain approached, Sergey looked up and smiled.

Holding Sergey's focus, the captain spoke in a clear, soft voice, "Hello, Mr. Kreftkova. I'm Captain Thomson. You are aboard my ship, the Coast Guard vessel *Ravenwood*. How are you feeling?"

"Well, Captain, I feel sore and confused. Where did you say I was? Aboard a ship? What kind?"

"It is a large, deepwater Coast Guard ship, about 120 feet long with a twenty-two man crew." The captain studied Sergey to make sure he was truly conscious.

Sergey smiled again and went back to sipping his

soup. The ship's doctor came over, pulled the captain aside, and whispered, "I'm not sure yet, but he seems to be suffering from a loss of short-term memory. It may well restore itself when he regains strength; however, for now he can't seem to hold focus for a conversation."

"Let him take his time, and do not pressure him for details. I'll call Crusoe and tell him the news." The captain waved to Sergey and left.

Sergey waved back as though he had just seen a friendly stranger.

At the other end of the infirmary, Augustus was recovering from blast wounds and minor burns on his left arm, none of which were severe. He had instinctively used his arm to blunt the explosion blast as flames shot out from the exploding deck on the *Mullet* and burned him. He appeared to be semiconscious, drifting in and out of sleep and on occasion mumbling meaningless words. Augustus, however, was faking it and was very much alert. Earlier his senses and memory returned when he overheard the nurses talking about a "Sergey." Only one Sergey, Sergey Kreftkova, could explain the use of that name. He reasoned that if he could delay the time when his rescuers felt it was safe to question him hard about the *Mullet*, Tarasov, Sergey, and the missiles, the better chance he had to devise an escape. He knew his ship and perhaps the entire crew were gone. He recalled the F-22 flying over the *Mullet* at two hundred feet and the attack from the Apache helicopter. He closed his eyes for a moment and tried to recall the last few seconds before he lost consciousness. He drifted back two days earlier, saw the F-22 coming over his bow, heard the Apaches, and witnessed his crew of military rejects and mercenaries shouting and firing back. He tried to envision the bridge, where he had stood when the first missile attack hit the hull just above the waterline then the major explosion ripping apart the deck and knocking him down the ladder. The scenes replayed in his mind again and again like short, surreal flashes of explosions and gunfire mixed with genuine reality. He kept straining to recall more detail. Augustus's eyes opened wide, and he gasped at the last image he recalled. He whispered to himself, "The euro attaché, the euro attaché."

Then he remembered just before he was blown down the ladder serving the bridge he grabbed the locked and watertight metal attaché, which held his €4 million from Yuri. He panicked and began to jump out of bed stopping when he saw a nurse talking with the ship's doctor at the opposite end of the infirmary. He held his emotions in check and, like witnessing a miracle, looked around the room and saw reflecting in a mirror fixed to the outside of a bathroom door a small, metal attaché. He could see only the top edge of it. Following the boat's slow roll in the sea, the door moved an inch back and forth. It was *his* attaché; he was sure of it. The team rescuing him must have found it clamped in his hand as he fell and brought it with him to the infirmary. It was locked, of course, and could be opened with a three-number combination. He challenged himself then recited the combination in his head to check his memory: *12, 34, 09.* He muttered again to himself, "Yes, that's it."

Trying to appear sedated and semiconscious was much harder now as Augustus's mind ran in high gear to check the attaché and plan an escape. He faked falling off to sleep as the nurse walked by his bed.

Augustus sensed the approach to land moments before the *Ravenwood* came within sight Miami's first evening lights. His eyes opened slowly as he heard the infirmary door close behind the nurse. The porthole revealed the horizon, sparkling in a backdrop of blue haze beneath a sky showing an approaching sunset producing brilliant red and orange hues. Soon the boat would be docked at the Miami Coast Guard base.

Dalton received a call from the Captain Thomson, who explained the news on Sergey's condition. Dalton requested that the two men in sick bay be held there until he could arrange a team of NSA agents and physicians to escort them from the vessel and provide transport in a medical helicopter to NSA headquarters in Washington.

The *Ravenwood* was quiet now and very few crew members were on deck. A young medic was overseeing the infirmary as the big cutter passed the first seawall before the dock location. As he made his last check on the two patients in his care, he first found Sergey asleep, showing signs of restlessness. Noting his condition, he moved down the hallway some thirty feet to Augustus's bed and found the curtain pulled around his patient. As he entered to check on the sleeping man, Augustus grabbed at the medic's neck, pulled him onto the bed, and thrust a table knife into his chest just below the sternum. The young medic struggled briefly then succumbed to the severed artery exiting his heart and died. Augustus rolled the limp medic into the sheets and blankets on the bed, went in the bathroom, and put on the clothes he had been wearing during the explosion on the *Mullet*. They had been cleaned and were hanging on the door hook.

RICHARD TREVAE

Two minutes later Augustus had gotten to the ship's stern and hid in a life raft suspended over the boat's rear railing. As the engines cut off to allow the *Ravenwood* to drift the last twenty feet into the dock, Augustus rolled out from the raft, falling fifteen feet in silence to the water, clutching his metallic silver attaché. Side thrusters on the *Ravenwood* provided plenty of white noise to mask the splash Augustus made when he hit the water.

20-ONE

THE WHITE HOUSE

THE press coverage was beginning to approach that of a summit meeting held during the Cold War era. Blinikov had arrived midmorning on Saturday and was whisked off for an early lunch with President Conner. The lead story for the networks prime-time news was that of the two men, standing at identical podiums displaying their presidential seals, taking questions from a press corps suffering from a feeding frenzy.

Blinikov was very easy to like. Unlike earlier Russian leaders, he spoke English well enough that his translator, always at his side, seemed mute. The two powerful leaders shared an obvious respect and burgeoning friendship for each other. They spoke in platitudes about the need for cooperation on a variety of fronts: energy, terrorism, arms control, financial policy, and human rights. It was as if a post-Communist, adolescent democratic society woke up one day energized, elected a true democratic reformer, and pursued the United States of America as a real partner. The political pundits were extrapolating the first seven hours of interaction between the two men as a breakthrough of Herculean proportions for the entire world. Even the president's wives hit it off at their first meeting.

Following the casual lunch in the Oval Office, Mrs. Conner took Mrs. Blinikov on a White House walking tour followed by the landscaped grounds. The women talked at length about their childhood years in their seaside towns in North Carolina and Lithuania, respectively. The weather was fresh, warm, and mildly humid under a fantastic, blue sky. The press corps followed like puppies seeking a handout, clicking their cameras and shoving microphones in their faces every time they stopped to make a comment to the press. The coverage was made even more interesting since both women were in their late forties, slim, well dressed, and attractive.

Dalton and his team watched all the reporting from a secure conference room beneath the White House that Ed Kosko had reserved. The intense media fascination with the meeting and planned sailing activity made the stakes very high to abort if the danger were not verifiable and imminent. The entire agenda for the visit was now mainstream news, and the media was setting up portable broadcast trucks around the White House and various sites in the Capitol area as well as the sailing route on the Chesapeake. Dalton knew he had to make some very tough decisions within the next several hours to safeguard the two presidents from an attack; and he hoped and prayed he could find and save Carolyn in the process.

As Ivana heard the large Coast Guard helicopter lift off, she came out from the secret passageway, where she had held Carolyn at knife point. Aaron was able to assuage and divert the impressions Dalton's team had about the yacht and its mission because Yuri was not on board and the warheads had been moved out. Without anything to claim as evidence that a security risk existed, the *Lady Cadence* was given a pass. Ivana looked out from the bridge, saw the chopper moving fast toward shore, and commented, "Good work, Aaron; Yuri will be very pleased."

"Thanks Ivana. It did go well didn't it?" Aaron stood proud with his arms crossed.

She strolled over to the young, athletic Russian, touched his cheek with a gentle pat, and offered a seductive smile as she moved on.

Carolyn was taken back to her cabin and told to relax. When Yuri returned, Ivana warned, he would want to know everything she knew about Dalton's work as well as her relationship with him. She feared she would never be rescued and that the Yuri Ivana mentioned, would be ruthless in his questioning about Dalton.

NSA Headquarters, Washington, D.C.

Dalton reviewed the *Lady Cadence*'s movements, albeit small, through the latest satellite images, and the *Amersythe* freighter heading out in the Atlantic. He felt a bit bogged down with his failure to find any clues on the yacht about Yuri's efforts to locate and recover the Russian warheads. Nevertheless, he plowed ahead with plans to intercept the *Amersythe* at sea and scour the eastern seaboard for any indication a bomb was planted for the Labor Day weekend. Staying focused was a rare problem for Dalton, for his intellect and fast mind seldom had trouble staying on mission. Something about the yacht inspection kept bothering him. He replayed the events and images he recalled from the boarding. Aaron was too slick, too well prepared; someone—no doubt Yuri—had coached him well.

Walking over to Cotter's station, he asked, "Do you have the Seal leader's video recording of the *Lady Cadence* inspection loaded into the computer files yet?"

"Yes, I entered it about ten minutes ago and filed it for reference, in case we need to return."

THE TARASOV SOLUTION

"Please play it for me . . . from the beginning." Dalton was following an instinct, a feeling he could not explain. Twenty-three minutes through the filming, Dalton yelled, "Stop! Right there."

Cotter pressed the computer keyboard, and the screen paused in the last cabin checked by Dalton and the Seal leader. He began a methodical scrolling around the room once again.

"What are we looking for, sir?"

"I don't know yet, but I believe we're looking for it in the right spot."

A few seconds later, Dalton said, "Stop the video and amplify the image." Pointing at a roll of gray tape resting on a small bookcase about three feet tall, Dalton said, "That is duct tape, perfect for binding things like mouths. On a yacht in tip-top shape like that one is, they wouldn't need that for repairs or anything." Dalton could think of no reason it would be there except for silencing Carolyn just before he and the Seal team arrived at the *Lady Cadence*. Feeling vindicated and brimming with fresh ideas, Dalton said, "Check to see if Carolyn's cell phone is on."

Cotter earlier navigated through several computer screens and came up with the status of her phone. It had been in a sleep mode for a short time then, powered off. The recent GPS history then showed it had been moved from the beach house toward a location at Cove

Point, Maryland. The beacon signal was still off. Dalton examined a local map and reasoned Cove Point would be a perfect landing point for Yuri's small helicopter to have picked her up and taken her to the *Lady Cadence.*

Looking to Cotter with a forced smile, Dalton said, "Maybe we've found her. She's on that yacht somewhere . . . I hope."

Under his breath, Dalton whispered, "I'll find you, honey."

20-TWO

INTERSTATE 95, SEVEN MILES NORTH OF MIAMI

THE fourth trucker proved to be the lucky one. Augustus had taken a cab to the first rest area on I-95 and waited for the right trucker to ask for a ride north to the Chesapeake Bay area. He had just arranged a ride all the way to Baltimore with an old trucker who spoke some Italian and was very happy to take €500 for the trouble. With any luck, he would be in the Chesapeake Bay area by noon the next day.

The warm weather allowed Augustus to dry off an hour before he presented himself at a cab stand to get out of central Miami. Now he was comfortable and dry, although very tired, and needing serious sleep time. However all the weathered Italian long-haul driver wanted to talk about were the "old days," when he could siphon a few cases of good Italian wine from his load as a "bonus."

Augustus had calmed down following his dangerous escape from the *Ravenwood*. He feared he might have been spotted or perhaps even drowned in the big vessel's wake as it came into dock. However, the plan worked and he was able to swim past the empty docks and climb ashore on the dark, northern beach. Once he got into the cab, he sat relaxed in the backseat and held his breath while dialing the combination on the attaché lock. It cracked open. All the euros were still in neat, little packets. Each packet, bound with a one-inch-wide, white strap of paper, held one hundred bills in €100 denominations. All were there and dry. Either the *Ravenwood* crew ignored the case, or they were waiting for Dalton to order its opening. In any event, Augustus had what he needed, cash to fund his escape from the States and retire from the smuggling business. His problem—how to make his escape to Europe. Contacting Yuri was not Augustus's first choice however the possibilities were few. Yuri would be somewhere near the bay the weekend before Labor Day. If he could let him know he survived the attack on the *Mullet* and kept the €4 million in his possession he might be able to buy Yuri's help.

Just south of Washington, D.C., the trucker pulled into a truck stop for coffee and a bathroom break. Augustus took the opportunity to call Yuri's cell phone number, which he tried to recall. As the phone rang, Augustus hoped he remembered the number.

THE TARASOV SOLUTION

Yuri heard his satellite phone ring although he didn't recognize the number. He let it go to voice mail. A few moments later, a voice message notification popped up. He listened to it. "Yuri, it's Augustus. I'm safe and near the bay. I have the attaché with Euros. Can you get me aboard?"

Yuri played the message again and twice more. He recovered the phone number and had Ivana call back.

The pay phone rang, and Augustus picked up on the first ring. "Yes, this is Augustus."

Ivana covered the phone and told Yuri who was on the line.

"What? It's really him?" Caution controlled the moment as Yuri thought. Then he said, "Ask him if he has run across any deep-sea treasures lately." This was a trick that only Augustus could figure out, and it would establish his identity if he could answer it.

Augustus, sneering a partial laugh, said, "Yeah, I found some treasure, sold it, and then dumped the two empty boxes in the sea."

Yuri grabbed the phone from Ivana. "How did you survive? The last call I had from you sounded very terminal."

"You can thank the U.S. Coast Guard for that, but I grew weary of their hospitality and left yesterday. Can you pick me up?"

Yuri did not want to do it, although he had little

choice. Augustus knew where many the "bodies were buried" and he could not let the U.S. Coast Guard or Dalton Crusoe interrogate him. Unable to stand the delay in Yuri's response, Augustus said, "I have Euros to pay with."

Yuri did the math and saw the opportunity to tie-up some loose ends. "Give me your location, and I'll have Ivana bring our tender to you."

Ivana and Augustus discussed a quiet pickup location. Then he asked to speak with Yuri again. "Yuri, they are on to your plans."

"Yeah, although I'm ahead of them. Don't worry," Yuri bragged.

"They've got Sergey. I'll explain later." Augustus hung up.

Yuri shut down his satellite phone, hoping he had not been tracked or heard. He feared Augustus's last words foretold a derailing of his plans for Blinikov. Yuri despised surprises and never accepted defeat. A mental slip was unacceptable to the Yuri way of doing things. Slamming his fist into the granite bar top on the *Lady Cadence's* aft deck, Yuri lit a small cigar and drew a deep breath. He looked to Ivana and said, "Take Taros along to the pickup point, and don't bring Augustus back with you. Understood?" A definite chill came over the discussion, and Ivana nodded acknowledgment.

Ivana looked back at Yuri for several seconds, felt her

hip pocket for her knife, smiled, and said, "Oh yes, I understand."

Leaving Augustus alive only hurt Yuri's chance to escape clean from his little endeavor. He could learn about the attack and dumping of the missiles, however what did that matter if Crusoe already knew he had recovered the warheads? No, it was better for all if Augustus disappeared. Besides, with Sergey still alive and in the hands of Crusoe, it left only one critical question: What was the plan for the bombs? Only Yuri knew all the details.

It was 12:45 p.m., and the sleek tender boat *Flipper II* drifted near shore, the crew looking for Augustus in the forested area leading to the water. Taros was driving while Ivana searched the shoreline with binoculars.

Augustus saw the craft and emerged from the woods carrying his metallic attaché.

"There he is. Turn around and head back about a hundred meters," Ivana instructed.

Taros looked back and saw Augustus, waving like a lost child.

The distant traffic along this Chesapeake shoreline was moderate, and the water was quite calm. The boat slid within five feet of the shore, and Augustus waded in up to his knees. He grabbed the boat rail.

Ivana said, "No, come around to the stern, where we have a swim platform and steps to help you."

Taros held the boat motionless and put the engine in neutral. Ivana moved to the back to the boat's stern while Taros kept a watchful eye out for any intruders.

Augustus grabbed the hand grip near the stern. Unable to lift his weight with one arm, he said, "Please take this from me while I get on board."

Ivana smiled, took the attaché, and said, "Of course, let me help you."

Just as Augustus slid his right foot onto the swim platform, Ivana plunged her knife deep into his left-side jugular and pulled it sideways. Augustus never even let out a scream as his throat and larynx were severed in a swift, accurate cut. He was dead in four seconds. He fell backward, sinking into the shallow water, and Taros put the boat in gear and sped back to the *Lady Cadence.*

Back aboard the yacht, Yuri took the silver attaché Ivana offered him as she said, "Got a little case for you. Look familiar?"

Yuri took the attaché and knew what it once contained. He opened it with the combination he had used for Augustus. It contained the money just about as it appeared when Yuri had loaded it. Delighted at what he saw, virtually all €4 million were still neatly stacked, he said, "Did you know what you had here?"

"I assumed it was the original attaché you gave him but didn't realize it held almost the entire amount you paid him." Ivana and Taros looked stunned at the amount of money still in the attaché.

"Here." Yuri tossed a taped bundle of €100 bills to both Ivana and Taros. "Consider this a bonus to you two for a job well done." Closing the attaché, Yuri said, "Did he present any trouble?"

"No, he didn't and he won't ever again. So much for honor among thieves." Ivana laughed at her own sarcasm.

"Get prepared for tomorrow. We need to be 100 percent coordinated to arm the bomb and escape before 4:00 p.m.," Yuri warned.

Ivana had been with Yuri for the better part of eight months now, and she knew his moods pretty well. She knew he was tense and unnerved by this Crusoe chap. Taros had gone below to check on things, leaving Ivana and Yuri alone in a lounge area behind the bridge. She pulled close to Yuri, who was lost in his own thoughts. A long, wet kiss seemed to have no effect. She sat on his lap, unzipped her top jacket, revealing her full breasts, and pulled his face into them.

At first he withdrew then kissed her and hugged her warmly. He began to calm down and said, "You really are starting to scare me, you know. I'm beginning to think you care for me. Is that possible?"

They headed off to their luxurious cabin for the next few hours. Ivana could play about any role the situation demanded; Yuri knew it yet still welcomed the attention of his beautiful, assassin mistress.

20-THREE

The White House, the Oval Office

ED Kosko had called the meeting, this time in the Oval Office. President Conner had only one hour Sunday afternoon to get briefed and make a final decision on the sailing plans for Labor Day. Ed wanted Dalton to personally lead the briefing and let the president weigh all the options before changing the itinerary.

Ed and Dalton sat outside the Oval Office and waited for the president's chief of staff to come for them. Just down the hall were Cotter and Wilson, who would join them later. It seemed to take forever, and Dalton wrestled with what the intel told them. He was still not convinced Yuri had not sold the two bombs to Zahid. He ran over in his head the recorded conversation and text message that Zahid had left for Tarasov and hoped he was wrong and the bombs were both outside the United States on Zahid's freighter. The submarine intercept Kosko had ordered was under way and the boarding would begin soon enough. Zahid's reputation left little doubt he would not give in to an *Amersythe* boarding.

Dalton reasoned that Zahid and his men were taken on as passengers to the freighter, not as the captain and crew. Zahid was a street fighter and terrorist, not a seaman. Still, a conflict was inevitable, and Ed and Dalton were glad it would take place out at sea. In a few hours, following the boarding, they would know the details of what transpired between Tarasov and Zahid.

The formal-looking assistant chief of staff opened a door and called for Dalton and Ed. As Dalton walked in, his focus drifted as the office's majesty overwhelmed him for a moment. Thankfully, the president was quick to approach Dalton, shook his hand, looked him in the eye, and said, "Dalton, I'm very happy with the work for Ed. I can only say that we would not be on top of this situation had you not gone to Cuba and acted on what you learned."

He waited for Dalton to speak, as Ed jumped in and said, "Mr. President, I've asked Dalton to lead the briefing today. Is that satisfactory?"

Looking back at Dalton, the president said, "He's exactly the person I would like to hear deliver the briefing."

Despite the serious subject at hand, a photographer snapped a dozen photos showing the president and

Dalton as they shook hands and moved to opposing couches in the Oval Office.

As everyone sat down, the president said, "Dalton, have you found out anything new on Carolyn McCabe?"

The mention of Dalton's love interest even before the briefing began was a warm and heartfelt concern on the president's part that Dalton appreciated. It calmed him down as he began to lay out the findings to date. Dalton thanked the president for his concern and assured him efforts were under way to locate her.

Ed nodded his approval of the sincere yet brief acknowledgment Dalton made regarding the president's inquiry.

Dalton suggested they go downstairs so he could show the president and the others the satellite images that would help him explain the situation. The entire group, led by the president, headed to the subterranean Situation Room dedicated for his exclusive use. On the way, they picked up Cotter and Wilson; Pickler; Dan Jefferson, Head of the Secret Service Presidential Detail; and Josh Pearson, Deputy Director of the CIA. They all took seats around the conference room table. One wall was covered with large screens displaying various scenes throughout the world.

Dalton began with what they knew at this moment. The *Lady Cadence* was still drifting around Chesapeake

Bay, causing no harm that anyone could detect. Tarasov, while gone during the Seal boarding and inspection, was now back on board. His reason for taking the short three-hour trip to the eastern shore was unknown. Ivana Yenko had slipped out unnoticed on one of the tenders for unknown reasons and returned in about an hour when satellite coverage showed the tender returning with her aboard.

Sergey Kreftkova was still in sick bay on the *Ravenwood* and had partial physical recovery although suffered amnesia and was of little use for information until, and if, his memory returned. Augustus, the *Mullet* captain and mercenary acquaintance of Tarasov, had escaped from the *Ravenwood* sometime in the hours just prior to the Coast Guard cutter's return to port, despite the fact that his medical chart listed him as not fully conscious. He had without a doubt faked the extent of his injuries to have later attacked and killed a ship's physician's assistant. Captain Thomson had begun an investigation without much evidence to go on.

Recorded satellite phone conversations revealed that Zahid, the terrorist leader, had purchased at least *one* of the two warheads recovered by Tarasov. His location in the Atlantic was being monitored, and soon he would be stopped by a navy submarine and boarded.

Dalton tried to put all the intel into an action plan for the group.

Pickler tried to interject a point, however President Conner said, "Dalton, how would you describe our security risk now?"

Pickler withdrew to his chair.

"The issue now, it seems to me, is how do we continue the planned sailing schedule with the you and President Blinikov without confirming the second nuclear bomb is not nearby, in place now, armed and set to detonate and kill both presidents." Dalton paused and surveyed the room.

All heads were up and listening with full attention. Pickler broke in like a storm to make his point, which was that if even a remote possibility existed that a nuclear bomb of ten kilotons could be exploded over the Labor Day period, precautions needed to be taken now to evacuate people within a ten-mile radius of the bay. He concluded by asking the resident to consider canceling the sailing event.

President Conner glanced at Pickler and again held the floor. "Dalton, this meeting with Blinikov has been a godsend in terms of establishing solid relations with the Russians that we haven't had since the Gorbachev era. I do not want to lose this momentum in our relations because of a false alarm. And furthermore, I don't want to initiate pandemonium."

Pickler twitched in his seat.

"I appreciate that, sir," replied Dalton.

The president stood to indicate the meeting was nearing its end. "We continue with the announced schedule until we know more about the real risk. However, if by 9:00 a.m. tomorrow we have not located the second bomb and are confident it poses a threat to us, then we cancel. But, if we find and secure the second bomb or know its location is not a threat to the weekend sailing, we hold to the original plan of events. Clear?" The president looked around for objections. He stood, shot a look towards Pickler, and was followed by Josh Pearson and Dan Jefferson out of the oval office.

Kosko sensed Pickler was not pleased yet kept his silence. Dalton stood as Kosko approached and said, "I'll speak with Pickler; the president does not want the entire matter made public and evacuations begun, yet."

NSA HEADQUARTERS, WASHINGTON, D.C.

The presidential briefing went well by all accounts. As a practical matter, Dalton had his hands at the NSA controls, a Navy Seal team, and the Secret Service through the president's commands. The message was clear: *Do what you have to, within the broad authority of national security, to find the weapon, or weapons, and protect the two presidents in the process.* The meaning not expressed in words was *do not violate the law, however don't let it stop you from doing what needs to be done for national security. And keep the press out of the way by not provoking their involvement.* The strong vote of presidential support and the intention to keep the matter as contained as possible gave Dalton several aggressive options. His next move against Yuri Tarasov was going to be clandestine without the formality of search warrants or a safety inspection. Time was running out, and playing strictly by the rules was likely to cost Carolyn, the two presidents, and many others their lives. Kosko knew the president's mind and assured Dalton he would not be left out alone to face any critics of his plan. In six hours, at 10:00 p.m. Sunday, the mission plan was to start.

While in the Situation Room, Cotter got a call from NSA surveillance that the nuclear sub *Dakota* intercepted the *Amersythe* four hundred miles northeast of Puerto Rico and boarded her. Brief gunfire erupted, although it was put down in seconds by Special Forces personnel aboard the *Dakota*. Zahid's men were overpowered by the navy and surrendered. Seven hard-core terrorists were captured, some of whom had been pursued for years based on prior reports and intelligence.

Zahid was quiet and admitted nothing. He demanded he be taken to Lebanon, where he could be properly charged. Dalton and Kosko were going to have nothing to do with that idea as they assumed Zahid could provide valuable information on Tarasov. The *Dakota* was making arrangements to transport Zahid back to NSA headquarters as soon as they were within helicopter range of the East Coast. One of the two nukes was located unarmed and fitted with a very sophisticated detonator system. The boarding results supported a key assumption that Yuri still held the other bomb and had not tried to sell it. The *Amersythe* was impounded by the navy, and the *Dakota* escorted the ship back to Wilmington for additional inspections.

The Seal team indicated that only the four of them should board the *Lady Cadence*. Dalton, however, had a personal reason to join the team, and Cotter then insisted he accompany Dalton. The discussion tilted back and forth until Dalton finally said, "Look, guys, you heard the president. This is my plan, and it's going down the way I explained it." Dalton looked to Cotter, who shook his head, indicating there was no way he was letting Dalton go without him. Knowing the expert training and experience Cotter represented, he adjusted his plan and said, "All right, Cotter, you may join the team."

The Seal leader knew Dalton could handle the physical and combat part of it, however he was trying to isolate the key decision maker and strategist from getting killed. Nevertheless, it was Dalton's call, and the president had made it clear that Dalton was in overall charge. Dalton admitted to himself that if Carolyn were on the *Lady Cadence,* there was nothing on this earth to keep him from the mission.

By 9:40 p.m., the sky had darkened to about 10 percent light, and it was fading fast as the sunset formed over the western horizon. Every one on the four-man Seal team, as well as Dalton and Cotter, were equipped with full wetsuits, assault weapons, radiation meters, and COMSAT gear for communications with real-time video and voice. They slipped into the water more than a mile from the *Lady Cadence* in an inflatable raft under paddle power. The bay was too quiet for even a small motor, and they did not want to risk being seen or heard. As they approached, the decks looked clear, and very few lights were on inside the yacht. The four Seals tied off the raft under the stern and climbed a nylon cable line thrown over a mooring cleat near the starboard side. Close behind were Dalton and Cotter. Once on deck behind and below the bridge, the team was careful to avoid being caught by one of several security cameras scattered about the yacht. Catching Yuri by surprise and taking control of the *Lady Cadence* was the objective. A more exhaustive inspection using more persuasive methods than words was certain.

Aaron and a navigation crewman were on the bridge. The Seal team came in from the port side and tried to drop the two men to the floor in a fast assault. The navigator dropped to his knees and was secured with plastic ties and tape in seconds. Aaron bolted and headed to the starboard side and ran into Dalton's incoming fist, which knocked him flat to the floor, unconscious.

"Good job, sailor," commented Cotter, looking at Aaron, who lay groggy on his back and moaned in pain.

From the bridge, the team headed out with quiet steps and staged themselves for the next move. One Seal remained on the bridge and monitored the video cameras surveying the ship while chaperoning the navigator and sleeping Aaron.

Dalton and Cotter moved back along the starboard side while the three remaining Seals moved down the port side. The ship was far too quiet and dark; Dalton was concerned he had overlooked something. He felt certain Carolyn was there somewhere. Faint sounds of a mechanical nature seemed to flow from the lower decks. Dalton reasoned the engine crew could be doing some maintenance. Cotter had just stepped into a darkened passageway to the yacht's center main deck when sounds of a struggle broke out then stopped abruptly. Dalton approached with caution, stopped, and whispered into his COMSAT head gear, "Cotter, where did you go?" Seconds passed and he was startled as Cotter was pushed in front of him. He was bleeding from a head blow and near unconscious. Propping him up was a stumpy-looking man with a 9-mm H&K rifle pointed at Cotter's head. Dalton remembered the hardened man's face from the earlier inspection.

"One more step, and he dies one second before you do."

Dalton knew the man was serious and close to a panic mode. Dalton said nothing, listening for any contact from the Seal team opposite his position on the same deck. The seconds dragged on for hours, it seemed, he and the man waiting for the other to make an aggressive move. Cotter was pulled back along the cabin wall by his assailant, now looking for an escape route. Dalton followed at close range, his assault rifle in front of him and held at shoulder height. Then the sound of a powerful engine starting filled the air. It was followed by a woman's scream, and Dalton reacted, glancing to his right. The stumpy man flinched to see the Seal team outside the port windows. Dalton took the distraction as an opportunity and fired one shot into the man's right temple, dropping him to the floor like a wet towel. Cotter caught himself before he hit the floor, shook off the head pain, and took aim at the dead man at his feet.

Dalton then realized he had been cheated again in his attempt to recover Carolyn. As he looked out to the east, the sleek *Flipper II* was screaming toward the ocean. On the stern deck was an unmistakable image: Carolyn held by a man and a woman with a large knife to Carolyn's throat. He raised his assault rifle in vain; the boat was more than a hundred yards away. Looking through his night-vision binoculars, he could see the fear in Carolyn's eyes.

A few minutes later, the Seal team controlled the yacht and confirmed the raft was destroyed and that no bomb could be found on board. Unable to make chase and trapped on the yacht, Dalton felt like a freshly fused piece of steel as he watched his Carolyn being taken away by a madman.

Yuri jammed the throttle forward, and the sleek Scarab jumped ahead, pointing the nose skyward until it leveled off. He enjoyed the head rush provided by out-maneuvering Crusoe again. Taros, Ivana, and Yuri had returned from their task of arming the bomb to receive a detonation signal when they came across the raft tied up to the *Lady Cadence*. They sabotaged the raft, retrieved Carolyn, and sped off. Streaking along at close to fifty-five miles per hour, Yuri had to make the next bay inlet before satellite surveillance could locate him. Ian was waiting in the small bay less than two miles from the *Lady Cadence*, sitting in a rented Cadillac SUV at a small marina. As the Scarab rounded the point of land announcing the little bay, Taros stripped the name *Flipper II* from the hull and added the clear plastic sheeting displaying *Rumors* as the new name for their escape boat. Canvas was added to further disguise the boat's original look. When finished, Taros said to Yuri, "How is it you always manage to escape this guy Crusoe?"

Revealing a slight smile, Yuri said, "Like I have done in all my major business dealings, I consider all possible outcomes and create alternative options. The disguises for my boats are only one of several schemes that have served me well."

It was dark and the thirty-slip marina was closed. No one was in sight as the boat, *Rumors,* tied off. Yuri, Ivana, and Taros with Carolyn in tow walked off to the SUV.

20-FOUR

EARLY MONDAY MORNING, WASHINGTON, D.C.

The second inspection of the *Lady Cadence* was a bit more intense. The secret passageways were found, computers were removed, and several crew members, including Aaron, were questioned rather unceremoniously. Despite the persuasive tactics, Aaron was not giving up any information about bombs; he was steering master for a powerful businessman's yacht . . . period. The rest of the crew claimed a lack of English speaking skills and appeared to be deckhands for the yacht operation, not henchmen for Yuri's business dealings.

Again, Dalton felt cheated. The sickening feeling in his stomach was as much frustration in stopping Yuri as it was finding his beloved Carolyn. The fear he saw in her face through the binoculars was unforgettable. He began to feel guilty that he had ever suggested she plan a rendezvous with him after the Sergey interview. Had they not made the plans to spend the weekend together, she would have been occupied with activities at the university, surrounded by faculty and friends, not isolated at the beach house, worrying about his tardiness.

THE TARASOV SOLUTION

Another frightening thought was why Yuri felt he needed to kidnap her as part of his plan. If his plan was to sell the bombs, then Carolyn had no direct role to play. If he planned to use the bombs, then her capture must be related to the investigation and pursuit Dalton was carrying out. His head hurt at the thought of losing her. He again choked down his fears and did what his innate skills always forced him to do: focus, analyze, and solve the problem.

The blast radius studies were frightening enough to make Pickler's evacuation recommendation seem pretty sensible. The problem, apparent to everyone involved, including the president, was that Dalton's speculation was just that, speculation, and all the efforts so far could not support or disprove it. Something had to change and fast. Nevertheless, Yuri had escaped again and this time with Carolyn visible in his grasp.

Aaron was a tough case. He argued that unless he and his crew were charged with a crime, they should be freed and the *Lady Cadence* released out of quarantine. Dalton resisted the demand out of hand and envisioned a way to draw Yuri out from his hiding place. Besides, the yacht searches revealed nothing that one could claim as a terrorist or even criminal act. After six hours of interrogation, Aaron revealed nothing about Yuri or his plans. Aaron just stated again and again that he was the steering master for the *Lady Cadence* and the owner had come to enjoy the fall weather before heading off to the Caribbean for a week of cruising among the islands.

Dalton instructed Wilson to keep a satellite targeted on the yacht's movements then allowed Aaron and the crew to return to the *Lady Cadence*. NSA lawyers were checking every angle to find a defensible reason to continue the detention of Aaron and the crew, although the evidence was all circumstantial at this point. NSA counsel and the administration didn't want to have some hot-shot liberal lawyer jumping in with a media army while he fought to protect his innocent client from the government's big oppressive arm . Besides, the issue now was not one of legal correctness; it was one of getting information fast and having Yuri believe he was not a target after all.

Cotter and Wilson were all over the arrest of Harith Zahid and recovery of the second bomb. Zahid was flown back to an NSA holding room near Andrews Air Force Base for interrogation. Staff who spoke his language were trying to break him down all evening and into the early morning. He was tough and had been in a situation like this before with Mossad before being rescued by his men at the Lebanese home of an Israeli mole.

NEST, the Nuclear Emergency Search Team, was dispatched to the returning *Dakota* in an effort to determine the nature of the detonation controller Yuri had placed on the bomb. A mistake, even four hundred miles out in the Atlantic, could mean devastating results to hundreds, if not more, innocent people in addition to the *Dakota* crew.

The satellite phone lit up, and Cotter took it. "Yes, he's here. I'll put the message on speaker." He motioned to Dalton.

"Mr. Crusoe, this is Johnson with the NEST team. We have analyzed the controller that Tarasov's scientist installed on the warhead. It's made to be an operational bomb from as far away as twenty miles."

"How is it set up?" asked Dalton.

"The device is very sophisticated, employing several different commands to commence varied methods of detonation, destruction, or disarming based on the order of keypad inputs."

The entire group around Dalton listened in utter amazement.

"Please give me some more details, Johnson. Can the controller detonate the bomb instantaneously, or must a timer bring the weapon to the detonation point?"

"Actually it can be set off either way, instantaneous or immediate through a delay command."

The room let out a collective moan and shifted about in their chairs.

"What about the destruction command? How does that work?"

"Well, as we understand it now, any wrong command entered once a timed detonation is begun will throw the controller into immediate detonation."

Wilson looked at Cotter and said, "Good God! What do we have here?"

Dalton thought about the predicament the complex detonator created for him. Finally he said, "Johnson, is there a command to disarm the bomb regardless which state it is in?"

"There appears to be a disarm function; however, it could take weeks to analyze the software behind these commands. Without the proper sequence and entry keys, anything could happen . . . from disarming to detonating the weapon." Johnson paused. "There is some good news here, however. The core is virtually depleted, and I'm doubtful it would detonate into a full nuclear explosion. It would not be nice to be around as it blew, but the core is compromised."

Dalton thought again for more than a minute while the room erupted in chatter and doomsday scenarios. Then, quieting the room with his raised hand, Dalton said, "Johnson, how fast can you get that detonation controller to me in Washington?"

Johnson posed the question to the sub commander, who took the phone and said, "This thing is quite light. We could package it in a watertight bag and suspend it from a retrieval balloon three hundred feet above the sub. A slow-moving Harrier aircraft could snag it and bring it to you in less than ninety minutes."

"Make it happen, Commander." Dalton handed the phone back to Cotter and asked him to get Ed Kosko on the line. General Rusk was notified of the request and dispatched a navy Harrier jet to the *Dakota* for detonator retrieval.

Looking to Wilson, Dalton said, "I want to interview Zahid before we go any further."

20-FIVE

NSA INTERROGATION CENTER

HARITH Zahid was the classic Jihadist terrorist. A rabid hater of Western culture, he despised everything about free, capitalistic societies. He purported to be an advocate of a theocracy form of government, however the only way he could achieve it was by a totalitarian dictatorship. His own organization of Jihadists was outcast from moderate Islamic groups and had to establish their own interpretation of Islam to justify their actions and policies. Labeled any other way, they were still cold-blooded terrorists capable of inflicting atrocities on their own people to achieve their ends. The vast majority of sensible Islamic political leaders declared them radical outcasts; however, some turned a blind eye to their actions.

This particular terrorist had seen his fair share of atrocities from his early teen years. Raised in Saudi Arabia and well educated in the Muslim tradition, he took a radical stance when his parents were killed while praying in a Mosque during an Israeli missile strike to wipe out terrorists in Lebanon. He never forgave the

THE TARASOV SOLUTION

Israelis and the decadent West that supported them. He committed his life to abolishing them and ridding the holy lands of infidels. Once before, eight years ago, he tolerated Mossad's interrogation of him and nearly died just before his followers rescued him. Since then, no measure was too extreme to punish Israel.

Zahid came to believe this interrogation was not all that difficult. The Americans had lost their appetite for serious grilling, and if he were to die, the West would be blasted by the rest of the free world for their extreme methods. That would be enough to ensure his martyrdom forever.

Dalton entered the room and looked at the half-naked prisoner shackled to a chair. He was defiant, as expected, and still concerned for his fate. Dalton asked the guard to leave the room and give him some privacy. Zahid did not sense Dalton was the blood-and-guts type; rather, he appeared calm, logical, and informed. This led to some confusion at first, however then Dalton began to explain his presence. "I'm not here to inflict pain on you to get answers; others are available for that. I'm here to tell you that you were duped out of a large sum of money for a phony warhead."

Zahid smirked at this weak attempt to frustrate him.

Dalton examined every facet of the man's demeanor. "No, it's true. The warhead had the radioactive core removed before you obtained it. It looked real, tested real, although it had no punch." Dalton looked for any reaction from the terrorist.

"Once we obtained the bomb, we scanned it for radioactivity and there was some, however not from live, fissionable material. Your scientist admitted your tests could not distinguish different radioactive isotopes. Correct?"

Zahid showed slight concern at Dalton's statement, although he remained quiet and subdued.

"This warhead couldn't blow up a newspaper stand, much less an Israeli police headquarters."

Zahid snapped his eyes toward Dalton then away.

"To make sure, we tested your detonator on the 'bomb,' and it did nothing except sit there as a reminder of your stupidity. You were taken, Zahid, for a lot of money."

"You are lying! The bomb is real!" Zahid erupted.

"No, I'm telling you what we discovered. And because we found no crime on your behalf against the U.S., we cannot hold you. We will return you to the *Amersythe* so you can continue your journey . . . *without* a nuclear bomb. Then you can explain how you paid so much for a toy bomb."

Dalton gathered some papers, stuffing them in a folder, and stood up to leave. "You are free to go, Mr. Zahid."

Dalton's Dalton would wait to see if his plan was

working its way to fruition.

Zahid was taken aback by the results of his interrogation. He was free to join his terror group again after having been taken at sea by the Americans? As he walked from the NSA headquarters, the thought of having paid €15million for a fake nuclear bomb consumed him. He couldn't believe his Pakistani scientist missed the efficacy check on the bomb. Zahid was boiling with thoughts. Perhaps the Pakistani was faking, having been paid off by Yuri, or maybe he was incompetent, or Yuri's men could have tricked the readings to false positives. Things were moving fast, he recalled, as the *Sammie* wanted to spend no more time than necessary tied to the *Amersythe*. The reactions of his financial supporters and fellow terrorists would be unbearable. Far worse would be the shame at being duped by Yuri Tarasov, the top man in the world among merchant arms dealers. Yuri could deny the bomb was defective, make it sound reasonable, and cast aspersions on Zahid's reputation as a savvy leader. A severe blow to any influential Jihadist.

The Americans had returned all his belongings to him, including some euros and dollars along with change for cab fare to reach the shipyards where the *Amersythe* was being held. Less than a mile away from the shipping port, he yelled to the cab driver, "Stop the cab a moment. I have to make a couple of calls." His first call was to his Pakistani scientist's cell phone.

RICHARD TREVAE

Nothing, not a sound . . . the phone was dead. "Damn! He must be running from me." Next he entered the number he recalled for Yuri's satellite phone and hoped he would answer it despite the minute risk of being recorded when it originated from a hard line. The phone rang several times, followed by a jump to voice mail.

"Yuri, it's Harith. You bastard! You sold me a useless nuke. I want my money returned. Call me on this hard line." Zahid repeated the phone booth number twice and hung up.

Twenty seconds later, the phone booth rang with an incoming call. Zahid picked it up and asked, "Yuri?"

"No names, my friend. I won't stay on long. What the hell are you talking about?"

"The bomb, it's no good. The core was removed, you prick. I want my money back or your second bomb as a replacement, and I want it now." Zahid was fast getting angry and irrational the more he thought of his situation.

"The nuke was fine. What did you do to it? And the first bomb is already positioned and armed. Its time is very near. I can't upset my plans."

"I want to meet to discuss this problem!" Zahid was almost screaming into the phone.

"I'll meet you in a few days, as planned. Calm down. Your bomb is fine." Yuri ended the call.

THE TARASOV SOLUTION

Back in NSA headquarters, Dalton and his team were all wearing headsets and listening to Zahid's call. They were watching a large wall screen of the Washington, D.C., area, which displayed a blinking red dot showing Zahid's location. The button-sized recording bug was transmitting as planned, so well, in fact that its location, embedded in the collar of Zahid's denim shirt, picked up Yuri's words as well. The ruse had worked, and Zahid had been manipulated into confronting Yuri and making him disclose the fact that first bomb was armed and in the D.C. area.

Cotter released the agents following Zahid from a distance to close in and arrest him again on conspiracy to commit terrorism.

Now Dalton had to find the first bomb and disable it.

Master arms merchant Yuri Tarasov always—*always*—had a follow-up or alternative plan to achieve his objectives. Harith Zahid was an unwilling accomplice in the current plan, yet he performed his role to perfection. When they met in Cyprus, he would explain and make it up to Zahid.

RICHARD TREVAE

Yuri's scientist and his team removed the core from the bomb sold to Zahid and replaced it with a spent core from a similar device Yuri had acquired several years earlier. An arms merchant such as Yuri was always hearing of weapons for sale, as well as buyers looking for specific items. He maintained a boneyard of outdated although still-lethal weapons from the dismantling of the Soviet military arsenal. Now the fresh core was installed in a detonator package similar to a metal attaché not unlike the one holding euros for Augustus, except when this case was opened or penetrated in any way, a three-kiloton nuclear explosion would result. Hidden on the *Sammie,* the lethal attaché would make its debut on Labor Day.

NSA Headquarters

THE conference call was set up in record time; it had taken about eighteen minutes to collect the president, Pickler, Ed, CIA Deputy Director Josh Pearson, and Dalton's team. The big wall screen in the NSA operations room was split into three sections: the president, Kosko, and Pearson. On separate, smaller screens were Pickler and Dan Jefferson of the Secret Service Presidential Detail.

Dalton began with a summary statement to catch the collective state of mind up on what had transpired over the past several hours. "We have been able to confirm in the last half hour that a second bomb is in position and armed in the Washington, D.C., area. It also seems, based on tangential data, that the bomb may already be in a countdown mode, although I must emphasize that has not been confirmed."

Each individual began to voice concerns and questions at once, and the president waved his hands, trying to gain control.

Ed Kosko bellowed through the voices and said,

"Dalton, will you please proceed? I will direct the incoming questions first after the briefing has brought us all up to speed. Is that all right, Mr. President?"

The president nodded his approval.

Dalton said, "I'm now recommending that we alert the D.C. police, the Coast Guard, and the navy only and specifically on a low-impact search mission. Any broadscale, visible effort with a high military presence could alert the target, Tarasov, to initiate an immediate detonation."

Ed had his hand raised to attract everyone's attention. He carried Dalton's thought further and said, "Dalton's team has also obtained the detonator from the second bomb, which is now in our control and has been disarmed. We believe the detonator is identical to the one planned for controlling the second bomb we need to locate."

"That is correct but we must not risk accidentally detonating the bomb while trying to disarm it. We do not know enough about how the programming works within the remote detonator to employ it yet." Dalton paused for reaction, yet none was forthcoming. He continued. "Yuri could have delivered the bomb by a smaller boat to the Chesapeake Bay area and either parked it with the bomb or moved the bomb on land to position it closer to its target. Our search must focus on the marinas and numerous docking facilities all along the bay's coastline."

THE TARASOV SOLUTION

The president was deep in thought about the new information he had been given. He said, "Dalton, can we have confidence a ten-kiloton device would . . ." The president paused, searching for the right words. "Achieve its objective anywhere in the Chesapeake?" All eyes were on the president as the grim potential reality set in.

Dalton looked to Wilson, who handed him a handful of photos covered with red, yellow, and orange circles. "The bomb's location is critical to that answer, Mr. President, but since the route for your two-hour sailing trip has had worldwide coverage, we can narrow down where a bomb must be placed to . . . achieve its objective." The words were hard for Dalton to deliver, even in a disguised vocabulary. Everyone loved this president, and no one wanted to see him become the casualty of a madman.

"You mean that because the sailing route is known, Tarasov would be limited by the bomb's blast radius to specific locations?" asked the president.

"That is exactly what we're speculating, sir." Dalton referred the group to an inset screen in which he brought up a satellite photo highlighting the proposed sailing route. Only two locations were close enough to deliver the maximum impact.

Looking over all the areas the sail intended to cover,

Ed said, "Dalton, if this logic holds, where are the probable locations?"

Using a laser pointer, Dalton identified the two points on the photo. "We believe the highest probability of finding the bomb is in an area, along the shoreline, beginning five miles north and south of Cove Point, Maryland, and extending east to the Delmarva Peninsula. This calculates to a search area of about forty square miles, however, only about fifteen miles of shoreline."

"Dan, isn't that about the turnaround point in the sail?" The president looked to his top Secret Service man for an answer.

"Yes, sir, that is right."

"Assuming a favoring three-knot wind, when should we arrive there, if we take off at eleven in the morning as planned?"

Shuffling through a pile of notes, Dan Jefferson looked up and said, "Right around 2:15, sir."

President Conner was not one to be intimidated and followed the logic of Dalton's analysis. He then leaned forward in his oversized, leather chair and said, "We will have the maximum time to locate and disarm this thing if we don't alert Tarasov we are this close to nailing him, so I propose we ready *Marine One* to fly over and pick up the crew, President Blinikov, and me at two o'clock if we haven't stopped this damn problem before then."

THE TARASOV SOLUTION

Heads, hands, and mouths were reacting in wild emotion at the suggestion the president offered. Raising his hand to silence the group, the president said, "If Dalton is right—and I feel he is—the bomb has to detonate in that narrow time slot to assure a kill. If it is there and explodes, *Marine One* will have me and the others thirty miles away. If it is not in the prime location, then Dalton's team will still need all the time available to locate the bomb."

Dalton drew a deep breath and reflected on the wisdom and courage of this president. The suggestion saved Dalton at least another twenty minutes getting that idea out to the group. It was not a popular alternative; however, the only other opposing option was to try an immediate evacuation of the entire Chesapeake Bay region before Yuri learned they were on to him and initiated an immediate detonation. The group was stalemated on what appeared as a no-win set of options.

Ed Kosko spoke up and asked if President Blinikov should be advised of the situation. Looking every bit the commander in chief, the president said, "I will talk to Georgi in person and let you know if he wants to cancel the sail." Pausing to collect his thoughts, the president looked at the men surrounding him in person and through video means and said, "Gentlemen, give Dalton your immediate and complete attention so we can end this nightmare."

20-SEVEN

A RENTED BEACH VILLA NEAR THE ATLANTIC OCEAN

YURI and his group, along with Carolyn, arrived at the small, isolated beach villa set aside for escape from his yacht if needed to ready the bomb. Ivana overheard Yuri's words as he took Zahid's call. "What are you going to do about Zahid?"

Reflecting for a moment, Yuri mentally replayed the phone conversation. "He called from a hard line, so he was not on the *Amersythe*. I'm worried about what he's gotten into. Our Cyprus meeting should tell me more." Yuri smirked at the skill he had in manipulating single-path thinkers such as Zahid.

Carolyn sat exhausted in a soft chair tied at her feet and hands. The SUV ride from the small bay where Yuri beached his *Flipper II* tender, now labeled *Rumors*, took more than ninety minutes, and very little discussion went on among Yuri, Ian, Ivana, and Taros until Yuri's phone rang. Carolyn was packed into the flip-up third-row seat and left to lie on her side the entire way. Ivana took the second seat along with Ian, who remained quiet, as she kept an eye on Carolyn. Taros drove and Yuri took the passenger seat. The call must have been a problem for Yuri as he didn't want to talk to the man on the other end and concluded the call by saying he would meet him in Cyprus. Following that call, Carolyn could hear occasional words as Yuri and Taros spoke in quiet tones for around a minute about...a Labor Day timetable.

It was approaching midnight, and Carolyn was in need of sleep; however, the adrenaline pumping into her system kept her awake and concerned. She was placed in a bedroom and chained to the bed frame. Weary and nervous, she tried to rest and fall asleep. As time dragged out, she fell into a slumber that allowed her to stay asleep. About 2:18 a.m. she became aware someone, or something, had moved her door. The room was dark and appeared empty and she felt a cold chill come over her as she looked about. The beach side awning window was open an inch at the bottom and allowed the mild breeze to produce a slight fluff on the side curtains. Again she began to drift off into semi-consciousness and thought of Dalton. Oh, how wonderful it would be if she would wake in the morning to find Dalton beside her and realize all this was just a dream. She stretched as if to nudge his body when a hand touched her leg and ran up along her hip. Involuntary shaking tried to warn off the frightening feeling as her eyes opened; it was Taros leaning over her and clamping his hand around her mouth.

"Be still and I'll let you live," Taros whispered near her ear.

Shaking, Carolyn tried to scream, however no sound emerged through Taros's tight grip over her lips. Taros tried to climb into the bed as Carolyn managed to swing her tied hands into a powerful arc and caught Taros across his left eye with her long nails. She could feel the penetration her fingers made into his eye and the flesh on his cheek. Taros pulled back, falling into a dresser and yelling in pain. She screamed as loud as she could at that point, and within seconds, both Yuri and Ivana were in the room. Ivana jumped on the bed and had her knife pressed against Carolyn's throat. Yuri followed her in and saw Taros lying on the floor in pain.

"You stupid shit! What the hell are you doing? I need her alive to manage Crusoe." Yuri grabbed the Ukrainian by the hair, raised him to his knees, and then slammed his head into the bedpost knocking him silly. Grabbing his hair again, he pounded his right fist into Taros's temple, cutting his face with the stone on his large ring. He then made four swift kicks to his groin and abdomen before pulling his Glock 9-mm automatic and pressed it to Taros's bloody temple. Glaring at Taros, he said, "Next time you need company at night, find a goat. Understood?"

THE TARASOV SOLUTION

Taros managed to stand up, holding his groin and his bloody head, and sputtered, "Understood. Sorry."

Carolyn was crying nonstop until Ivana released the pressure on the knife blade against her throat. "Get some sleep. You have a big day tomorrow." Ivana scowled at Carolyn. Over the next thirty minutes, Carolyn tried to collect herself and think of Dalton. She feared she would never see him again. She faded into a restless sleep.

A strong gust of wind swept the curtains far from the sides of the beach window. It was showing 2:46 a.m. on the small alarm clock sitting on the dresser. She rolled over and took a deep breath when she felt something under her hip. This was not a man's hand, so she resisted the impulse to scream. As she moved aside, she saw her cell phone. It was off, lying there between the sheets. She could not understand why it was there then remembered Taros had taken it when they left Dalton's mother's beach house. He must have lost it in the bed during the struggle with her and Yuri. Grabbing the phone with both tied hands, she was able to power it on. She threw the covers over her head to muffle her words. She made three key strokes: contacts, Dalton, talk. The phone rang. She prayed he would answer, however it rang and rang before going to voice mail. In a quivering, soft voice, she spoke. "Dalton, it's Carolyn. I've been kidnapped by some crazy named Yuri along with a Taros and a frightening woman named Ivana. I don't where I am except it's on the beach. Please, please come and find me, darling." She left her phone on, hoping that the cell signal would help Dalton locate her. Awake and alert, Carolyn began to allow herself thoughts of a rescue.

20-EIGHT

EVENING AT ED KOSKO'S HOME, WEST SPRINGFIELD, MARYLAND

DALTON was tired and worn out from the stress and tempo of the day. Ed had invited Dalton to his home for a late-night drink and a good night's sleep. Comforted with a scotch served neat, Dalton began to open up about Carolyn and share his worst fears concerning her fate. Ed had been a mentor and surrogate father at times to Dalton, since his dad's unexpected passing. Tonight was a good time to have a close friend to help absorb the pain and guilt Dalton was feeling. He began to talk about all the plans and dreams he had for Carolyn. Dalton yearned for the guidance and support a father provides a son although having not enjoyed those feelings in almost seven years. He recalled a talk with his father prior to a high school tennis match, where his school's trophy was dependant on his beating his opponent, a player he had never beaten before. Jonathon Crusoe was a man of great insight, and he spoke with his son about the importance of giving 100 percent to every test of life. Without spewing endless praise on Dalton's game strength or his physical skill, he reminded JD that if he could manage his fear of losing, the training and mental discipline to remain competitive would prevail and his opponent would fail. Always provided with the genuine belief his son had unique physical and intellectual talents, his father's soft-spoken style allowed his love to show through.

Ed sat and listened, sipping his brandy, while Dalton gave aimless reminiscences about his memories of his father. Kosko and Jonathon Crusoe had been friends and shared many special times together, however business had seldom been involved. The friendship tended to be that of country club buddies who would play a round together, plan a fishing trip, or spend an evening out with their wives. Knowing both the senior and younger Crusoe men very well, Ed realized that Dalton needed a father; however, he could not and would not assume that role. Ed's instincts told him he fell into the mentor role, which in an ironic kind of twist, repaired some of Dalton's loss felt from his father's death. Dalton wished he had the strong emotional veneer his mother had shown following the loss of her husband of twenty-eight years. She became stronger, taking immediate charge over family affairs, Dalton's education, and getting on with life. At the time, Dalton was a very young man and took more time to digest the loss.

Dalton stopped for a moment and said, "I'm sorry, Ed. I guess I'm boring you to death rattling on like this."

"Not at all, Dalton. I do the same things at times. Your dad was a fine man, and it's OK that we all still miss him so much."

Dalton looked up, showing an artificial smile to mask a threatening tear, and commented, "Ed, you are a good friend. I guess the prospect of losing Carolyn is what started all this. She is so important to me, and I think of my dad when trying to work out all these intertwined issues."

"JD, I would not have asked you to take this effort on, nor would the president have agreed, if it weren't evident you have abundant skills to carry this off." Ed took his last sip of brandy and continued. "It is not a sign of weakness to experience the things you now feel. And I'm here to help."

Dalton nodded his head in agreement and remained silent, stirring the last of his scotch.

Recognizing the late hour and using subtle caution, Ed directed the discussion away from Jonathon Crusoe. "JD, has the man Wilson assigned to investigate Carolyn's disappearance reported anything new?"

"No, I spoke with Wilson and his man, Cherney, earlier, and they have no new information. Yuri just grabbed her and still has her as some kind of leverage, I guess, over me." Dalton stared into his glass and found no answers.

Ed moved the evening along at a comfortable pace,

yet it wasn't until 12:30 a.m. when they called it quits and headed off to bed. Dalton fell fast asleep, aided by the scotch, sincere friendship from Ed, and a long day. He was convinced of one thing, however. They had to allow the search teams prowling the Chesapeake Bay shoreline even at the late hour to complete their work without alerting Yuri. The president's decision to let Dalton's strategy play out, although painful and dangerous, was the right one.

Several hours later Dalton woke and lay in bed, again thinking about Carolyn and what she must be going through. His eyes drifted closed then opened for a few seconds as he tried to fall back to sleep. For some reason unknown to Dalton at the time, he grew very alert and surveyed the room. It was a large, upstairs guest bedroom that Arlene and Ed kept for guests and friends when in the D.C. area. It was quiet and comfortable, although he remained very alert. Then he noticed a faint blinking light every few seconds near where his clothes were piled. He sat up in bed and looked at it. Then it hit him: his satellite phone was still on, and a call had come in. He got out of bed, felt his way in the dark to his clothes, fumbled around in his coat vest pocket, and retrieved his phone. Pressing menu to see the message, he could not believe his eyes: *Incoming call from Carolyn McCabe 2:47 a.m. Today.* He listened to the captured voice message on the phone and offered a short prayer; Carolyn was alive.

His mind ran into high gear as he laid out a recovery plan. He didn't want to bother Ed at the late hour, so he called Wilson and told him the details. Wilson called Cherney, still at NSA headquarters in the situation room, checking for information about Carolyn's kidnapping, and had him begin a new search to locate her phone. Wilson said he would meet Dalton at NSA headquarters in twenty minutes. He would call Ed in the morning to explain his absence.

Dalton walked in wearing jeans and the same white shirt he had worn all day, open at the collar and covered by a light leather jacket. His face was supporting a day and a half's beard growth. "I appreciate you following up on this right away, Wilson."

"That's no problem, sir. I know how I would feel if someone important to me was kidnapped to distract me from my primary effort. We'll find her, sir."

Dalton shook Wilson's hand while showing his appreciation through a light pat on his shoulder.

Cherney was at a computer console and looked up at Dalton with a full smile. "I've found her, sir, about twenty-five miles by air from here, near the water."

Dalton looked at the satellite map, enhanced to great

detail, and zeroed in on a beach house facing the bay near Crocheron. An exploding red circle flashed, identifying the exact phone location. The image was clear enough that even in the dim predawn morning light, Dalton could make out the house, a deck, and a light-colored SUV parked in the driveway.

Yuri awoke and sat up in bed. It was just after 7:00 a.m., and the sun was already flashing off the water and warming the mild, fall air. He looked around and hoped Taros had not tested his patience again during the night. If he had, he would be dead in short order. Ivana's hand reached his back and gently rubbed his right shoulder, relaxing him somewhat. She was waking and now moving into her sensuous part of the day—morning. Each time they were intimate, he marveled at how this thief and accomplished killer could show such tenderness and caring then, just hours later, use lethal skills to take a life without any remorse. Yuri knew her general background, although certain details were missing. She had never been married and, at nineteen, fulfilled a contract killing on a man it was reported she was engaged to wed. She had used her beauty and youth to attract her victim, a thirty-four-year-old corrupt politician, who was extorting money from a crime syndicate controlling much of the loan sharking in Moscow. The death was so surgical, it was assumed a fellow rival had eliminated him with an ex-KGB assassin, so she escaped all scrutiny. After that relationship, she moved about the former Soviet states for ten years, taking on a dozen or more assignments. In time, Yuri contracted her to investigate and eliminate a bodyguard suspected of exposing his business dealings to the Blinikov regime. After the assignment, they became close as casual lovers. When he hired Taros as the replacement for the bodyguard role, Ivana was elevated to the status of confidante and sometime partner in Yuri's business dealings. He trusted her, however only as long as he could control her with money and a rich lifestyle.

Her naked body aroused him, although he knew there would be time later for pleasures. Now, however, he had to make his gradual retreat from the blast area once the presidential sailing trip got under way on the expected route.

Entering the Atlantic Ocean

The *Lady Cadence* was moving slowly to the southeast in no particular hurry. Yuri had prepared Aaron in the event the big yacht was taken over by the

Americans. Only a few select crew members were privy to Yuri's entire plan, and most spoke no English, so questioning them through a Russian translator revealed nothing important. Aaron, Yuri's nephew, could be trusted more than others because Yuri had been a provider and surrogate father to his sister's son for the better part of eight years, after his father died from lung cancer. Yuri had no family other than his sister, although they were very close. Aaron was eighteen when his father died, and he was very despondent and cynical. Yuri stepped in and helped his sister and nephew out of financial trouble, arranged for her to get a legitimate job, and paid for Aaron to learn navigation skills while working on a fishing trawler. By twenty-two, Aaron knew that he wanted to work for Yuri, become his right-hand man, and learn the arms merchant business from an expert. Yuri had made a decision to shroud much of his illegitimate business in the cloak of his lavish lifestyle gained through fast dealings in the Russian oil business. The *Decadence* became his mobile command and control center. Aaron was made steering master, an ancient term similar to a bridge captain. The crew did not know Yuri was Aaron's uncle, a secret he was happy to keep. Pathologically neurotic, Yuri wanted Aaron to have unfettered access to the crew and Yuri's bodyguards, assuming any plot against him might rise to Aaron's attention if he were not obviously beholden to Yuri in any way.

All the years of learning seamanship and navigation paid off when Yuri brought Aaron aboard the first test run of the *Decadence*. He was told he could have a job with Yuri if he wanted it. The only requirements were complete confidentiality and absolute loyalty. Aaron jumped at the chance, even though he knew beneath the smooth exterior of Yuri's facade was a disciplined criminal running a huge arms merchant business extending all over the world.

Four years had passed since Aaron took over as steering master, and he felt his skills were being noticed and appreciated by Yuri. The confrontation with the Americans was not unexpected, however there were several split-second decisions that Aaron made to free the *Lady Cadence*. A complete manifest and cruising itinerary locked into the navigation computers revealing a plan to cruise up the eastern U.S. seaboard, hang out at Chesapeake Bay for the Labor Day weekend, and continue on to the Bahamas gave critical support to Aaron's claims about Yuri's intentions. Maintaining his poise when Dalton's team had boarded his vessel at night also was smart. The death of a crewman during the yacht's defense was problematic for Dalton, and Aaron knew it. No search warrant, Coast Guard inspection, or announcement that federal officers had boarded in a clandestine midnight raid on the yacht presented itself during the ordeal. Without probable cause and a sign-off by the proper authorities, the raid was illegal, and Aaron concluded Dalton must have known that during the interrogation. The lack of any visible criminal or terrorism activity on the boat made the death of a crewman and the raid indefensible. Aaron had won the *Lady Cadence's* release using a combination of cool-headed skills, combined with a poor legal basis and bad luck for Dalton.

Two miles east, off the entrance to the Chesapeake, Aaron called Yuri on his encrypted satellite phone. Aaron knew to disguise the conversation to eliminate any of the NSA experts' attempts to capture and decrypt the call. "This is Aaron. I have the yacht headed to international waters as scheduled. Is your return time still as planned?"

Yuri retrieved his phone and examined the caller ID. He let the phone proceed to voice mail. Always cautious about phone use, Yuri listened to the message then sent a text message back: *Our plans have not changed; expect us at the scheduled time.*

Aaron stood on the bridge of the *Lady Cadence* and surveyed the horizon with his powerful binoculars. No visible helicopters or Coast Guard boats were within sight. He checked his watch then noticed the text message light was flashing on the satellite phone. The screen revealed Yuri's message, which was received at 9:22 a.m. The helicopter carrying Yuri was to arrive at about 4:00 p.m. Until then Aaron was to make a south-southeast heading toward Bimini at only four knots and remain in international waters. The crew had settled down following the past events only twelve hours earlier and were glad to be back aboard the yacht, tending to their usual chores. The night raid was explained as a false alarm by Coast Guard intelligence expecting to find illicit drugs on the vessel. The death of a fellow crewman, however, was not easily forgotten, and Aaron claimed it was an accidental shooting.

The more Aaron recalled the details of his capture and interrogation, the more he felt like Yuri at the controls. He smiled and thought, *Maybe someday I'll own all this.* One more critical assignment from Yuri remained on Aaron's to-do list. It was a clever backup plan to ensure Yuri's problems with the new Russian president were finally quelled. The *Sammie* slid back into the Chesapeake without anything more than a casual fly-over by the Secret Service as they felt its cargo had been off-loaded to the *Amersythe* out at sea. The crew would be questioned, although they were not expected to yield

RICHARD TREVAE

much information as they were simply delivery contrac-
tors for Yuri. A trusted mercenary from the *Decadence*
had been placed on the *Sammie* crew for the Labor Day
weekend and had locked the special attaché case in his
storage locker.

20-NINE

DALTON wanted to move in fast with the Seal team and take down Yuri and his team and rescue Carolyn. It was tempting to set aside the primary mission and move out to retrieve his beautiful lady; he had to fight the impulse every second. He now knew the location; it was less than ten minutes away by helicopter, and Yuri would not expect that Carolyn had been able to make a call on her cell phone. The evening clouds lingered throughout the night yet by an hour after daybreak, the sky cleared to a bright blue. Dalton thought to call Ed before setting up the rescue, however then decided not to initiate a full-scale discussion of the pros and cons of taking this risky action. He reasoned if Yuri sensed capture, he could detonate the bomb as a simple diversion to aid his escape, or his pure rage at being discovered could trigger a reaction leading to thousands of deaths. Just as he convinced himself it was time to act and move out with the Seal team, he glanced at the satellite images refreshing every two minutes and noticed the SUV was gone. Again fueled by the thought Yuri had outmaneuvered him once more, he called out, "Wilson, please replay the last thirty minutes of satellite coverage on the beach house."

"It will just take me a minute to access the downloaded files. Hang on." Wilson never even looked at Dalton, for he knew the request was high priority. "It's coming up now. I'll zoom down for more detail."

The time clock at the screen's lower right edge ticked off time in hours, minutes, and seconds, the latter stretching into what seemed like hours. Dalton said, "There! Look at that. It is 7:23 a.m. and they are loading up the SUV."

The images were painful to watch. During less than eight seconds, four individuals left the house, got in the SUV, and drove away. After thirty seconds, the SUV was out of range for the narrow-field zoomed-in satellite. The screen images revealed Carolyn held close by a woman as she forced her into the vehicle. Dalton's heart sank to his stomach and he felt weak. It was Carolyn's light brown, medium-length hair and faded denim jeans Dalton loved to see her in. The rage boiled up again in Dalton as he missed, or wasted, in his critical view, a chance to rescue Carolyn.

The room of NSA technicians and the Seal team were dead silent. Dalton was hurting and they knew it. Dalton looked around the room and saw all faces staring at him. He looked distraught, turned to Wilson, and said, "Let's try tracking her phone again; maybe she was able to hide it in a pocket before they left the beach."

THIRTY

THE WHITE HOUSE, 10:00 A.M., LABOR DAY

THE president had just finished taping his brief Labor Day address to be broadcast later to the nation. It contained the same kind of patriotic messages of prior presidents, praising the American worker, although this one had a real sense of optimism for the upcoming year. Jerome Conner had been in office only a few days more than seven months, yet his aggressive administration had already garnered broad bipartisan approval for his diplomatic initiatives and steady fiscal policy. There was a general sense of hope for improving relations with former allies who had taken a backseat during the Iraq war debacle. His counterpart in Russia, Georgi Blinikov, had a similar aura surrounding his spectacular rise to power and his firm stance on the tough issues he was addressing. One major issue concerning both men was that of rogue Russian arms merchants buying up vast military supplies and weapons and selling them through secret transactions all over the world. Terrorist organizations could order anything they desired for their missions if they were well financed, and many

Jihadist groups had money donors in the Middle East who were wealthy from oil sales over the past twenty years. This issue alone was enough to suggest an early meeting between the two new presidents who both wanted to trust each other's country again.

President Conner stood near the Oval Office entrance and saw Blinikov, accompanied by the White House press secretary, strolling over to meet him. Trailing close behind was the Russian security team.

"Good morning, Mr. President," said the Russian in near-perfect English.

"And good morning to you, Mr. President," replied Jerome Conner. Both men chuckled at the formal addresses they were forced to use when not in a casual setting.

Once within the Oval Office, the president shut the door and said, "Georgi, I have to discuss something with you about today's sail."

The Russian president gave Conner a teasing look and said, "Jerome, you are not going to tell me you get seasick, are you?"

"No, no, I assure you I can handle the wave action on the Chesapeake. It's more of a sensitive political nature." Conner glanced at this chief of staff and the Russian security team. Blinikov noticed the glance and looked back at Conner. The implication was clear: Conner wanted to speak alone with his counterpart. At first the lead Russian security man resisted in polite discourse. However, after Blinikov uttered a few words in Russian, he motioned him out the door. The president's chief of staff followed the Russian security head out of the Oval Office.

The two men sat down opposite each other on the twin couches separated by an antique coffee table. Blinikov, relaxed and comfortable, reached for some orange juice set before him.

President Conner began, "Georgi, we have been able to track a yacht to the Chesapeake Bay area. Over the last few days, we have come to believe the yacht owner located and recovered two submerged SS-5 nuclear warheads dropped in cocoons years ago off of Cuba."

The Russian president froze his gaze on President Conner. This was not what he expected to hear from his new friend and counterpart while preparing for a sailing trip. "Jerome, are you sure about this? I mean about the missiles, for we never were able to confirm those stories at the Kremlin."

"All our intelligence suggests an arms dealer somehow discovered secret knowledge showing the order was given. In a recent interrogation of a Sergey Kreftkova, who served under Captain Demkin during the Cuban missile crisis, we confirmed the deployment of two SS-5 nuclear-tipped missiles." President Conner paused to let the weight of his remarks settle into Blinikov's mind.

The Russian president followed up. "Yes, I recall the name Kreftkova from investigations years ago. Our findings indicated he knew nothing of the alleged order from ... Admiral Sarkov, I believe, to drop the missiles. The Kremlin summarized their report and closed the file decades ago."

"Kreftkova is seeking asylum in the U.S. because an arms merchant, Yuri Tarasov, is pursuing him. He was hiding in Cuba until my men met him and learned of his story. So yes, we believe the story is real and that the nuclear warheads were recovered and configured as bombs."

Blinikov slammed his fist into a couch pillow and swore in Russian. He regained control and calmed himself, apologizing to Conner. He then set down his orange juice glass, wiped his mouth, and said, "I'm committed to exposing this guy and stopping his dangerous business of selling military weapons. He arms anyone who can pay, even those who attack Mother Russia." The anger in Blinikov's voice was evident.

"That brings me to my real point, Georgi. We have a theory we're working under that he has planted a nuclear bomb along our sailing route today. I felt I had to inform you so we could cancel if you'd prefer. Our various security teams are searching the area now for the bomb's location . We learned it is perhaps triggered by any one of several methods to avoid being disarmed."

Blinikov showed signs of concern as the president explained the danger to them and the civilians within the blast radius. "Jerome, the entire world will be watching our sailing this afternoon. It is a stepping stone for the healthy relations our two countries seek, is it not?"

"Yes, indeed it is. That is why some in charge of this search feel the safest route is to proceed with the sail as our security teams try to locate the bomb and then disarm it before we're in a position where it would, by all estimates . . . take us out."

Blinikov caught the delicate terms employed to mask a direct mention of death.

"My personal security detail could evacuate us from the *Windancer* by helicopter at least fifteen minutes before our safety could be compromised."

The Russian president also was not easy to intimidate. He folded his hands, looked at Conner, and said, "I'm willing to follow your plan if you are, Mr. President." The formal title brought both men back to the realization that a successful assassination would leave both their countries leaderless.

"All right, then. Let's get ready to sail."

30-ONE

TAROS drove the Cadillac SUV to a small business park with a heliport for pilot training, aircraft maintenance, and medical evacuations. The *Lady Cadence* helicopter was stored there and had been repainted and fitted with plastic decals to look like a local news helicopter. Ian had been given the task of monitoring the tender, *Flipper I*, until the *Windancer* left its slip under sail with the two presidents. Then he was to arm the bomb through the remote detonator for a delay of two hours and twenty-five minutes. He would then leave the area in the SUV and wait at the heliport for Taros to pick him up and head to the *Lady Cadence.* Yuri, Ivana, and Taros were going to monitor the event from the air in his helicopter with enough separation to avoid drawing attention. Once the sail was under way and Ian had entered the proper detonation time delay, Yuri and his men would reunite on the *Lady Cadence* in international waters, far from the blast area.

THE TARASOV SOLUTION

Carolyn Katrina McCabe was a fortunate grab for Yuri. At first he wanted to persuade her to reveal useful information about Dalton's job and capabilities in the NSA. It became very clear early on in her interrogation that she knew very little of his job and far less about any mission he was on. Carolyn told them that she reasoned that unless he had to reveal something about his assignments, the less Carolyn knew, the safer she would be. Only after more than an hour of questioning and threats from Ivana Yenko did Carolyn appreciate the true safety in knowing nothing about Dalton's mission. However now with the *Lady Cadence* inspected and boarded twice then released, Sergey Kreftkova still alive, and Carolyn McCabe his long lost niece who just happened to be Dalton Crusoe's girlfriend, a final step to conceal his acts and escape emerged. Yuri discussed the plan with Ivana, who liked the idea and saw it as another opportunity to build on her reputation as a fearless, well-paid assassin.

Carolyn sat motionless in the backseat of the SUV with everyone except Ian. His absence caused her to question what was about to transpire. She was taken to the small helipad check-in area, which was empty except for her, Taros, and Ivana. Yuri remained outside and went over his instructions one last time with Ian, who had been waiting nearby after he took a cab from the marina to the abandoned heliport.

Yuri spoke with renewed intensity. "Park near but not too close to the marina. We need to confirm *Flipper I* has not been discovered nor had the bomb removed. From the SUV, you can determine if the local detonator is receiving commands from the remote. When I call to confirm the *Windancer* sail has begun, you enter the delayed detonation time and head back to the helipad. We'll allow you five minutes after you leave the marina to get back here, and we'll all fly back to the yacht. Got it?"

"Yeah, I have gone through this a hundred times. We're good." Ian was annoyed at being addressed as if he were a child. In his mind, he was the technical genius making Yuri's plans possible.

Yuri fumed. "Don't screw around with me. You are well inside the blast zone here at the helipad. You get a flat tire, stop for a beer, or get lost in traffic, we're not waiting and you'll die. Now do you have it?" Yuri was right in Ian's face, who knew enough to not respond with defiance.

"Yeah, really, I know what I have to do. Don't worry."

Ian pulled away alone in the SUV, and Ivana tugged at Carolyn's arm to pull her into a small mechanical room behind the heliport waiting area. She sat her down in a folding chair and taped her hands and feet together and behind her to a four-inch-diameter building support column. She felt that whatever Yuri was trying to achieve was about to come down very soon. The room was dark and smelled of oil. There was one small light and one tiny window with permanent metal louvers to allow ventilation.

Ivana finished her work by connecting a wire cable around Carolyn's neck and pulling it taut against the round, metal post. Carolyn grimaced in pain as the cable pulled her to the support. Ivana looked at her and said, "Well, this is it. I guess we're not going to be friends after all." She left the small room.

Yuri spoke in a whisper to Ivana and Taros in the outer lobby area for a moment; however, Carolyn could not make out the words. She did hear the unmistakable sound of an automatic pistol being loaded with a clip and a bullet sliding into the chamber as the breach was released. She shuddered with fear and strained to see, yet could distinguish only shadows of movement in the thin stream of light coming in under the door to the room. Her only hope, she felt, was that Dalton had heard her distress call early in the morning and that he would track her cell phone, still on in her front jeans pocket. She felt isolated and helpless at that moment. It was all she could do to keep focused on staying alive. Dalton was coming; she knew it.

RICHARD TREVAE

Beyond the small back room door, Taros was busy. He planted wired bricks of C4 sufficient to devastate the flight office, Carolyn, and anyone within twenty-five feet. Yuri needed to make a short phone call to detonate the C4 bricks after he lured Dalton in to rescue his girlfriend. The plan was coming together.

30-TWO

AT THE *WINDANCER* SLIP, LABOR DAY

THE Secret Service team arrived at the marina four hours earlier and closed it to the public. Only a few well-known and connected political insiders were allowed to be at the marina when the two presidents arrived to begin their sail. The Russian team of security agents made their own inspection and signed off on the marina and the sailboat. A few members from the large network news teams were allowed to be present at the dock when the *Windancer* headed out to sea, although no reporters were allowed on the boat. The sky had been buzzing for hours with a dozen helicopters from all over the East Coast providing nearly continuous coverage of the historic meeting and Labor Day sailing trip. Meteorologists and the Weather Channel experts were on the television networks, explaining the weather conditions at the slip and in the Chesapeake and what the men could expect farther down the bay for the balance of the afternoon. Graphic displays tracking the intended route were popping up on everything from computer screens to Blackberrys to the local news cov-

erage. Estimates were spewing forth as to when the
Windancer would be at various locations along the sailing route, assuming the mild, two-knot wind held in
their favor and the full sails were let out. It was going to
be a great day and a historic event unfolding as the
world watched.

The top man in Georgi Blinikov's security team was
brought into the loop concerning the threat. Blinikov
noted his objections to proceeding, however the plan
remained unchanged. Likewise the lead man for
President Conner's security team was also briefed on
the situation and had arranged for an immediate
removal of the two presidents by *Marine One* if the
threat was confirmed and the men were in danger or by
2:15 p.m. if, as Dalton had theorized, the bomb would
be detonated very near 2:30 p.m. The surveillance teams
on the shoreline were busy yet appeared calm, checking
every dumpster, outhouse, marina, and boat found within the blast radius models.

President Conner, followed closely by Blinikov,
climbed aboard the *Windancer*. Three security men for
each president were already on board, dressed like
sailors except for the sophisticated communications
equipment and array of defensive assault weapons and
handguns. In the end, the president insisted Blinikov
and he be allowed to operate and truly sail the boat for
a time. After all, if they were viewed as sailing the boat

together and sharing the load, what better imagery to show a working relationship on the political stage. Neither man wanted to be missing from those photo ops. At least fifteen other boats were out in the main sailing channel used by the true racing crafts. All the boats allowed to be within two hundred yards of the *Windancer* had been approved weeks earlier by the FBI for this very day. All others were warned through the media to remain at least a half mile away or be fired upon if they failed to comply. The day was nice and warm, approaching seventy-one degrees, as they boarded the fast sailboat. A full sun and low humidity made the air feel fresh and invigorating. Both men wore Nautica-style lightweight jackets, each embroidered with their country's presidential emblem on the left chest. Navy blue ball caps displaying the name *Windancer* were provided to all the members of both presidential teams.

Dalton held his satellite phone in his right hand and listened to the latest intelligence from Cotter on the ground searches progress. A prank call from a college fraternity resulted in no bomb discovery, although three sophomores at American University were locked in a holding cell at NSA headquarters and were being interrogated using persuasive methods.

As they were preparing to tie off and begin the sail,

President Conner came over to the port side rail and motioned to Dalton. In a low voice, he said, "I'll see you for drinks later with Ed; go prove your theory and solve the problem."

The president smiled as if nothing were out of the ordinary, although Dalton felt sick to his stomach. Not only had he used convincing logic to persuade the two most recognizable and powerful men in the world to embark on this potentially disastrous sail, he still had no new information on Carolyn's whereabouts. Dalton smiled with confidence and said, "I look forward to that time, sir."

The *Windancer* looked sleek and powerful as it slipped through the low chop near the docks. It reminded Dalton of a thoroughbred racehorse, in the prime of its career, being led to the gate, positioned to vault out onto the track and lead a following pack of lesser competitors. Once in the channel, the sails were unfurled, and the *Windancer* listed about four degrees as it caught the wind. Nearby boats were also hoisting their sails as if responding to the challenge of a race. Dalton's trance was interrupted by his satellite phone ringing.

Cherney said, "Dalton, I've located Carolyn's cell phone again. The signal is weak, although she is not far from here, approximately seven miles closer than she was earlier at the beach house."

"Excellent work. Tell Cotter to meet me here in five minutes with two Seal team members, fully armed." Dalton was not about to wait for some local sheriff's deputy to meander over to her location and blow the opportunity. He was more determined now to lead his team and rescue Carolyn.

NSA Headquarters

Dalton's phone rang again. "Dalton, this is Cotter. We apprehended Yuri's scientist, based on a call from a citizen who noticed a suspicious man parked in an SUV in her neighborhood. Maryland State Police called NSA based on our earlier alerts, and we grabbed him."

"Has he revealed anything about where the bomb is and if it is armed?"

"No, he has said nothing except that his name is Ian and he was resting before the planned fireworks along the shore this evening."

Dalton thought for a moment. "How are you sure this is Yuri's scientist?"

"This is really cute. He has an electronic device on the front seat. He claims it is a new style TV/DVR controller. It is an exact replica of the detonator the *Dakota* retrieved for us. I recognized it right away and suggested I try the buttons and he freaked. It is another detonator; that's for sure." Cotter also found rental agreements for the SUV and a beach house where Carolyn must have been held.

"He's been fingerprinted and we're running a search now, and we have him in a mobile unit headed your way," Cotter announced.

"Where did you find him?"

"In the exact area you figured. It is about six miles south, near a cluster of small municipal marinas at Cove Point."

"Make sure no one touches anything on the keypad. Got that?"

"Yes, sir. I've got it in my hands now, and I'm shaking in fear along with our new friend Ian, but I'll be OK."

Dalton allowed himself a brief smile at the good fortune in capturing the detonator. He looked at his watch, 11:46 a.m., less than two and a half hours from the presidents' forced evacuation from the *Windancer*.

The NSA mobile unit arrived with Cotter, two

Maryland State troopers, and Ian. The modified Lincoln Navigator had the latest in satellite communications, GPS tracking, computer interface with NSA headquarters, and camera coverage of the SUV's interior. Ian was handcuffed to one of several stainless steel rings anchored to the floor to secure equipment and suspects. He was very quiet and looked pale.

Dalton entered the van from the side double doors and sat next to Ian. "Are you working with Yuri Tarasov?" Dalton asked, studying the sweating scientist.

Ian shook his head and said in poor, accented English, "No, I don't know this man."

Dalton knew that was a lie, and he didn't have time to play the interrogation games Ian may have learned from Yuri. Resting back in his seat, Dalton smiled and said, "We have the second bomb. We also have its detonator. Sergey Kreftkova is alive and talking, and neither of the two presidents are on the sailboat *Windancer.*" Dalton didn't have to wait long for a reaction.

In a voice that sounded terrified, in near-perfect English, Ian starting spewing information. Yuri's well-thought-out plan had been compromised, and Ian knew he could not stall or lie his way out of his predicament.

Dalton sensed Ian's weak commitment to carry out a suicide and said, "Now we're prepared to leave you chained in your Cadillac SUV where you were waiting while we vacate residents from this location and watch from a safe distance as the ten-kiloton bomb explodes and takes you with it."

Ian flushed and tried to explain he was just a technician for Yuri and only helped him for the money. Ian straightened in one last attempt to gain bargaining leverage. "I know where your friend Ms. McCabe is and can take you there."

Dalton didn't take the bait however looked the man directly in the eye and said, "I know where she is also and we don't need you to recover her." Ian deflated at the statement then looked up and said, "How would you like to capture Yuri . . . on U.S. soil? I would tell you everything I know of his plans. He's to fly me back to the yacht when it is in international waters just prior to the detonation."

"Where is the exact bomb location? Tell me now."

"It is close. You cannot retrieve it without Yuri knowing. He's watching it." Ian's lips were shaking as he spoke. "If you try to disarm it manually, it will detonate."

"Can you disarm the bomb from the remote detonator?" Dalton held his breath, awaiting an answer.

"Yes, although it is a complicated process. I have to enter the disarm code from the remote; then Yuri must confirm the code from his satellite phone, or the timed detonation continues." Ian wiped his sweaty face with his sleeve. "You must have Yuri's phone to stop the detonation."

THE TARASOV SOLUTION

Dalton performed a fast mental analysis on the information gained, looked at Cotter, who remained quiet, holding his sidearm pointed at Ian's chest. "We have to capture Yuri to make this work, is that right?"

"Yes, it is, so will you help me if I help you?" Ian looked at Dalton, the troopers, and Cotter for sympathy. None appeared. Dalton said, "When are you supposed to return to the helicopter pickup point?"

"Yuri should call soon and confirm the sailing trip has begun. Once he does, I enter the final timed detonation commands and leave for the pickup. I have to be there within five minutes of his call, or he leaves without me."

Dalton looked at his watch then Cotter and Ian and said, "You may have just given me an idea that will save your life."

Dalton stepped outside the van with Cotter and called Ed Kosko. One hour and twenty minutes remained to put the plan together, rescue Carolyn, and stop the assassination of two world leaders.

The idea of removing the bomb was too dangerous. It had to be disarmed soon, or the evacuation of the central blast area would be mayhem. A cell phone rang, and Dalton saw Cotter reach for his jacket pocket. I was Ian's phone; Yuri was calling. Ian was trembling as Cotter handed him the phone and leveled his 9-mm Glock at his temple.

Dalton said, "Keep it simple and according to his plan."

Ian swallowed hard and took the phone. "Yes. I'm monitoring the marina . . . No one has approached the bomb . . . OK, I'll enter the final detonation commands in thirty seconds. I'll be at the pickup point soon."

Yuri closed his phone, ending the call. He was convinced the call had been far too brief to be caught and recorded by the NSA. His helicopter, painted to look like the Channel 2 NBC News chopper, was circling the armada of ships following the *Windancer's* route from a radius of about a mile. Each turn to the west flew Yuri over the marina where the bomb hidden inside *Flipper I* was docked. He scanned the area with binoculars to look for flashing police cars or signs of an evacuation. He rejoiced that his plan was working so well and he soon could get back to the business that brought such financial success and power.

One thorn remained and that was Dalton Crusoe, for he had challenged his intellect and daring. Crusoe had some luck finding Kreftkova floating in the sea, and he discovered the *Mullet* and destroyed it, yet Yuri's plan to assassinate the two presidents aboard the *Windancer* was still moving along. Yuri also came into some luck locating Carolyn and learning she was Kreftkova's niece and Crusoe's lady. She would be a compelling force to bring Crusoe to her where he and Ivana could eliminate them both. The plan continued to unfold and gave Yuri a rush.

30-THREE

DALTON directed Cotter and the Seal leader to fit the new NSA tracking and SatCom equipment into the Cadillac SUV driven by Ian into the marina. Cotter hid in the far back cargo area, while Dalton and the Seal leader crouched in the backseat with weapons drawn. Ian was driving as Yuri would expect. They were going to surprise Yuri at the pickup point. Dalton would have preferred an assault team of ten men, although he had no time to assemble such a force. Based on Ian's claims, Carolyn was still bound there as bait for Dalton.

The small back room behind the flight office felt like a tomb to Carolyn. She fought back tears, although in the end she feared she would still be here when the bomb went off. For a few minutes, she just sat, bound to the round, metal support post, and tried to avoid thinking of death. For a moment, her thoughts turned to utter despair, and she felt her will weakening, almost welcoming death to free her from this bondage. Trying to imagine death, her survival instincts kicked in and she focused on her love of Dalton, knowing that despite no word from him, he was searching for her. She then committed herself to escape or die trying. Her face reddened and rage took over. She struggled against the cable chain, kicking at the floor, and discovered her foot reached a small, capped oil pipe valve. It rose only a few inches above the floor and looked as if it were unused for years, probably due to an upgrade to gas-fired heating. The stub pipe and valve were rusted shut. She felt leverage against the stub and pushed hard with her left leg, yelling out loud to increase her strength. The round column shifted a bit. Twisting her neck to see the floor, she noticed the square plate beneath the round column had moved about a quarter inch. She noticed there were bolt holes in the base plate and no bolts; it simply stood on the concrete floor, held in place under the roof's load. Her energy level rose to new heights, and she pushed again; the column moved another small fraction of an inch. She pushed again and again until it slid hard almost two inches. The roof creaked under the lack of support. Determined to get free, Carolyn pushed again with all her strength, and the column toppled to the ground, dragging her with it. The roof beams shifted and dust from years of neglect drifted down around her face, stinging her eyes. She slid along the floor and was able to free first her hands then her neck from the column. Still bound, she dragged herself to the door and pulled herself up to a standing position. From there she was able to wiggle the tape loose on her hands then pull off the tape on her feet. She was free.

The sunlight refreshed her as Carolyn looked outside the office and saw no one around. She checked and her cell phone was still in her jeans. It was on however the battery was weak. She opened the cover and pushed the auto dial button for Dalton.

Dalton looked puzzled when he heard his phone ring. Setting down his Colt Armalite .223 caliber assault rifle, he grabbed the phone and saw Carolyn's name appear *Incoming call Carolyn McCabe.*

He ordered Ian to stop at the side of the road a moment.

"Carolyn, is it you?"

"Yes, yes, thank God you got my call. Dalton, I escaped and I'm near some small airstrip near the shore. Please come and get me."

"Move to any cover close by; I know where you are, and I'm on my way. Keep your phone on. I'm in a white Cadillac SUV. A state trooper vehicle is behind us." Dalton looked over to Cotter, who gave him a silent thumbs-up and a broad smile. Visibly relieved, Dalton said to him, "Call the Maryland state troopers to follow us and pick her up." Cotter made the call.

Dalton felt a rush of adrenalin as he thought about

Carolyn and what she had endured because she was in his life. He promised himself to better protect her as the thought of losing her was painful. The SUV was about two minutes from arriving at the heliport when Dalton saw Carolyn waving to him from behind a covered bus stop bench. She looked scared although unharmed. He hoped it was so. He held her close for a moment then told her to get in the trooper vehicle pulling up behind him. She questioned the reason until she saw the weapons Dalton and Cotter were holding. He was trying to protect her.

Ivana sat behind Taros, who was piloting the helicopter. The aircraft had just landed and the engine left to idle as the Cadillac SUV approached. Yuri sat in the copilot seat and checked his watch just as Ian came around the corner and into the parking area for the small heliport. Ian stopped the SUV and sat motionless for some reason Yuri could not fathom. Yuri looked at him first assuming he was collecting his small equipment items—a phone, the remote detonator, and a jacket—yet he was motionless. On an impulse, Yuri opened the chopper passenger door and began to get out, cursing under his breath. Ian then opened his door and shut off the engine. Yuri stopped and studied the vehicle only fifty yards away. Something was wrong. He asked Ivana for the binoculars from the rear seating section and brought them to his eyes. Ian was still motionless; otherwise all looked normal. He then waved to Ian to come over to the helicopter. Ian nodded his head and started to exit from the open driver's door when Yuri noticed a small roof antenna connected to a thin cable running along the rear side window; he focused in tighter with the binoculars and saw the reflection of a small, bright circle. He was perplexed at first then recognized it as a rifle scope. He lurched back, slid in the chopper, and said, "Get us out of here fast! Ian's got company."

Taros looked out to the SUV and saw nothing unusual. "What? Ian's coming now."

"Go now!" Yuri repeated. "He's not alone!"

Taros flipped two toggle switches, and the engine roared as the chopper began to lift off. It made a fast, low circular spin and darted over the SUV. It flew not more than twenty feet above the top of the Cadillac. Ian stood outside the SUV. The rear doors flew open and out jumped Crusoe and another agent, weapons in hand. In the two seconds it took them to exit the vehicle and position themselves for a shot the chopper was moving out towards water. Taros was two hundred yards away and turning fast to the east. Unable to hit the fast-moving helicopter, they withheld firing to avoid alarm in the nearby homes. Dalton looked to the sky and said, "I have the tail numbers, 347 AH," He pulled his rifle sling his over his shoulder and freed his hands, reaching for his phone. Noting the size, direction and markings on the helicopter Dalton scrolled for Wilson's phone number at NSA headquarters. He watched in disgust as the bird headed out to open water.

Looking back at the heliport, Yuri turned on his phone, called up a stored number labeled *Surprise,* and pressed send. A second later the heliport burst into an orange fire ball, engulfing the flight office, the SUV, and a thirty-foot zone around the wood frame building.

"I think we may have killed them all." Ivana smiled as she surveyed the damage.

"Yeah, and I didn't even have to lure Crusoe into the trap. He drove into it by himself. I guess he's not going to be a problem anymore. Too bad about Ian," Yuri remarked with a cold, blunt expression.

The blast was powerful yet confined to about a hundred-foot circle. The rapid rate of detonation from C4 produced a shock wave as lethal as the blast fragments. Ian was hit in the throat by flying debris and fell to the ground, bleeding and unconscious. He had been standing outside the vehicle and unprotected. Dalton and

Cotter were partially protected by the open doors between them and the blast center. They were knocked to the ground, suffered minor cuts, felt disoriented and sustained a temporary hearing loss, although alive. Dalton's phone was blown from his hand and landed hard on the pavement smashing it to bits. The Maryland state trooper car pulled up a minute after the explosion. Carolyn jumped out and ran to Dalton, still kneeling on the ground, trying to get his bearings. She grabbed him and threw her arms around him in a forceful embrace. Still on one knee, Dalton held her face and said, "I'm so sorry, darling. Are you all right?"

"Yes, I'm OK now. I thought you were killed in the explosion." Carolyn wept, traumatized.

"We're all right . . . very lucky. I think the explosion was meant to take us all out. He must have thought I would track you down." Dalton gave the chopper tail numbers and description to Cotter who called Wilson to alert the security aircraft covering the presidential sail. Yuri's helicopter was out of sight and headed east.

Carolyn would not leave Dalton until he explained the full gravity of the situation. He ordered her taken to the NSA headquarters some twenty miles away to stay with Ed Kosko's unit until the crisis was ended. She was exhausted from her ordeal however otherwise all right. Her principal concern, she told him, despite the bomb prospect, was Dalton. He was under tremendous pressure, and while supported by a talented group of people, the events were unfolding so fast any effort to expand the leadership situation beyond Ed, Dalton, and the president would never have sufficient time to gain traction. No, Dalton Crusoe was alone at the top of the decision tree. As Carolyn left Dalton to go with Ed to NSA headquarters, she whispered to him in a last-minute embrace, "Please be careful and call me when you can. Promise?"

Dalton looked into her eyes and said, "Yes, I'll call. And please get some rest." This time he knew he would not fail on his promise.

Dalton checked his watch. Less than two hours remained until the mandatory evacuation of the two presidents from the *Windancer*. A mass evacuation or nearby communities within the ten-mile blast radius was near impossible now, so the bomb had to be removed or disarmed. Ian described the *Flipper I* after his capture and capitulation under Dalton's interrogation. They knew it was at the last marina south of Cove Point in berth C21. They did not know how Yuri was monitoring the bomb and boat. The news helicopter masquerade Yuri employed might not have been his only option. Dalton feared Yuri had placed local surveillance cameras to thwart bomb's retrieval and not told Ian. Dalton got Ed on the SatCom and filled him in on the past hour's activities. Ed alerted the president, who had seen the heliport explosion from the *Windancer* some twenty-five miles away and assumed it was related to the pursuit of Yuri. Both the Russian and U.S. presidents said they would wait until the last minute to seek evacuation from the sailboat.

The problem became clearer although no less complicated. The basic issue was they had the bomb but could not approach or move it or attempt to disarm it without its detonating in the process. Ian was willing although physically unable to guide them through the disarming steps. And they needed to obtain the disarm entry code from Yuri's satellite phone, which by best estimates was now somewhere heading east toward international waters, soon to connect with the *Lady Cadence*. An attack on the *Lady Cadence* was still no guarantee Yuri's phone could be obtained. If Yuri were about to be apprehended he could simply destroy the phone or permanently delete the disarming code. Surrendering to a boarding at sea would be a hollow personal victory yet still a devastating one for the presidents. Dalton was no communications expert, however he was surrounded by them at NSA, and he had a clever plan to get the code from Yuri. He summoned Cotter and Wilson along with Cherney.

THE TARASOV SOLUTION

The FBI took Ian to Presbyterian Hospital near the capital. The president had given Ed Kosko temporary authority to marshal any resources from the CIA and FBI along with the Maryland State Police to make Dalton's final move. Crews worked at a frantic pace to set up the software and programming functions Dalton needed to carry out the next critical step of his bold plan. Carolyn was nearby, keeping tabs on Dalton, and knew better than to burden her man with the emotional issues she was dealing with. Time was the critical factor to avoid a horrific fate at the hands of a ruthless, corrupt Russian businessman.

Verbal mapping was applied to the recorded call from Yuri when he ordered Ian to enter the timed delay commands for a detonation just prior to the planned pickup. If enough clear words were recorded on Cotter's mobile equipment, then certain phrases using Ian's voice print could be compiled to trick Yuri into thinking he was alive. The deception went along with other software protocols, which would take control of Yuri's phone once he was connected to a bogus call from Ian. It was becoming clear to all involved they had only one shot at this approach. As the team of twenty-six technicians, software experts, communications engineers, and a host of NSA agents waited for the experiment results, Cherney came to Dalton and said, "Well, we have a pretty good voice map on Ian. We also have Yuri's satellite phone number and the download software to control Yuri's phone . . . *if* he answers it and hangs on for at least five seconds."

Dalton looked at the weary team of technicians facing him and said, "Good. Let's go with it in five minutes. I'm calling Kosko and the president right now to confirm their plan's approval."

30-FOUR

NSA Headquarters, Director's Level Situation Room

THE room was much larger than the one Dalton, Cotter, and Wilson had operated out of for the past several days. Dalton had never seen this situation room, although he had communicated to it a few times when teleconferencing with Ed Kosko. It looked much like a small theater except that the situation manager, a title to designate the person directing the console operators who were positioned in a recessed floor, walked a raised semicircular mezzanine platform overseeing every console and faced opposite the twelve-foot by six-foot plasma wall screens covering two-thirds of the elliptical room. The room was quite dark, the only light coming from the wall screens and miniature floor lights to guide one around the walkway and down corridors to the thirty console operators. Eight screens could display different information at once and, with a merging command, overlay one on another to display a picture-in-picture format typical for showing an individual's ID alongside a rap sheet.

One screen had a satellite view featuring the

Chesapeake Bay area with a blinking red dot identifying the *Windancer's* location. Another was a live video feed from a couple of F/A-18s circling from a mile out, capturing every roll and heave of the sailboat as it cut through the waves at about five knots. The real-time images of the presidents were sharp as they were enjoying the day and their time together. One screen scanned through the national and international feeds to major networks every thirty seconds, all trying to get the best coverage of the historic event and narrated by senior reporters. The satellite coverage shifted just far enough south to reveal a second blinking red spot on the screen, the Cove Point marina position now known to hold the bomb. The distance between the sailboat and the marina seemed frighteningly small, although the blast radius studies confirmed the *Windancer* was still not in the kill zone. It was time to put Dalton's plan in action.

The situation manager called out the operators' functions and awaited confirmations they were connected and ready for their assignments. They were all ready. Dalton received a look from Kosko, still holding a cell phone that was connected to President Conner, as evidenced by the satellite images showing him with his cell phone open to hear Ed's commentary on the upcoming events. Dalton nodded his approval to make the call to Yuri. Technicians on the recessed floor started the process.

Wilson directed additional satellite surveillance and found The *Lady Cadence*. She was moving at twenty-three knots, near her maximum speed, toward the Venezuelan coastline. As the imagery appeared as a screen-in-screen inset to the *Windancer* coverage, Yuri, Taros, and Ivana landed on the *Lady Cadence* deck. Dalton watched numbers spread across a console computer screen and flash as the call to Yuri went out.

Aboard the *Lady Cadence* Yuri read the message on his phone: It read *Ian satellite phone*. Yuri did a double-take at the caller's name. He confirmed it was the phone he gave to Ian for this very mission. Doubting Ian survived the explosion, he hesitated, yet he had to satisfy his curiosity. He pressed *Talk* and, without greeting the person on the other end, listened for a moment. Finally he said, "Ian, are you OK?"

The software kicked in and said in a contrived voice, "Yuri, it's me, Ian. I was injured in the explosion but was able to crawl away and hide in a vacant garage. Can you come and get me out of here?"

Four seconds had passed, and the computer consoles

were flashing download after download to Yuri's phone. Then the main center screen flashed vast amounts of data transmission under the pulsating heading *Capturing Data,* and the situation room went ballistic with cheers.

Yuri held his thoughts a moment, formed a question, and asked, "Ian, what is the number I gave you for your phone?" The phone was silent; Yuri listened for an instant then slammed the phone closed. He looked to Aaron and said, "Find somewhere to hide us in the Caribbean until nightfall."

30-FIVE

NSA Headquarters

THE mood inside the situation room was a mixture of euphoria and panic. The software continued to grind and produced a wealth of information taken from Yuri's phone. Hundreds of files and bits of information streamed across the main screen and collated to isolate certain numbers into a file named *Examine*. After six minutes, the search of the phone contents came up with five possible numbers. Dalton's technical experts were all openly discussing their reasons a particular number should be the first one tried. Two had person names attached to a number file, while the rest had numbers as file names. Ed Kosko kept the president informed about the successful download and disabling of Yuri's phone and the ongoing effort to determine the right phone code to disarm the bomb.

Cherney put the three files names suspected of containing the disarm code on the large, middle screen:

02040816
04091500
03092781

RICHARD TREVAE

Dalton looked at the three file names for the possible disarm codes and wondered if any were alternate rearm codes or immediate detonation codes. The room of technicians, computer experts, administrators, and NSA agents all stared in silence, awaiting a revelation. None came forth. Dalton decided to pull back from the numbers and educate the group about Yuri.

Asking for their attention, he said, "There are things we've learned about Yuri you should know, which may help solve this puzzle. First of all, Yuri is no one's fool. He's fifty-two years old and has survived and prospered in the arms business for over twenty years. At six foot one, 210 pounds, he's an impressive man with a lean, strong physique and exercises twice a week. He has no children, although he was married for several years in his late twenties. His wife is deceased for reasons yet unknown. He has some higher education although never completed college as they view it in the Russian educational system. Hobbies include sailing, cruising, and anything that involves getting out on the water. This is apparent by the use of the *Decadence,* a floating arsenal and command center for his business. He also enjoys hunting large game animals, mostly in Russia, and bird hunting in eastern Europe. His mind is very sharp and he has demonstrated a near photographic memory, which he uses on occasion to play chess and other mathematical games. He worked for a short time in the war games section at the KGB and wrote some impressive research papers on first-strike strategies. However his greatest strength is his ability to foresee every option in a conflict situation and devise an escape plan. He has never been caught in an illegal arms deal. He has shown us some of these skills in the last few days." Dalton paused and looked again at the screen displaying the three files names. "Let's figure this out, people. Think outside the box."

The room erupted in a clamor of words and computer keypads managing hundreds of new keystrokes. Assumptions were made about birthdates; none worked for either Yuri or his deceased wife. His KGB ID numbers were entered in every conceivable order to no avail. Cherney noticed one common aspect in two of the file names. The first and third number groups were progressive sequences of number powers. In other words, 2 squared is 4, the third power is 8, and the fourth is 16. The same applied to the third number: 3 squared is 9, cubed is 27, and to the fourth power is 81. The room breathed a collective acknowledgment concerning the interesting sequence. Dalton said, "That is exactly how a mathematical mind like Yuri's may work to simplify memorizing data. Keep working along those lines."

The activity defaulted back to noisy keypads and rambling conversation about mathematical tricks to recall data. Dalton studied the numbers for a long time then pulled Ed aside, saying, "Ed, today is the fourth of September isn't it?"

"Yeah, that's right, the fourth." Ed looked at Dalton, waiting for a reason for the question. Extending his arm and pointing to the middle number, 04091500, Dalton said, "This has got to be it. He used the European style of recording a date: day first, followed by month . . . then he added the hour."

Ed said, "Fourth of September at three o'clock. Right?"

The room of techies all agreed that the middle number was the most logical to disguise the disarm code phone number. Ed Kosko called the president, who gave approval to try the number to disarm the bomb.

It was 2:10 p.m., and the evacuation by *Marine One* was ready to proceed if the plan didn't disarm the bomb. As Dalton waited, the technicians set up the computers to create the call and enter the number in the file coded as 04091500. He hoped he was right because no time was left for hundreds of citizens and perhaps the two presidents sailing south in Chesapeake Bay.

A gentle touch on Dalton's back caused him to turn and look behind him. It was Carolyn, looking beautiful although very concerned for her man. He put his arm around her and said, "If this works and the bomb *is* disarmed, so we can safely retrieve it, we'll have a squadron of attack helicopters pursuing Yuri and his yacht. With the discovery of a real nuclear bomb on U.S. soil armed to detonate and kill our president, he will be a war criminal and we'll go after him whether in international waters or wherever. He's going to pay for what he put you through."

Carolyn hugged him and kissed his cheek.

The situation room fell quiet as the computers dialed the selected number behind the naming code. They heard the phone ringing: three times then a click. The silence deepened to terrifying levels as all awaited the images on all the wall screens to reveal the results. The *Windancer* was sliding along at a comfortable four knots under an exceptionally brilliant blue fall sky. Both presidents were enjoying the day, though expecting any moment to be evacuated, vaporized, or told the device was disarmed. The news media were covering the sail live with a worldwide audience approaching 150 million.

The helicopter and F/A-18 cameras focused on the small marina containing *Flipper I*. No change appeared. Maybe it had been disarmed. Dalton strolled around the walkway, relieving nervous tension; Ed Kosko lit a bummed cigarette for the first time in years, fully aware smoking was not allowed within the situation room. The images remained steady, and no detonation occurred. A full three minutes elapsed before everyone began to breathe easier and the room once again became raucous with yelling, laughter, and cheers.

Ed was on the secure satellite phone, telling the president the disarming effort seemed to have worked. A NEST team was dispatched immediately to the marina, where they quarantined the *Flipper I.* A working perimeter two blocks around the marina was set up, and civilians were asked to move out because a large diesel fuel spill might ignite. This gave citizens a plausible reason to leave and understand why all the security and men in hazmat suits were taking over the marina following the explosion.

When Ed finished his call to the president, he, Dalton, Cotter, and Wilson huddled around a vacant console and strategize the capture of Yuri Tarasov. Carolyn stood behind a thick, glass viewing panel, watching them. It provided visual, though not audio, activity observation in the situation room from a separate anteroom. She saw the satellite and aircraft coverage of *Flipper I* as the NEST team moved in and boarded the boat. Shaking, she wrapped her arms around herself, trying to preserve warmth as a chill ran through her body.

THE TARASOV SOLUTION

Stowed in a canvas cargo bag in a conference room used earlier by Cotter, Wilson, and Dalton, the remote detonator taken from Ian was blinking in rapid pulses. The flashing letters spelled out *Press Enter for Immediate Destruct.*

30-SIX

ABOARD THE *LADY CADENCE*

THE broken cloud cover helped conceal the big yacht's movements. Just as they entered the straits near Bimini, Yuri sat glued to his twin TV sets, observing the events in the States on Labor Day. He was tuned into BBC News and Sky News on one split-panel television and CNN on the main plasma screen located in the center lounge and bar on the main deck. As three o'clock approached, Yuri sat back in his favorite leather chair with Aaron and Ivana on either side. Yuri was so confident that his plan would succeed despite last-minute failings such as Ian's apparent death that he poured a Cognac for himself and relaxed as the news coverage followed the day's events. He checked his watch for the third time in less than a minute, and still nothing unusual was showing on the screens. He thought about the call on his satellite phone. It probably hadn't been Ian, likely a weak attempt by Crusoe and his team to locate him through the satellite signal. Anyway, he was sure he had not stayed on long enough for any trace to yield results. If they had Ian, which was doubtful judging by the blast at the heliport, he was dead anyway and they mimicked his voice to attempt the trace. The minutes stretched out for Yuri as he watched with building anger and frustration that his plan had not produced the small however lethal nuclear explosion. In a final rage, he threw his drink at the wall and ran for his satellite phone. He looked at it with absolute disgust for a few moments then punched *Redial*. The phone did not respond with a dial tone. No sound, no screen image of a number, nothing. He shut it down and went to the starboard rail. He looked up and, through the thickening clouds, he could see some stars appearing. In an hour it would be totally dark unless the horizon permitted a thin glow of red sky to the west.

Aaron knew best to avoid questions when Yuri chose to think. Ivana strolled to the rail and looked out to sea.

"They somehow took over my phone and used the disarm command call to stop the timed detonation at three o'clock."

Ivana looked puzzled and said, "Can they really do that?"

"Hell yes! But I didn't give them enough time to find that number among the hundreds that are in the phone contacts." Yuri continued to struggle with the facts before him.

"Maybe they got what they needed from Ian's phone." Ivana tried to be helpful.

RICHARD TREVAE

"No, his phone never had the disarm number, only my phone. That's why he had to call me just as we picked him up, so I could call if necessary to reprogram the detonation. But everything was on schedule." In a moment of clarity, Yuri said, "Wait a minute." He powered up his phone again and pressed *Menu,* then *Contents,* and checked every file. All were void of content—no names, numbers, contacts, dates, events, or codes.

"Damn, they took over my phone, copied the entire contents, and then deleted its programming and memory. It's worthless now." He tossed it in the Atlantic. After a minute of silence, Yuri began to laugh.

"The fun may not yet be over for them." Yuri shot a wink at Ivana as he smiled with confidence. "Remember the reboot commands?"

Aaron had studied a dozen maps revealing hundreds of deep channels leading to sheltered harbors and bays all along the Bimini coastline and knew where he could hide the yacht. Sunset came early at this time of year, and it was even sooner than usual with the increasing cloud cover coming in from the west. A quiet, low scrub island, one of hundreds in the area, provided ideal sanctuary for the *Lady Cadence* until about eleven that evening, when they would make a fast run to Caracas.

THE TARASOV SOLUTION

Yuri watched the *Windancer* return at about 5:30 p.m. EST on the CNN coverage and knew that his *first* opportunity to take out Blinikov was passed. He recalled Ian explaining how the bomb controls had a default reset for a twenty-four-hour delay of detonation unless the remote were turned off within five minutes of the disarm call. The active remote, after a five-minute period following disarming, simply rebooted to a twenty-four-hour delay in detonation.

Yuri was not about to concede that Crusoe had succeeded in spoiling the plan until the next two days were history—a history Yuri believed he had already written.

30-SEVEN

CHESAPEAKE BAY

THE entire day was perfect to the casual observer watching as the Russian and U.S. presidents enjoyed a five-hour sailing adventure before the world. The inferences from the images showing the two men, sharing a role in navigating and steering the boat, working the sails, and appearing very happy working together, were worth a dozen treaty signings and trade cooperation agreements. This marked a visible and emotional change in the relations between the two countries. Finally, after emerging from the fallen Communist political and economic system, to *perestroika,* to true democratic reforms, the two countries now had a basis to accomplish some good things together. Rooting out terrorists and terrorist supporters such as Yuri Tarasov was a prime example. The news coverage was hailed as some of the most-watched news of international significance since the 2008 Olympics in China. Both men were pleased they let the drama of Yuri Tarasov's assassination attempt play out privately while Dalton and his team foiled the plan. Alerting the news media, mobilizing the local police to effect an evacuation, in the short time available, would have caused a panic. The backup presidential evacuation plan allowed the day-sail to end successfully.

Back on the White House grounds, the two presidents walked about before dinner, and they discussed the details of the recovery and disarming the bomb. Both men agreed that at a later time, when Tarasov was apprehended or dead, they would issue a joint statement summarizing the events were thwarted that day.

Cotter had been in contact with the NEST team leader and asked that before any contact with the bomb was made, they brief Dalton on what they found. Meanwhile, waiting for that call, the hospital group tending to Ian's injuries called to indicate that he would live and, while critical, was conscious. He wanted to talk to Dalton. Wilson took the request and was arranging for a conference call from NSA headquarters when Ian said, "Has the bomb been disarmed through Yuri's phone?"

Wilson informed Ian that Dalton had conceived a plan to capture the disarm commands from Yuri's phone and disable it from further use. The uploaded commands were evaluated, a selection made, and when tried, it worked.

Ian looked cautiously at Wilson and, struggling to speak through his damaged throat, asked, "Is the remote still powered?"

"I don't know. We didn't feel we needed it once the disarm command was completed."

Ian began to sputter something in Russian, then English, in a very emotional tone. He blurted out, "The bomb can still detonate without the remote being shut down in time."

Wilson went pale and fumbled around for his secure satellite phone. He got Cotter on the second ring. "Tell Dalton, Ian says the bomb may still be active despite the phone command to disarm."

Ian coughed up blood. The nurse alarm went off, and six nurses and doctors were all over him, trying to control his coughing and bleeding.

Dalton heard what Wilson told Cotter and said, "Where is that damned remote?"

"I'm sure it was stowed with our weapons pack when we returned from the heliport, However I'll check now. I left it in the small conference room outside Kosko's office."

Dalton's phone rang and the number had no name associated with it. "Hello, this is Dalton Crusoe. Who is this?"

THE TARASOV SOLUTION

"Mr. Crusoe, this is Phillips, NEST team leader. We're over the bomb now, and it has been fitted with one hell of a detonator system. It appears dormant although there is electronic activity inside. Do you have the remote?"

Dalton spoke with extreme clarity. "Yes, we're retrieving it now. Don't touch the bomb at all until we get you the remote and we learn more. I repeat, *do not* touch the bomb. Our captive scientist who developed the detonation system is in the hospital, and we must hear what he has to say about the device before we mess this thing up and it explodes."

"Yeah, I hear you. We will hold for your call."

Five minutes later Cotter returned to Dalton with the weapons pack. Dalton had just informed Ed of what he had learned and decided, depending on what Ian revealed, they must move the bomb out of the bay area.

Inside the weapons pack, amid guns, SatCom equipment, and hand radios, was the remote. It was flashing at a rapid pace, *Press Enter for Immediate Destruct.*

Dalton looked at the device and said, "Let's get over to the hospital wing and hope Ian lives."

Ian was not doing well; he kept coming in and out of consciousness. Several times he tried to speak and had to stop as the bleeding increased. As Dalton walked into the room, he whispered, "Pencil," to the doctors. Wilson gave him a pen and handed him a clipboard with his medical status sheet turned over, revealing a blank sheet of paper. Ian took the pen and wrote, *24 hours till reboot. Bury it soon. It's not*— He passed out again, dropping the pen and clipboard.

The doctors frantically ushered everyone out of the room, as Wilson kept yelling to Ian, "Is it arming again? Is it arming again?"

Ian looked up, raised his left hand, fell limp, gasped a deep breath, and died.

Dalton took the remote from Cotter again and looked at the flashing message; it had not changed. Dalton shook his head in disbelief. The bomb might actually be rebooting and could then detonate. With a note of discouragement in his voice, Dalton said to Cotter, "Get me maps of West Virginia coal mines and a military helicopter fueled and ready at the NSA helipad."

30-EIGHT

NSA Headquarters

WEST Virginia was often considered a place where a dangerous nuclear weapon could be disposed of without undue risk to civilians. Scores of old, abandoned coal mines were scattered throughout the remote eastern and northern end of the Appalachian range covering the state. Some had already been converted to store radioactive waste from power plants in the southeast. Local objection was at first loud, although as time went on and no catastrophes occurred, the waste sites were accepted. A quick study by the NEST experts revealed that a ten-kiloton nuclear device could be contained and sealed in a mine at least a half mile deep and five miles from any population areas.

Wilson reported to Dalton, "Here are four possibilities, all within fifty miles of our bomb location near Cove Point."

"Good. Let's have a plan ready to go on very short notice to transport the device by a helicopter lift to one of the mines. Find the one that is easiest to evacuate the nearby civilian population."

"You got it. I'll have something in a couple of hours."

Carolyn was outside the situation room, waiting for Dalton to come out. The circumstances seemed to be stable now, and she needed to see Dalton. In an ironic twist, she now was not worried about him and all the pressure he was under to protect the president and neutralize the threat. Less than six hours earlier, she feared for her life, although Dalton had found her and came to her rescue. Now she felt a responsibility to him. Dalton came out and walked with purpose, probably to brief Ed Kosko, when he noticed Carolyn. He almost ran and pulled her into an embrace.

"Are you OK? I can't tell you how glad I am you were not hurt."

"Yes, JD, I'm fine, thanks to you. But now I want you to know how much I prayed my life would not end without me telling you how much I need you in my life." A small tear flowed down her left cheek. "The thought of not being together was unbearable. Please be careful. I learned a little about Yuri and his friend Ivana, and that is they will do anything necessary to achieve their evil ends."

Dalton hugged her again and held her hand as they walked down the hallway to the cafeteria. "I've got a few minutes before Ed is able to see me for my briefing. Let's get some coffee." Welcoming the time to spend with Dalton, she smiled and held his hand like high school sweethearts.

The coffee was refreshing and provided a nice break in the tension Dalton and his team had been under. Carolyn brushed her hair from her face and looked Dalton in the eyes. "What's wrong? You look a little flustered," Carolyn said as she held her focus on him.

Dalton smiled although wouldn't comment.

Carolyn took a deep breath and began her rehearsed warning. "My concern, dear, is that Yuri is still a serious threat. He always has an alternate plan, an escape or new obstacle to throw in your way. I can tell from his behavior that I was only useful as a way to get to you. He wanted to learn how you think. My only value in the end was to get you trapped rescuing me while the flight office was blown up. He has enormous research on you, your background, friends, co-workers, and career."

Dalton looked at her with renewed intensity as her words sank in. Carolyn continued. "You have challenged his intellect and beaten him. He will not let that go unchecked. So please be careful . . . for me." The concern on Carolyn's face was undeniable; Yuri wanted Dalton dead.

RICHARD TREVAE

NEAR GRAND BAHAMA ISLAND

Aaron was successful in dodging surface radar by hugging the islands' shorelines making up the Caribbean archipelago. During the night, he moved the *Lady Cadence* toward Venezuela, cruising just thirty miles west of Barbados among a distant sisterhood of ocean-sized yachts on similar courses. By 7:30 in the morning, Yuri was up and on deck, doing some exercises. He was at his creative best when he was working his muscles, and he liked to work his muscles early in the morning to jump-start his mind. His thoughts were consumed with Dalton Crusoe. Regardless of how Crusoe and his men handled the bomb intended to solve another problematic situation—Russian president Blinikov—Yuri felt certain that Dalton Crusoe was not about to yield his pursuit.

The governor of West Virginia, Willy Boone, was caught off guard when NEST officials called him to explain the plan Dalton created to bury the bomb before it presumably rebooted its detonation controller. The danger if the mine did not contain the blast and potential radioactive leaked in his state made for political suicide, and he refused to proceed without more information. He demanded to talk to the president, who took his call and explained the events over the past several days. He insisted on confidentiality until both the United States and Russia could claim the issue was settled, meaning they had captured Yuri Tarasov. The governor still did not agree with the plan and wanted the president to come up with an alternative. Politely putting the folksy governor in his place, President Conner made it very clear he was dealing with a matter of national security and that he had no other choice available. The governor's tone changed then mellowed to acceptance as the president explained that when all this was made public, he would be certain to provide numerous photo ops for the two of them to take questions on the event. The governor knew that being presented as a partner in the president's plan was worth hundreds of spaghetti dinner fund-raisers. He told the president he would stand in full support his plans.

Dalton had been reviewing Ian's last words as he tried to explain his comment about the bomb rebooting. He understood the detonation device was complex and able to be commanded by several methods: phone call, direct entry on the detonator kcypad, or through the remote. Ian had explained before the explosion at the flight office that only a command from Yuri's phone could disarm the bomb, although he had neglected to tell them that without shutting off the remote, the disarmed bomb would reboot and become active again in twenty-four hours. The thought occurred to Dalton and others looking at the device that trying to remove the nuclear core when disarmed might still result in a nuclear detonation if the wrong steps were taken during disassembly. As a result no action was planned to disassemble the bomb or its detonator. The best course of action, Dalton felt, was to dispose of it in a secure setting where even a nuclear detonation would be contained. As horrible as the result would be for areas of West Virginia, it would be far worse if the device were to detonate on the shores of Chesapeake Bay.

Dalton again thought about Ian's words just before he died, *"24 hours till reboot. Bury it soon. It's not—"* Then it occurred to him that the remote was known to be effective only within a two-mile radius of the bomb. Commands manually entered could be set for time-delayed detonations, so the terrorist could escape the blast. A ten-kiloton nuclear bomb would almost guarantee a kill for everyone within a two-mile radius. However a nuclear bomb might be exploded without going nuclear and kill no one beyond three hundred yards. The flashing command, *Press Enter for Immediate Destruct,* could only be effective within a two-mile range, so the explosion would *have to* be non-nuclear.

THE TARASOV SOLUTION

Dalton's logic assumed the terrorist was not planning on becoming a martyr, a reasonable theory considering the power- and money-driven Tarasov.

Dalton had pretty much convinced himself that Ian was trying to say the bomb was not going nuclear. Ed and the president listened to Dalton's explanation about the detonation scenario. The logic finalized the decision to drop the bomb in a West Virginia mine, the clear option to minimize the bomb's devastation, and detonate it with the remote.

The huge heavy-transport helicopter was crewed by six men, all from the NEST team, and Cotter who insisted he, not Dalton, be the one directing the flight to West Virginia. Ed and the president stepped up and made clear Dalton was not to be on the aircraft. The helicopter left the ground at the Cove Point marina, amid increasing press coverage and nosy reporters talking to residents about the explosion at the flight office a short distance away. Public speculation began that a bomb was targeting the president, although he was nowhere near and unharmed by the small yet powerful explosion. Wilson arranged for separate department memos from the Secret Service and NSA that confirmed the marina explosion was the result of a leaking diesel fuel tank and faulty electrical controls. Television coverage from a quarter mile away showed the transport lift off, carrying a package on a wire tether amid speculative reporting on what had actually happened during the president's Labor Day sail. It was 12:37 p.m. when the helicopter left the marina and headed west to the mountains. Two military F/A-18s were flying close support, only leading to more speculation as to the true events past and present. Again the NSA released a press memo stating that spent radioactive waste was being disposed of at a deep well burial site in the mountains of rural West Virginia. Governor Willy Boone added his supportive commentary to the unusual airlift on the local evening news.

The twenty-two-minute flight went smoothly, and at 12:59 p.m. the bomb was dropped into an abandoned mine in West Virginia. They used the remote to detonate the bomb, and the NEST personnel were able to confirm that it was not a nuclear explosion, rather a conventional detonation. Several NEST team specialists were left to sample for any radiation leakage; however, the explosion itself was unremarkable and little more than a typical gas explosion that occurs on occasion in mines.

The president, who was with Ed and Dalton, heard the news and said, "Dalton, your instincts and strategies were impeccable, and I and the country owe you a tremendous debt of gratitude. Unfortunately it must be a personal thank-you until the country is prepared to hear the entire story. Agreed?"

"Of course, sir, and thank you for the kind words."

Ed smiled in similar appreciation for all Dalton's skill and leadership.

The president reached out and shook Dalton's hand. "Now why don't you and that attractive girlfriend of yours take a little time off? The NSA and CIA men working with you will handle Tarasov, I'm sure."

30-NINE

CARACAS, VENEZUELA

THE *Lady Cadence* made Venezuelan waters and was harbored off shore about a half mile out to sea. Yuri wasted no time once on land renewing old contacts from prior business dealings. Franco Kindros, a Greek investigator and occasional contractor for Yuri when he needed to know the background of all players in a massive arms deal, accepted $50,000 cash for a week's work in the States investigating the whereabouts, work habits, and travel plans for one Jameson Dalton Crusoe.

The Labor Day Sailing Summit, as some political pundits were calling it, was a huge publicity feast for both the Russian and U.S. presidents. Their respective popularity rankings rose, and the entire world saw the makings for a strong working relationship between the two countries based on the friendship developing. President Blinikov wanted very much to participate in the capture of Yuri Tarasov now that the United States had evidence to brand him a terrorist. This was the exact kind of damning evidence the Russians had lacked up until this point because of Yuri's careful maneuvering. President Conner assured the Russian president he would keep him updated on the pursuit and allow him to share in the apprehension and eventual extradition to face similar charges in Russia. Now with the Americans after him, the capture was expected soon, and even for countries against extradition, the pressure to turn him over would become unbearable.

Yuri figured that the Americans somehow managed to permanently disarm the bomb, whether through sweating it out of Ian or just plain luck. Whatever the reason for the failed detonation, the meeting on the Chesapeake was not overshadowed by a bomb killing two powerful world leaders. In fact, Yuri was hunted now by both countries. He had to disappear for a while, and that was always accomplished on Cyprus. He used the island as a sort of field office. It had a corruptible government with no particular sense of duty to seek justice for what went on there. Yuri had concluded many sizable arms dealings on the island without any interference. It was easily accessible from all over the Mediterranean, Europe, and Africa. Banking connections were crude and unreliable in general, yet a client the financial size of Yuri Tarasov was able to demand security, secrecy, and performance. He gave instructions to Aaron regarding the *Lady Cadence*, which would change her look once more, restock supplies and fuel, give the crew a few days' shore leave, and head straight to Cyprus. Yuri and Ivana chartered a private jet to take them to Cyprus, while Taros waited in Caracas for information about Dalton's plans before intercepting and isolating him for assassination.

The old resort at Cyprus had been updated a few years earlier retaining the panoramic southern view of the Mediterranean from a hill region that was used for centuries as a lookout for invaders. Yuri had kept the five-room, five-hundred-square-meter penthouse for his retreats from the cold Russian winters. Ivana had never been invited until now, and she felt this was a definite status move up in her relationship with Yuri. It was equipped with the latest wireless communications provided in part by Yuri's bankers to facilitate his financing needs. Satellite antennas were perched at inconspicuous rooftop locations to catch several news services from Europe and the Arab states. When Yuri arrived, he activated new satellite phones and discarded others that were involved with the failed assassination attempt.

FORTY

DALTON had done some very serious thinking about the president's advice. Not only had he had a harrowing week, although Carolyn was very understanding about his attention to the national danger while she was in the hands of madmen capable of atrocities. A few days alone in one of their favorite vacation spots might be very curative. On an impulse, Dalton arranged to fly a private jet to St. Thomas for a five-day period of relaxation with Carolyn. They were to leave the next morning as a surprise, after Dalton had cleared the way for her to be gone from her graduate assistant duties at Wharton. At dinner Dalton would explain the trip, a gift from Ed for his efforts to defuse the crisis. He had one last issue before starting out on his plans with Carolyn. Sergey had regained full consciousness, along with his memory.

Franco Kindros was very good at clandestine fact-finding and had been trailing Crusoe as he flitted about the D.C. area, tying up loose ends, while the CIA and NSA began a serious search for Yuri Tarasov. Posing as a cab driver put him in the perfect position to record Crusoe's conversation as he spoke with Ed Kosko from his cell phone.

Crusoe told Kosko he was on his way to visit Sergey Kreftkova and mentioned the escape with Carolyn to St. Thomas in the morning. Kosko was insistent he use his personal aircraft for the journey. Crusoe reasoned that with the government jet standing nearby, he could rejoin the game if needed, and regardless the venue, he had to be in contact with Kosko and the teams pursuing Yuri. Kosko didn't want to keep Dalton on the phone. He knew he was on his way to meet with Sergey. "Try to have a relaxing time with Carolyn in St. Thomas. We'll keep you apprised of any new information we get from Zahid or the NSA efforts."

Crusoe finished the phone call by saying, "I truly appreciate the support you and everyone at the NSA gave to locating and aiding in the rescue of Carolyn. I was afraid we had lost her."

"No, thank *you*, Dalton. You led an effort to disrupt a horrible tragedy that would have marred this nation for decades. Have a great time in St. Thomas. I'll see you in a few days."

He closed the cover of his cell phone and ended the call just at the Franco pulled up to the side entrance of

NSA headquarters. "How much do I owe you?" he asked with a smile, completely unaware that his conversation had been recorded.

Franco replied, "Eight fifty, sir."

"Here are ten bucks. Thanks for the lift." He exited the cab and strolled to the infirmary.

Franco played back the recorded phone conversation and again heard the entire dialogue between Ed Kosko and Dalton Crusoe. He pulled away and decided to return his rented cab. The information he gained in three days was exactly what he had hoped to learn. He thought, *Yuri is going to love this bit of intel.*

Dalton walked into the waiting room and saw the elderly although able and alert man he'd met over a week ago in Cuba. Sergey stood up and greeted Dalton.

"Mr. Crusoe, I'm so glad to see you again. I understand I owe my rescue at sea to you and your associates."

"Well, that's very kind, Sergey, although in fact, it was Captain Thomson and his watch commander who first saw you and picked you up. I was down in the communications center trying to track Yuri Tarasov. By the way, I believe it's time you started calling me JD; that's what I encourage all my friends to do." Dalton extended a hand to the old sailor.

Sensing the blend of joy and tension in the Russian, Dalton then spoke to his primary concern, the asylum issue. "We have been able to verify your information on the missiles very conclusively, although it has not been without its ups and downs."

Sergey smiled and said, "I'm very pleased. Have you recovered the warheads?"

"Yes, although one warhead was within minutes of detonating before we located and disarmed the bomb. It could have killed the U.S. and Russian presidents. Tarasov got to them first, as you know, and planted one near the capitol. Because your information was valuable and correct, your request for asylum has been approved, and officials from the immigration department are completing your paperwork."

Sergey lit up with a broad smile and a visible sign of relief. He reached for Dalton's hand again and pumped it like a well handle. Tearing up, Sergey said, "I'm so glad you took the time to hear my story. I've been burdened with it for many years. And I'm very pleased to hear Tarasov's evil plan was stopped."

"There will likely be more interviews about the details of the missile releases back in 1962, but they won't be interrogations, I assure you." Dalton smiled, looked at him, and asked where he wanted to live.

Sergey retrieved a photo of his niece taken about eight years ago. "This is my niece, who lives in the U.S., somewhere on the East Coast, I believe. I want to find her and explain my story."

Dalton took the photo and studied it for a full twenty seconds, looking back to Sergey frequently. Finally he said, "What is her name?" Dalton knew immediately he recognized the woman in the photograph and waited nervously for Sergey's answer.

"Actually it is printed on the back." Sergey pointed to the reverse side of the small, black-and-white photo. Dalton turned the photo over slowly and saw the name *Carolyn Katrina McCabe.* He looked up at Sergey with a fanciful suspicious eye and said, "How old is the photo? Have you ever met her?"

"No, I'm afraid I have never met my lovely niece, although she must be about twenty-four or five now since the photo was taken eight years ago when she was sixteen, according to my sister. She is all I have left of my family as my sister passed away in the last three years and her husband died many years ago before her death."

The photo was old and worn yet there was no mistaking the image was that of Carolyn when she was in high school. Dalton had seen photos of her in yearbooks and other photo albums she kept at her apartment. The irony of the discovery left Dalton speechless for a moment and thankful he was the one chosen by Ed to investigate the Russian's story. Carolyn's kidnapping was now clearer than ever to Dalton; Yuri wanted more information and leverage, which the niece of his adversary and Dalton's girlfriend could provide. He wondered if the CIA and NSA teams had located the *Lady Cadence* and apprehended Yuri.

Looking to Sergey, Dalton said, "I would like to buy you dinner tonight and have you meet someone who might have an interest in your story."

Sergey looked perplexed although accepted the dinner offer from his new American friend with gratitude.

Dalton thought, *Carolyn is not going to believe this coincidence. It is time to acquaint Carolyn with her uncle.*

Paganelli's Italian Restaurant was not very busy even for a weeknight. Sergey had been told to arrive at about 7:15 p.m. Carolyn was simply told this was a quiet evening alone to make up for the tension and trauma felt over the past week. He also said he had a new friend he wanted her to meet for drinks before dinner. It was 7:05 p.m. when the couple sat down at the window table, Dalton ordered his usual scotch and soda and Carolyn selected a glass of merlot wine. He then said, "Have you ever wondered about your extended family?"

Carolyn was more than a little curious why this question popped up as dinner out with Dalton usually involved catching up on each other's schedules. Their lives, while seriously intertwined, didn't have much time for such issues. More often, the first questions and answers dealt with when they could get together again. Dealing with the question as seriously as Dalton seemed to present it, she remarked, "Well, I don't have much family to trace. My dad died when I was just a kid, and my mother passed away just before we met. My dad was a small-town banker and married my much younger mother after she emigrated here from Russia almost forty years ago. She was trained in ballet although never got the chance to pursue it professionally. What's got you curious about my long-lost family?"

Carolyn looked at Dalton while the server poured water and handed them menus. She waited for his answer and noticed his eyes seemed to be smiling.

"What are you up to, JD?" Carolyn was completely unprepared for what happened next. Dalton reached in his coat pocket, retrieved a small photo, and handed it to her.

"Is this young woman familiar to you?"

Carolyn looked at the photo of her taken more than eight years earlier by her mother at a girl's summer tennis camp.

"Where did you find this?" Carolyn turned the photo over and saw her name written in her mother's handwriting. A smile held back tears as she recalled the summer camp experience.

Dalton held her hand and said, "Do you recall hearing of your mother's brother?"

"Yes, his name was . . ." She paused to think. "Sergio, I think, but I never met him. I think he died in Russia or Europe somewhere; my mother never knew the details." Again, she pressed the question, "Now how did you come to locate this?" Her anticipation getting the better of her.

"It was given to me by your uncle, Sergey Kreftkova." Dalton studied Carolyn's face to see the reaction, which was one of utter disbelief and amazement.

"No. What do you mean? He's been gone for years."

"Actually he's is right behind you." Dalton spotted Sergey, who had just come in the restaurant and asked the hostess for Mr. Dalton Crusoe's table. As the old sailor cleared the corner to the main dining room Dalton waved him over to his table.

Carolyn looked at Dalton and knew he was not playing a practical joke on her. She turned and Sergey approached, smiling and standing tall. "Hello, Carolyn. I'm your uncle, your mother's brother. You look more beautiful in person than I could ever have imagined."

Carolyn looked at Sergey and saw her mother's features in his eyes and voice patterns. He extended a hand, grasping hers, then held hers in both his hands while he studied the beautiful woman in front of him. A couple of uncomfortable seconds quickly passed, and

THE TARASOV SOLUTION

Carolyn threw her arms around the stately looking, white-haired gentleman and began to sob tears of joy. Sergey held her; eyes closed, and thanked God for delivering him to this moment.

Dalton went on to explain how he and Sergey came to meet through his request to gain asylum in the United States and the horrific events that followed his meeting with Dalton. Dinner was delayed as the three talked about how stressful the past week had been. Carolyn's ordeal caused Sergey to apologize and renew his intense hatred of Yuri. Dalton lightened the moment by saying that Yuri was now a pursued criminal and assured them he would soon make a mistake, leading to his capture. Dalton finally called a time-out and they ordered.

Sergey left the restaurant just before Dalton and Carolyn were finished to give them some private time. All three promised to get together soon after the short getaway Dalton had planned and Sergey's formal process to gain asylum.

Franco, disguised with a false beard and thick glasses, shut off his mini recorder aimed toward Dalton's table, paid his bill, and walked out minutes after his targets left the restaurant.

Back at the hotel, Carolyn held Dalton in a tearful

embrace and thanked him for being the man who kept her hopeful during her captivity. "I'm not sure I could have survived the ordeal, JD, if I didn't have you in my life. I never want to leave your side."

"And I don't want to ever find you gone from my side," Dalton said.

Carolyn was exhausted and got into bed, awaiting Dalton, although before he could get there, she was asleep. As he undressed, he was relieved that things had gone so well, and the reunion of Sergey with his niece was a special gift. Sensing vibration in his vest pocket Dalton removed his satellite phone and saw a voice mail had come in. No name was showing on the screen, which typically identified callers whose numbers were stored in the phone. He looked puzzled and then checked his voice mail. It was Sergey. "Dalton, I remembered something not long before meeting you tonight. I thought I would tell you at dinner, although I didn't want to mention it in front of Carolyn and alarm her. As Yuri figured I would be dead long before his Labor Day events, he was not too careful about what he said and when he said things on the Decadence. I overheard Yuri say to his scientist, 'Configure the second core to the attaché as soon as possible.' It may mean nothing, however I wanted you to know."

40-ONE

LARNACA BAY, CYPRUS

TAROS checked his watch and did the math on when to call Yuri. He had received the call from Franco twenty minutes earlier on his satellite phone and made numerous notes. He knew only too well that anything as important as learning the travel plans for Dalton Crusoe had to be thorough. Franco had done his job well, as Taros and Yuri expected. He tracked down the mobile Crusoe, and had further bugged Carolyn's apartment while posing as a building maintenance man. The seven-and one-half hour time difference put Taros's late-morning call to Yuri into Cyprus at 4:00 p.m. local time. The fresh satellite phone Taros was using rang into voice mail at Yuri's penthouse. Standard operating procedure for Yuri was to let the phone ring, try to identify the caller, and let the answering machine record the call for later listening. He sat on a bar stool and let the message record then played it. "It's Taros. Our man has completed his assignment. Call me at this number."

Yuri looked at the message light and played the call

from Taros again. His face produced a brief smile as he heard the call.

Ivana was nearby when the phone rang and started to playfully tease Yuri as he prepared to listen to the message. He tried to ignore her, although she draped herself seductively around his neck to block his phone view as it played back the message. She maneuvered her body in front of his face to remove any question her thin, open shirt covered nothing except her bare breasts. Her left leg wrapped around his hips as she increased the close contact while feigning innocence. "Oh, did I disrupt your concentration? I'm so sorry."

Yuri smiled at her and looked around to see if the time of Taros's call was displayed; it was. "Yes, you are being a pest. Now let me talk to Taros, and I may be able to take you on another exciting kill. OK?" Yuri knew that controlling the situation with a knife or her body provided a similar reaction to Ivana. It was one of expectant ecstasy.

Ivana's eyes widened, as did her smile, and she kissed Yuri, saying, "I'll be waiting to hear what you have in mind."

Yuri paused another minute and called the number Taros used. After a few moments, the satellite connections clicked in and Taros answered. "Yeah, it's me. I talked with Franco about twenty minutes ago. He's been tailing Crusoe for a day and a half. It appears he has handed off most search efforts to the CIA field agents with help from the NSA. But the best part is, he's heading to St. Thomas in the morning, and get this: he's with that Carolyn babe. His boss, Kosko, is letting him fly an agency jet for the trip. He will be there about five days."

"Any mention of where the agents are searching?"

"No, just that they have been watching the *Lady Cadence* to see where it's heading and if you return to it."

"Tell Aaron to leave Caracas tomorrow and head to Cyprus. Assuming good weather, he should make it in about six days. During the first night at sea, have the name and canvas changed to the *Sea Rhythms* look. I haven't used that appearance in over a year. That will give him a little less scrutiny from surface and satellite surveillance. Then I want you to fly to St. Thomas today and stay ahead of Crusoe. Find out where he's staying and what his plans are on the island. I want to know his every move." Yuri checked his watch and concluded by saying, "Get back to Franco and tell him to meet me in St. Thomas in two days."

"Got it, boss. I'll get on it right now. Oh, I almost forgot; I think Crusoe has Zahid. He mentioned his name when talking in the cab Franco drove. Is that a problem?"

"Damn!" Yuri slammed his fist into the countertop,

bloodying his hand. "Yeah, it's more of the same problem . . . Crusoe." He hung up with Taros.

Ivana followed the conversation from the nearby sun porch and lifted her sunglasses to say, "At least he picked a nice place to die." Yuri could see the anticipation building in Ivana's eyes. "When do we head to the Caribbean again?"

"Soon, my dear assassin, soon, although we must be very careful with this one. He has shown us he's a very crafty guy. But he interfered in my plans, and that earned him top spot on my enemies list."

"Let me study the man and come up with a plan you will love, OK?" Ivana's teasing continued.

"Fine, although it had better be fool proof. I want him gone for good."

Ivana drifted off to her computer and began drafting details of her plan to add the death of Dalton Crusoe to her résumé. Yuri decided he had to make the call to Darien, who was still posing as a seaman on the *Sammie* as it worked the docks and cargo ship movements in the Chesapeake. Furthermore, he needed to confirm the plans he had put in motion before Labor Day were on track. Blinikov was completing his address to a joint session of Congress, and it was carried by all the major networks and broadcast around the world. It didn't capture the imagination and interest that the Labor Day sail did, although it was still a historic event and both leaders knew the image of a Russian president delivering a speech of new initiatives and interaction with the United States was priceless. Darien had a valuable secret known only to Yuri and a very few others inside Yuri's organization. Darien's identical twin brother, Daniel, was part of Blinikov's advance security detail and was ready to leave the humble service of the Russian government and join Yuri's organization. He had to earn his way in, however, so months earlier Yuri informed him there would come a time when he would have to carry out a dangerous task; a task that would forever cast his lot with Yuri Tarasov. Daniel was impressionable and anxious to live the good life he saw Yuri and other Russian criminals living as a result of their underworld activities. He was easily taken in, and with his brother encouraging him, the moment for changing his life was at hand. Yuri scrolled through his call directory and punched in the call to Darien.

"Yes? This is Darien," answered the young sailor.

"How is life on the *Sammie?*" Yuri typically did not use his own name in satellite phone calls, instead relying on the content of his statements to reveal his identity.

"Well, it's not bad work. Long, hard hours but not bad. I wondered if you'd call today."

"Tell me we are on track and that the package is in place."

"My man has the package, and it will soon be in place following the events today at the U.S. Congress." That was as much reference as Yuri wanted to hear over the phone about the plan in which Daniel would add the attaché bomb to similar metal suitcases used by Blinikov's aides to carry documents, computers, and communications equipment for the meetings and speeches the Russian president would deliver in the States. From there it would be loaded onto the president's plane for departure at 3:00 p.m. local time. A pressure switch would trigger the detonation as the aircraft climbed through twenty-five thousand feet. Yuri calculated the plane should be about twenty minutes out somewhere northeast of Washington, D.C., when it would explode and remove the problem of Blinikov from his life. Daniel would fly back to Moscow in one of two support aircraft always part of a major presidential trip such as this one to the United States.

"Excellent, my friend. I am impressed with your progress, and we will soon join up."

"Good. I'm looking forward to our next meeting."

40-TWO

ST. THOMAS, U.S. VIRGIN ISLANDS

THE prime vacation season had not yet started, although the airport was full. The renovated terminal had new small shops, liquor stores, slot machines, T-shirt vendors, and cabbies everywhere. Taros arrived on the first flight of the day in from Caracas, through San Juan, Puerto Rico. It was 9:55 a.m. under a sunny sky, and warming breezes waved away the cool, night air. The ocean was a brilliant sapphire blue as it rolled in, smoothing the beach for the next batch of sun worshippers.

Franco had followed Dalton from his Washington hotel near the numerous agency buildings a mile from the Capitol. Carolyn was with him, and they left directly for Ed Kosko's private agency jet. That was 6:30 a.m. and Taros estimated the flight for the Gulfstream G-5 would take about four hours. Taros was hungry and tired, even though his flight had been only about two and a half hours. He decided to wait around for the arrival of Dalton and Carolyn's flight, scheduled to land in forty-five minutes.

RICHARD TREVAE

A beachfront coffee shop looked appealing, so Taros took a table facing the water just beyond the runway. Within a few minutes, Taros was feeling very relaxed as the cigarettes, coffee, and croissant refueled his system. He dug into his jacket's breast pocket and retrieved his notes, scribbled on the back of an envelope. It was the critical stuff Yuri always cautioned him about. The list was standard for Yuri's MO: make initial visual contact before Dalton leaves the airport; follow in a rental car; obtain photographs of both targets from a safe distance; follow their movements and record every stop; check for security forces or bodyguards present or following the targets; and a critical last point, disguise yourself to avoid Carolyn recalling your voice or face. "Damn! I forgot the disguise," Taros muttered. Yuri was fanatical about details, and on a priority stalk such as this one, a screw up could cost him his own life. He threw some dollars on the table and left for a nearby beach shop. Ten minutes later Taros felt he was well disguised with a large, straw hat; sleeveless T-shirt; mirrored sunglasses; and his own day-old beard growth. He looked in a full-length mirror just before paying and thought, *Even his woman, Carolyn, wouldn't recognize me now.*

He learned they were staying in a beach villa at a high-end project called Frenchman's Reef Resort. Plenty of tourists were staying at the premier location on a cliff above the Caribbean looking southwest out to the sea. Taros set up a quarter mile down the road in an older hotel one block back from the. The magnificent beach formed a large, crescent cove with coral rock outcroppings on the west end and a shallow sandbar extending out some three hundred feet into the Caribbean before turning back sharply and heading north to another outcropping. Water sport enthusiasts were abundant on the beach and in the sea with personal watercraft, sail boards, and paddle boats. A few day sailors were anchored about two hundred yards offshore and sometimes tendered in to the beach about happy hour time. Taros sensed Dalton and Carolyn were planning a relaxing few days getting reacquainted, without concern for Yuri's status. The venue seemed ideal for a killing made to look like an accident, and that was the objective behind Ivana's plan.

Taros checked his watch again at 10:22 a.m. having returned to the beach café looking very much like a burned-out European traveler spending the last of his parents' estate spoiling himself in the tropics. He reasoned it was still a little early to expect the G-5 when he saw a small dot on the horizon lining up for an approach. He watched the dot emerge as a sleek, white G-5 coming in low and fast. Parallel to it, on a longer runway, was an American 757 passenger jet landing seconds ahead of the G-5. Both made the terminal area about the same time, although the NSA plane turned to a private hangar 250 feet from the main terminal and parked. Four people stepped down the G-5's staircase and waited for luggage handlers from the private terminal. One woman was youthful and strong with a shapely figure and medium-length, chestnut-colored hair. Taros instantly recognized her as Carolyn McCabe. He then focused his long-lens camera on the man near her and reasoned that he was Dalton, about six-one, fit, in a light sport coat, khaki slacks, and a dress T-shirt. The other two men looked like pilot and copilot types, both with aviator sunglasses and dark suits with white short-sleeved shirts and ties. The Nikon digital SLR camera took forty-five rapid-fire photos of Dalton and Carolyn deplaning and getting in the cab. Taros smiled, feeling he could report the pilots didn't appear to be security, merely pilots destined to take their own cab to a modest hotel similar to his own.

As the cab pulled away with Dalton and Carolyn, the 757 began to unload its 325 passengers. Taros moved quickly to stay ahead of the crowd and intercept Dalton's cab as it maneuvered down the two-lane road to the island's resort section. Stuck at a stoplight, Taros saw the cab drive through the green light and head east. No other vehicle followed close behind, again suggesting there were no security forces accompanying them. At the outside reception area of the Frenchman's Reef circular drive, Taros aimed his directional microphone at the bellhop helping Dalton and heard him inform the new guests that they would be staying in a water-front villa, D-44, and that the luggage would be taken by cart to their room as they checked in. Dalton hand-ed the bellhop five dollars and escorted Carolyn inside. Taros tucked away his equipment and checked his handwritten notes about Yuri's instructions.

While Taros drove away, Cotter texted Kosko's phone: *We just landed via commercial jet. Taros followed JD from the airport. We have him under surveillance. More later.*

Cotter looked to Wilson and said, "Ed was right to insist we tail Crusoe and Carolyn."

CHARLOTTE AMALIE AIRPORT, ST. THOMAS

The sky had just lost the visible sun, and the western horizon started its nightly process of blending colors of red and orange against the clouds extending from the water. Ivana spent the five minutes prior to landing looking out her starboard-side cabin window, following the end of the day. The expensive, chartered business jet was an impressive business tool Yuri frequently used to quickly get in, close a deal, and escape with his payment. He never personally carried the merchandise and avoided transporting it on the *Decadence* as well. The pilot and two bodyguards were all that joined Yuri and Ivana on the flight.

Precautions and multiple options were the mantra for Yuri, so he hired associates such as Augustus to do the fieldwork and make the physical transfers while his mercenaries and security people oversaw the process with heavy armament. This trip was to be no different. The flight took only six hours, and that included a stop in Sierra Leone for fuel. Franco had completed his assignment and phoned Yuri in flight with a complete report on the events in Washington as well as the plans Dalton had in St. Thomas. Ivana developed a plan to kill Dalton and still give Yuri the revenge and satisfaction he demanded. The impressive jet, free of any markings except its call letters, rolled to the end of the short runway and made a turnaround toward the private hangar used by high rollers. The pilot was to stay near the airport in a small ten-room hotel, colorfully decorated with local plants and flowers yet very much out of the mainstream tourist areas. Yuri wanted him in close contact with the aircraft and able to prepare it for flight on short notice.

The passengers walked to a loading zone, and there

THE TARASOV SOLUTION

was Taros, opening the doors to a Cadillac Escalade and stowing their small bags. The Escalade moved out quickly, however Wilson and Cotter soon caught up with them on their route leading up to the mountain-top areas where large homes and a few gated communities were located.

Cotter and Wilson had been sitting at the airport bar sipping lime-adorned Corona's when Yuri's plane arrived. The two NSA field operatives blended in like young singles trying to make a score at the bar. Dressed in casual, local attire, including silk, flowered shirts and baggy shorts, was a real change from agency dress code. A steel drum band played, and two dozen patrons were out on the dance floor, sweating to the heavy rhythms. They saw Yuri's jet arrive and park near the private hangars. It was just dark enough to capture some good photos without adding artificial light. When a woman and four men all got out, Cotter caught the group on his small camera.

Yuri had rented a five-thousand-square-foot private winter residence owned by a Swiss banker he had fre-quent dealings with on his financial matters. The white-washed masonry home's vantage point overlooked the entire string of islands comprising Drake Passage and spreading out to the east.

Ivana walked in and stepped out to the large wrap-around patio to take in the view. Dozens of small, lush islands dotted the blue Caribbean to the east. The infinity pool taking over a sizable portion of the backyard blended perfectly with the sea. Yuri walked up beside her, and she asked, "This is beautiful. How often do you come here?"

"I come anytime I want . . . a couple of times a year, I guess." Yuri removed his sport jacket to feel the last warming sun rays for the evening.

Ivana was puzzled by Yuri's answer. "Anytime you want? Doesn't your banker friend care that he may be planning to use the place?"

"No, he was only able to afford it using the fees I pay him each year to handle my affairs in absolute confidentiality. So he shows his appreciation by letting me use it whenever." Yuri smiled smugly.

"You like the power and influence afforded by your business, don't you?" Ivana asked playfully.

"Yes, I do. It works real well if I can keep the Blinikovs and Crusoes out of my life." Yuri's face tightened as he focused again on the failed opportunities over the past few days to right his business. Looking out to the west, he said, "I'll have another chance soon."

THE TARASOV SOLUTION

Beneath the horizon, virtually unnoticed, to Yuri and Ivana a car appeared. Yuri looked past it to the west focusing on the sunset. Cotter and Wilson had stopped at a curve in the road and took video of Yuri's extravagant setting and made note of the number of guards and security people he had brought along.

40-THREE

FRENCHMAN'S REEF RESORT

CAROLYN couldn't wait to get into a bathing suit. The two-bedroom beach bungalow had a modest kitchen and a large living room, which opened up to a patio half covered by a thatched, sloped roof. The window sliders were moved all the way back to the outer walls so the entire view and beach atmosphere took over the living and dining area. The early evening air was pleasant and calming. Dalton followed Carolyn out to the patio in a swimsuit and T-shirt. The warm breeze and melting sun felt soothing on Dalton's face as he relaxed in a lounge chair near Carolyn, who had already spread out facedown in her lounger, reading her latest novel. The seconds turned to minutes, which turned to hours, and Dalton found himself relaxing for the first time in a week. He drifted in and out of sleep, often daydreaming. Carolyn noticed his restlessness and concluded he was best left to work through it alone, although she kept a watchful eye on him. She looked over the brochure on activities available at the resort and saw a two-day, one-night sailing opportunity where a small, nineteen-foot sailboat with a cuddy cabin could be rented and used to explore the islands of Drake Passage. She learned the concierge would arrange for the craft to be reserved early in the morning, and a basket lunch would be provided for two, along with provisions to make breakfast in the sailboat's tiny galley. She thought she would surprise Dalton and set up the romantic sail over the next two days, marking the anniversary of their first date, after they had a chance to rest and take in the sun. She called the concierge desk and made arrangements when Dalton went inside to use the facilities. Her imagination exploded as she devoured the brochure and looked at all the hidden beaches and special sights they could see during two days of sailing.

Yuri and Ivana sat alone in the great living room near the patio and went over her plan to eliminate Dalton and Carolyn. She wished it were only Dalton that had to be dealt with, however Carolyn was part of the package and would become collateral damage. Ivana was not sloppy when it came to planning a kill. She played every step of the setup, the attack, and the escape in her head until she had it memorized.

Yuri liked the plan although he wanted to exact more

personal pain and suffering on Dalton than Ivana proposed. She was not about to underestimate Dalton and made certain her plan was not weakened by a prideful vengeance, which corrupted Yuri's reasoning. In this instance, Yuri yielded to Ivana, who said, "Look, I'm the one you hired to expose and assassinate your bodyguard who was preparing to sell your security off to a Turkish competitor cooperating with the Blinikov administration right?"

"Yeah, I suppose you're right. I'm too close to the problems Crusoe has caused me, and I want him to know I've defeated him as he dies." In an uncharacteristic moment, Yuri said, "We'll do it your way."

"Good. Now get some sleep. I want to make some calls to fill in the details of when and where we take him down."

Yuri was already relaxing in a lounger on the patio and sipping smooth Bacardi Select rum over a lump of crushed ice in his rock glass.

Ivana fired up a powerful laptop Taros had brought along at Yuri's request and began some searches. By midnight, Yuri was fast asleep on the patio under a clear sky displaying thousands of sparkling lights. A mild breeze held the temperature to seventy-two degrees. Ivana was able to get logged into the reservations desk at Frenchman's Reef and see the availability of water sports for the next several days. There, in full detail, were the plans for Dalton Crusoe and guest, villa unit D-44, to rent a sailboat at 8:00 a.m. for the next two days and instructions to provide a complete lunch basket and breakfast provisions for the guests to take with them. Ivana swelled at her resourcefulness and looked around for the ever-present security guards. Two men, both smoking, near the drive serving the front gate at the courtyard were playing some kind of card game.

Looking over at the sleeping arms merchant, Ivana smiled and whispered, "This one is going to cost you more than money." Ivana surveyed the large patio and saw Taros watching her from a distance lounger with a shallow effort at looking to appear asleep. Male attention was not an uncommon experience for Ivana, although Taros' interest troubled her. His careless advance on Carolyn revealed he could not be trusted to control his desires-a critical flaw. She worried about Taros' commitment to Yuri.

40-FOUR

Morning, Sailing Day, St. Thomas

DALTON got to the beach sailing shack before the water sports director arrived. It was about 7:55 a.m., and he was ready for a pleasant day sailing with Carolyn. She was on her way from the beach villa some two hundred yards down the shore. Dalton wanted to arrive early and check out the sailboats available. He had sailed a bit in college during the summers when his dad was alive and had not tried it since. Strangely enough, Dalton felt excitement, not sorrow, at sailing again. Perhaps it was having Carolyn with him or the relaxed pace he now enjoyed, yet the feelings were real, and he was anxious to get out to sea.

As Dalton studied the three rental boats anchored in about six feet of water, the largest of the three looked most interesting, and he had made arrangements for that to be theirs for the two day trip. It had a small flag that read *Reserved* dangling from the wheel, clean lines and plenty of sail area to catch the wind. The wheel area was sizable and surrounded with comfortable, cushioned seating. A forward cuddy cabin appeared to contain a small kitchen, a head, and a small bedroom. A five-horsepower outboard motor hung off the stern, just in case winds failed to appear.

"Sorry I'm late. Have you been waiting long?" asked Jason, the tanned, college-aged-looking sports director, wearing a knee-length bathing suit and a lightweight, long-sleeved, flowered T-shirt.

"No, not really. I just came early to check out the watercraft. We had planned on taking that one?" Dalton pointed to the largest sailboat, the *Ginger*.

"You can take any one of them. Although you did reserve the *Ginger*, right?"

"Yeah I did."

Jason looked relieved. "Have you sailed before?"

"I sailed years ago in Chesapeake Bay with my dad." A brief smile gave way to special memories. Dalton looked back toward the beach villa. Carolyn was coming, fumbling with a picnic basket supplied by the hotel. She wore a bikini covered with a teal shawl. The look was topped off with a large-brimmed straw hat and sunglasses.

"I'm ready at last," announced Carolyn as she smiled at Dalton.

"Good. I'll check the boat out for life preservers, radio, maps, and fuel while you review the paperwork. OK?" Jason walked into the cool water and waded out to the sailboat.

Dalton signed the paperwork and loaded the snorkel gear and other beach necessities into a small Zodiac for boarding the *Ginger*. Carolyn jumped in and took control of the two oars, rowing them out to the side ladder on the sailboat. The perfect day was starting out with a three-knot wind, calm seas, full sun, and seventy-six degrees. Carolyn looked radiant as she, too, soaked up the great weather.

Dalton let out the spinnaker a bit to pull away from the docking buoys dotting the shoreline a hundred yards out.

As the *Ginger* drifted to the east away from the buoy anchor, Ivana watched them through binoculars and called Taros. "They are in the sailboat now, heading in the exact direction I expected they would. Have Yuri meet me at the marina in an hour."

Jason stood nearby nervously as he awaited his payment from Ivana. She reached into her handbag and gave him an envelope of $750 for letting Ivana and Taros board the boat earlier in the morning. She had told Jason that they wanted to hide a cell phone in a gift basket from friends, celebrating the couple's engagement. For fifteen hundred, Jason would have let them steal the boat, however he was more than willing to assist in a surprise gift from friends. Jason was naive and unaware that his greed had allowed Ivana and Taros to set a death trap for Dalton and Carolyn.

"Thanks for helping us make their sail be a memorable one," said Ivana as she passed by Jason, still overcome by her generosity. Her broad smile was not flirting; rather, it was pride at her resourcefulness.

Dalton took the *Ginger* on a slow, easterly tacking wind down the center of Drake Passage for about three hours. Islands were visible in every direction, and the two were enjoying the delightful weather. Dalton had smothered Carolyn with suntan oil then got the return treatment from her with the occasional kiss and hug. She was losing the feelings of insecurity generated over the previous week.

Taros had called Yuri, and he met them on the slips at Sully's Marina, a high-end, yacht-dominated marina and ship's store catering to the wealthy who chose to boat on ocean-going vessels. Of the seventy slips contained within the marina, around two dozen held vessels available to rent while the owners were absent. Yuri had Taros rent a fifty-five-foot, diesel-powered Viking named *Intrepid*. When Ivana and Taros arrived, Yuri was just preparing to board the boat. Earlier, Taros had equipped it with satellite phones, scuba gear, and weapons enough to ward off any attack short of a military assault. The *Intrepid* headed out to sea, trailing the *Ginger* by more than a mile as the small sailboat moved farther out to remote waters.

Dalton moved in close to the private Peter Island and dropped anchor just after noon. Lured by the clear, turquoise water and sandy bottom, they swan off the boat in shallow water using their snorkeling equipment to examine many fish attractions. The exhilaration of swimming in the warm Caribbean water led to uncontrollable desires during a toweling off session once back on board. The small bed in the cuddy was just adequate for their passionate afternoon. After falling asleep, Dalton dreamed in vivid detail for more than an hour about Yuri and his assassination plans for the two presidents. Once awake, he was glad to realize he was dreaming and that Carolyn was busy in the small galley. Carolyn had awakened earlier and opened the picnic basket of goodies prepared by the resort. She and Dalton enjoyed lobster salad croissants, fresh fruit, and wine for the better part of an hour.

It was just after four o'clock when Yuri opened his satellite phone and entered the number given to the hidden phone traveling with Dalton and Carolyn connected to the electrical system on the *Ginger.* Ivana watched the distant *Ginger* though her binoculars as Yuri texted the numbers.

"I think it worked. Crusoe is looking over the side, trying to determine why steering is out." She smiled as evidence came into view of her successfully unfolding plan. Yuri called to Taros, "Are the air tanks filled yet?"

"Working on it now. They should be filled in twenty minutes or so."

On the *Ginger,* Dalton was unable to use the wheel to steer the sailboat. All power seemed to have failed at once. The sail motors were frozen, and communications were also out. The radar had ceased to rotate, and only a small generator operated, supplying limited lighting power. They were drifting aimlessly in the middle of Drake passage.

"What do you think happened?" Carolyn asked of Dalton.

"I don't know but we're without sail controls or steering for the time being. Check the radio and see if it's powered up."

Carolyn went to the lower cuddy area and switched on the mike for speaking. "Nothing here, JD."

"I would have felt it if we hit something big enough to jam the rudder." Dalton kept trying to determine the reason for the power failure until near dark, when he decided to put on his snorkeling gear and dive under the boat to look for problems. Carolyn was searching for flares when she noticed a large search floodlight in a wall cabinet in the cuddy galley. Opening the glass door, she removed the light and tested it. It lit up instantly, showering light into the cabinet. As she held the light, it revealed a small cell phone connected to an electrical device, which was attached by electrical clamps to the main circuit breaker panel serving the boat. The phone message light was flashing, and there was a burned electrical odor in the cabinet. Carolyn's face tensed and her breathing raced. The sense of fear and vulnerability missing over the past three days returned in an instant.

The sky had darkened enough to disguise the small, inflatable craft approaching the *Ginger* from the east. Taros held the raft steady while Yuri and Ivana slipped into the water with their scuba gear and weapons. At fewer than two hundred yards away, they covered the distance to Dalton in less than a minute. Dalton's powerful underwater flashlight directed the way for Ivana and Yuri. They came in toward the *Ginger's* stern, about twenty-five feet down. At less than fifteen feet away, Yuri took aim at Dalton's back left shoulder and prepared to squeeze the trigger. Ivana withdrew a seven-inch knife from her calf sheath and moved in slowly behind and alongside Yuri.

40-FIVE

ABOARD THE *INTREPID*

TAROS maneuvered the raft back to the drifting *Intrepid* and attached the Zodiac to its tow line. Two of Yuri's bodyguards were steadying the big motorboat in the water at a constant distance from the *Ginger*. He climbed aboard and looked out to the darkened sailboat resting on the mild sea. He saw Carolyn looking about the cabin for something with a flood light. No one else appeared on board the small sailboat. Once on deck, Taros looked around the horizon and saw a few boats cruising within a half mile of the *Intrepid*, although none of them were on a course that would interfere with Ivana's plan for Dalton Crusoe.

Taros stood on the main aft deck for a moment and lit a cigarette while he took in the cool, early-evening air. The lights of Charlotte Amalie were only a few miles west and outlined the island like stars in the night sky. Other less-inhabited islands were visible in every direction, each increasing its silhouette against the darkening sky as more lights appeared. The arm came from behind and to the right side of Taros with a jolting force. He was lifted off his feet, gasping for air. His mouth was covered, knocking his burning cigarette into his face, however before he could scream, he felt the mild prick of a needle penetrate his left jugular. In seconds, he lay conscious although paralyzed. However, his eyes functioned normally as he saw two men dressed in black wetsuits and hoods move away from him toward the upper bridge where the two bodyguards were sharing a bottle of rum and laughing it up.

Taros lay motionless although his eyes were flitting rapidly as he tried to assimilate what was happening. The two men in wetsuits moved with precision towards Yuri's bodyguards whom were still drinking and amusing each other with their stories. Each carried a sidearm and a satellite phone was positioned near their deck chairs stationed side-by-side looking out to the west. Approaching from behind, the intruders simultaneously knocked the two clueless guards to the deck, delivering several quick, targeted blows to disable their opponents. One body guard did manage to produce a knife and slashed at the smaller of the two attackers, cutting him on the arm. A moment later the second wet suited man delivered a crushing blow to the guard's face, smashing his nose and rendering him unconscious. After a few minutes searching the boat, one of the intruders spoke into a head phone extending from his ear to his lips and said, "Command, this is Cotter. We have immobilized the two bodyguards along with Taros and are now in control of the vessel."

Taros could make out the response.

"Any casualties to report? Are Yuri and Ivana in custody?"

Cotter spoke again, "Wilson was cut on the arm by one of the bodyguards. It's not severe and he has it bandaged."

Wilson gave thumbs up, pressed his earpiece and said, "I'm good to go. We find no one else onboard; however two sets of scuba gear are missing from the diving locker compartment...a man's and a woman's vest, mask, fins and tanks. Clothing for both is lying near the diving locker. Also two spear guns appear to be missing."

Cotter and Wilson walked back to Taros' location and propped him up in a deck chair. As Taros watched helplessly Cotter, produced a small black plastic case, opened it, withdrew a tiny hypodermic needle, drew in a clear liquid and injected Taros in the arm. Panicked at first, Taros quickly came around to regain some functions including speech. The man called Cotter asked, "Can you speak now?"

Taros tried and made some gurgling sounds for a moment then found the ability to form words. " A h , yes, yes, I think I can speak." Cotter reached down his right leg and grabbed his Glock 40, jammed it into

Taros's temple and said, "Where are Yuri and the woman?"

"Don't shoot please, don't shoot! They are in the water heading to that sailboat." Taros's flimsy arm and hand pointed to the *Ginger*.

The former seals were enjoying the opportunity to work in the field together again. The technical investigative and reconnaissance work was fine, however an occasional stint in the field pursuing real bad guys was always a welcome assignment for the two former Seals.

However now they feared their secret mission, mandated by Ed Kosko, to keep watch over Carolyn and Dalton from a distance was about to fail. They bound Taros and secured him to a handrail, slipped into the water, powered the Zodiac and double timed it to the *Ginger*.

Carolyn was desperate to get Dalton back on board and show him what she had found. She was certain it was some kind of sabotage to disable the sailboat and leave it helpless at night in the middle of Drake Passage. Waving her light frantically over the side of the boat, she saw the two swimmers approaching from below Dalton. The knife flashing in the water made Carolyn's blood run cold. She knew the woman and her skillful use of knives; it was Ivana. The man next to her was aiming his spear gun directly at Dalton's back. She waved her light through the water, hoping Dalton would notice her. She saw the spear shoot from the gun and streak toward the keel of the boat. Both divers escaped the light as they swam beneath the sailboat, leaving only erratic flashes of light diffused by air bubbles escaping from the sea. A violent light show seemed to go on endlessly beneath the surface while Carolyn moved from side to side, trying to locate Dalton. Near panic, she first thought to get in the water to assist Dalton although realized she would be powerless against Ivana and her partner. Without any warning the water became quiet. Desperate to defend herself, she ran to the small cuddy and dug through a storage bin beneath a seat cushion. There she found ropes, extra cleats, and a first-aid kit. Tucked in the far corner was a red, plastic container labeled *Survival Gear.* As she pulled at the container to remove it from the stowage cradle it was snapped into, she heard the sound of someone breaking the water's surface and heavy breathing. Scrambling to open the case, she heard someone set foot on the aft deck and remove swim fins. She grabbed a yellow flare gun and a handful of flares. Shaking uncontrollably, Carolyn relived the panic she felt when Ivana held a knife to her throat as Dalton inspected the *Lady Cadence.* The few inboard lights running on solar batteries provided just enough light to make out the form of a person. She instinctively wanted to call out Dalton's name yet withheld her impulse while she looked for more clues as to who had climbed on board. She lost the dark shape against the black sky, and realized if it were Dalton, he would have called out her name. Carolyn grasped the flare gun in both hands and moved stealthily toward the three steps rising to the aft deck. As her left foot touched the first step, she sensed movement and heard dripping water very close to her. Raising the flare gun to her eye level, she saw more movement and the flash of chromed steel moving fast down from over her head. Ivana lunged through the stairwell with her five-inch, serrated knife leveled to pierce Carolyn's chest. Instinctively rotating on her forward foot to avoid the thrust, Carolyn held her gun pointed at waist level straight up the staircase opening. The blast was loud and resonated throughout the cuddy. The reddish flash revealed Ivana dressed in a black wetsuit with a burning flare buried in her upper abdomen and searing her flesh as she fell down on her back midway up the staircase. Ivana let out a long, blood-curdling scream. Her expression, lasting for several seconds as the flare burned out, went from a fanatical rage to confusion to submission and finally to pain at her death. Carolyn was dazed and frozen stiff in fear from the attack. She dropped the flare gun and held her head to cry, though she had no sooner started to consider the results of her actions than the fate of Dalton consumed her. Retrieving the flare gun she fumbled opening the chamber when finally it opened and she dropped in another flare. She pushed Ivana aside and stepped over her legs to get to the aft deck. No sound of any kind came from the water; it was eerily still. She lit one of the hand flares and held it high. The other hand, shaking, moved the loaded flare gun around her perimeter. Then she thought she saw water stirring. Again, she stretched her arm with the flare to light the surface of the water and recognized Dalton lying face down, floating in the water some ten yards from the boat.

"Dalton! Dalton!" she screamed. There was no response. She reacted without fear for herself and jumped in the water, holding the end of a nylon dock line, which was secured to a cleat. Paddling out to Dalton seemed to take several minutes, although her athleticism allowed her to reach him in five seconds. She grabbed his shoulder to turn him over and sighed as he began to cough and spit water from his lungs. Gasping for air, his consciousness returned and he reached for Carolyn, very relieved she was alive.

"Are you OK? Did they find you? I'm so glad—"

Dalton grabbed his left shoulder, which was bleeding from the spear gun Yuri had used on him. Carolyn pulled him by his good arm to the boat with the help of the dock line. Once on board, she dragged Dalton as he pulled himself onto the sun deck at the stern. He looked over to the galley stairs and saw the woman diver still smoldering from the burning flare in her lower chest.

"Is that Yuri's girlfriend . . . Ivana?" Dalton stepped awkwardly on the wooden deck.

"Yes. That's the bitch that held me captive and just tried to kill me with that knife."

Dalton looked at the imposing knife then back to Carolyn, who was unable to assimilate all that had happened in the past ten minutes. Weak, exhausted yet alive, Dalton wrapped his good arm around her and hugged her, at which point she broke down and cried uncontrollably. He held her for a full minute before she regained composure and asked him what had happened under the boat.

"I had just come up to get a fresh lung full of air and clear my snorkel mask, and as I went under the water, I saw these lights fast approaching me. I turned toward them, not knowing what I was into, when the spear hit me high in the shoulder on the left side. I spun in pain and hit my head against the keel and nearly passed out although stayed alert to see Yuri approach again while trying to load another spear in the gun. So while he was using his hands to load the spear and attach the rubber thrust straps, I grabbed my ankle knife and cut across his chest, opening a deep wound. I slipped in and out of consciousness until you found me in the water." Dalton pressed a towel into the half-inch-deep channel cut through the top of his shoulder just above the collar bone.

"You never saw him again?" asked Carolyn.

"No, I was barely with it. How did you manage this?" Dalton pointed to the shapely woman smoking on the aft deck.

"I was so afraid, but I wasn't going to let her put that knife to my throat again." She began to sob and shook her head in disbelief at the brutal attack and her defense of her life.

The sound of a small motorboat startled both Dalton and Carolyn to their feet. It was Cotter and Wilson in their Zodiac. Dalton looked at them and said, "Where in the hell did you guys come from?"

"Ed Kosko felt you needed some backup. I guess he was right." Cotter threw a line to Dalton, and he tied off the inflatable. "We arrived just behind you on a commercial jet."

"Score one for Ed; I guess he knew if he had suggested a backup team follow, I would have resisted it."

"Yep, he definitely has your backside covered," offered Wilson with a smile.

"Did you guys catch Yuri?" Dalton had almost forgotten his attacker.

"No, we thought maybe you had killed him when the

flare went off." Dalton shook his head at the many lives Yuri possessed. "He's still out here somewhere."

As the four considered the possibilities the sound of a motor broke the silence. Looking back the four saw the lights come on the idling *Intrepid* yacht which powered up and sped off to the west.

WASHINGTON D.C.

The speech at the joint session of Congress was an epic event. The Russian president came across like no other Russian leader in history with a combination of honesty, wit, commitment, and a list of common goals he and President Conner were agreed on. The news coverage followed the Russian through the House chamber and out to meet reporters, where President Conner joined him in a final press meeting. The networks turned to various cities to determine the moods of viewers in New York, London, Moscow, and Tokyo. Each locale had hundreds of spectators charged up for the dynamic duo comprising the Russian and U.S. presidents. The Wall Street reaction was also very positive, with the Dow Jones rising 375 points in the last hour of trading for the day.

THE TARASOV SOLUTION

The coverage continued after the Russian presidential plane took off from a secure hangar in Andrews Air Force Base, followed several minutes later by the support team. Daniel called Darien via cell phone as he boarded one of the Russian support aircraft, and they, without revealing any details, congratulated each other on their success, which was soon to play out as a lethal, spectacular event.

40-SIX

ABOARD THE *INTREPID*

YURI jammed the throttle full forward, and the powerful yacht accelerated and planed out in less than fifteen seconds. Taros and the two bodyguards were slowly regaining motor functions, although their speech had returned earlier. They were explaining, in defensive, agitated tones, how they were taken over by two men. Yuri offered no slack and railed on the men for letting him down. He looked at his chest and the fourteen-inch gash that started just under his right shoulder and extended across to his rib cage on the left. Fortunately for him, the wound was only about a half inch deep at its worst. It had bled so quickly that Yuri had not been able to see Dalton for the blood diffusing through the water. He had dropped his underwater flashlight and spear gun when Dalton struck. He knew he had hit Dalton near the top of the shoulder, not five inches lower at his heart, which had been the intended target. He expected Ivana to join him in the water once finished with Carolyn, however when she failed to return, he swam away and returned to the *Intrepid*. Through powerful night-vision binoculars, Yuri could make out her left arm, visible at the galley staircase, lifeless, draped over the handrail and clearly revealing the two small, gold rings she always wore on her left pinky finger. The rage Yuri felt overcame his pain from the slash across his chest. When beyond *Ginger's* hearing range Yuri's emotions took control of his mind, and he howled a scream of rage for ten seconds. Taros and the two foggy guards stared at him in astonishment.

Yuri seethed with anger, for not only had Crusoe cut him badly, which could have killed him in the water, however he now knew Ivana had somehow been overtaken by Carolyn and died on the sailboat. He now had two more reasons to finish off Dalton Crusoe once and for all.

Taros regained control of his muscles and took over the boat's controls. The first bodyguard to come around applied a field dressing of sorts to Yuri's wound. He made a brief stop at the *Intrepid* marina slip and dropped Taros off to get to the airport and ready the aircraft for flight. Despite the pain and loss of blood, Yuri demanded his torso be wrapped heavily over the bandages, protecting his wound, and his men ready themselves for one last attack on Dalton Crusoe. The bodyguards and Yuri had one final chance at Crusoe that night, and it would happen at their beach villa. They anchored the large yacht offshore, out of sight, and took the inflatable raft into the beach at Frenchman's Reef.

Cotter and Wilson managed to attach the *Ginger* to their Zodiac and tow it northwest toward the resort. As they traveled through the dark, calm water, Dalton kept looking for Yuri, he hoped floating face down and dead. It occurred to him that Yuri may have died and that Taros and the bodyguards had regained motor functions and left, realizing Ivana was also likely dead. A careful area search within a hundred yards of the *Ginger's* location revealed no sign of Yuri. The sharks were present, however, telling Dalton that between his wound and Yuri's, a lot of blood went into the water. He wondered if the sharks had gotten Yuri before he could escape to his boat.

Two and a half hours later, the Zodiac reached the wide dock serving the beach at Frenchman's Reef. It was 12:32 a.m., and the resort was very quiet. Random lights shone from many rooms at the resort, and the beach villas had a few dim reading lights and televisions still on. Cotter held the Zodiac against the dock while Wilson walked with Dalton and Carolyn to their unit. He walked in ahead of the couple and, with his Glock

40 held in both hands, checked each room and declared the unit secure. Dalton thanked the men and said they would talk in the morning regarding the status of their search for Yuri.

Carolyn was tired yet not surprised she could not sleep. She decided to make a pot of coffee. Dalton went into the bedroom and checked his bag for the black, plastic case that held the Beretta 92 9 mm Cotter had given him for use when they first boarded the *Lady Cadence*. Once he located it, he opened the case and retrieved the weapon, held it a moment, slammed in a full clip and set it beside the bed on a small table. The clip sound caused Carolyn to halt as she carried two cups of coffee to the bedroom sitting area. The coffee was strong, as if either of them needed any more stimulation, although it did provide a relaxing activity as they discussed Yuri's surprise attack.

Looking nervously at the gun Carolyn said, "I hope you now understand what I meant when I said this animal will not stop until he kills you . . . and me." Carolyn wrapped her blanket tighter around her legs as if it were protection from the world.

"Yes, Carolyn, I do, and I did understand your message about the dangers of Yuri. I just never figured he would be bold enough to try to get to us down here when we have the CIA and others keeping him on the run. I assumed he would try to get to a country that would not grant extradition to the U.S. or Russia." Dalton sipped the hot coffee and set it aside. "Let's not worry about it. He may be dead. I sure tried to kill him. If he survived, which I doubt, he must be critically hurt."

Dalton looked at her and tried to not let her struggle with Ivana ruin their increasing sense of calm. After all, this was supposed to be a vacation from all that horrible stuff of last week. He stood up, sighed, stretched, grabbed Carolyn by the hand, and said, "Let's go to bed."

Yuri and his bodyguards were watching from the nearby beach towel shack only a hundred yards from Dalton's villa. The lights went out, and all they could see was the dim patio lights to highlight its edge. It was 1:18 a.m. when Yuri and his men approached the house, armed with silenced assault pistols. Dalton had fallen asleep after taking a handful of penicillin and painkillers however was restless and woke frequently. Cotter looked at the painful wound and saw it was a clean pass-through penetration. He would heal in time. Carolyn was in deep sleep with her right arm draped over Dalton's chest for security. The evening had cooled to a comfortable seventy-one degrees by the time they went to the bedroom, and Dalton lay in his underwear above the top sheet. Carolyn had one leg artfully thrown over the top sheet, while the rest of her body was under it. She was breathing very deeply, and Dalton feared she was dreaming. He, too, wanted to rest and sleep; however, the day's events and the struggle with Yuri keep drifting into his consciousness. The conflict had clearly become personal, and Dalton knew Carolyn's instincts were right about Yuri's pathological drive to even the score.

As he tried to think of happier times, a strange sound brought him to full awareness. Dalton sat up in bed and looked out to the sliders, which in the daylight, displayed a sandy beach and endless waves breaking on the shore. Tonight he saw and heard no wave action as the sea was very calm. He caught a glimpse of a shadow moving outside the windows. At first he thought it was the wind blowing a palm branch, however the wind was nonexistent. As he reached for the Beretta, he saw three men coming toward the seaside slider. They applied a glass cutter on a circular arm and cut out a small section of glass next to the latch securing the door.

Dalton's mind jumped into high gear in less than a second. He was awake, alert, and focused on the shapes outside his slider. He thought, *Can I be dreaming? Is this Yuri back from the dead, or is it Taros and his men come to complete the job?* He looked at Carolyn, who was still sleeping soundly. The cutter carved a clean, six-inch diameter hole next to the latch. A hand went through the hole and released the lock to open the slider. As the door moved aside in silence, two men came in and stood still when they motioned to the third man, apparently in charge, to enter. Dalton reached, over nudged Carolyn, and covered her mouth. She awoke in an instant; eyes broadcasting former terror when she recognized it was him. Studying the three body shapes and their movements a chill came over Dalton, *Yuri could be the third man,* he thought.

Once inside, all three moved in stealth mode silently toward the bedroom door, which Dalton had left open far enough so he could see through the crack created at the hinged side of the frame. Dalton could see the automatic weapons and felt outgunned and outmanned. He had to make fast, accurate shots to take these guys out, or they would spray the room with bullets. He took aim at the third man, assuming it was Yuri, and clicked the safety off just as four rapid, muffled shots broke the silence.

Cotter had taken the first shift to guard the house. He lay behind a beach chair, focused his laser sight on the first man's head, and squeezed the trigger. He dropped like a sack of sand just as the second man turned to raise his weapon. In response, two more shots caught him in the neck, and he collapsed in his tracks.

THE TARASOV SOLUTION

Yuri, the third man, sensed the danger and ran into the house, firing wildly into the bedroom. Luckily he did not have time to aim, and his shots went wide and over the bed. Dalton feared he may have a high-tech bullet-proof vest on for protection, so he took aim and blew out Yuri's left knee, dropping him into a screaming heap on the couch. Dalton dived across the bed and dragged Carolyn, frightened and shaking, to the floor. Yuri kept firing by reaching over the back of the couch, although every round hit high above the bed. He tried to stand for a better shot, and Dalton caught him in the side of the neck, severing a carotid artery, yet he continued to advance. Dalton covered Carolyn as best he could with his body and took careful aim. Before he could pull the trigger, Cotter unleashed ten rounds into Yuri's back, side, and head. He dropped to the floor, bleeding everywhere. As Yuri hovered within seconds of dying, Dalton stood over him and said, "Yuri, you asshole, your pride and arrogance killed you. I was just the delivery vehicle."

While Cotter ran in and checked to see if the other men were dead, Yuri looked up at Dalton and said, "I'll still have the last laugh, and you can't stop it." He gasped and died.

Carolyn lay on the floor, eyes glazed over and shaking; she was in shock. Her emotions could take only so much, and the past eight hours put her over the edge.

Dalton reached out and held her, saying, "It's really all over now. It's over."

EPILOGUE

DALTON and Carolyn flew home the next evening. Carolyn went to the hospital and received some counseling and medications to control her panic attacks and left with Irene Kosko to rest at her home while Dalton and Ed met with the president and his senior staff.

Their relaxing Caribbean vacation was not to be, and the events in Washington D.C. over the Labor Day weekend were being sanitized for release to the press. President Conner insisted, along with the concurrence of Blinikov that the claims and evidence concerning Yuri Tarasov, Ivana Yenko and the Tarasov arms dealing business be conducted in closed hearings and sealed until sufficient time was provided to root all off Tarasov's associates.

Throughout the day, Dalton kept replaying Yuri's final words in his mind: *"I'll still have the last laugh, and you can't stop it."* Were those the senseless words of a dying, neurotic killer, or was there a true message there? When the news came through of the midair explosion on the Russian Tupolev aircraft, Dalton feared he knew what Yuri had been bragging about.

Ed Kosko wanted Dalton and Carolyn to make formal statements about his attempts on their lives. Adding that to the evidence surrounding the assassination plan could be used by the Russian and U.S. governments to declare Yuri's organization an ally of terrorist groups, thereby branding him and his organization an international criminal. That would allow the residual elements of Yuri's group to be rounded up and prosecuted in international courts. The banks Yuri used would be ordered to open all his accounts and financial activity to review by Russian and U.S. investigators to see who had been buying things from the premier arms merchant. Both the Russian and U.S. prosecutors were prepared to issue arrest warrants and subpoenas for anyone whose name appeared in Yuri's business documents.

The *Decadence* traveling under the name, *Sea Rhythms,* was discovered near Ibiza, Spain, trying to blend in with other ocean yachts from Europe. It was recognized and seized by Spanish authorities based on preliminary evidence U.S. Justice Department officials shared concerning the role the yacht and her crew played in facilitating the foiled attack on Labor Day. Aaron was defiant, as before, although eventually started talking to save his own neck when he was told Yuri and Ivana were killed during their attack on Dalton Crusoe earlier in the day.

Taros made a dash in his rental car to get to Yuri's aircraft. He and the pilot were able to fly out of St. Thomas and were headed to Cyprus when Wilson discovered their escape. The NSA ordered F/A-18 jets from a carrier in the eastern Mediterranean to intercept and fly them to Ghedi Air Base, a U.S. installation near Milan. Franco Kindros was still at large although believed to still be in Caracas or the Caribbean. The CIA and Interpol were pursuing him. All the players, past and present, who participated in Yuri's Labor Day plans were either in custody, dead, or about to be arrested.

Russian leaders had the most compelling case for conducting an investigation, post mortem, on Yuri Tarasov's criminal empire. They had lost a dozen senior elected politicians and several more administrative support staff as a result of the midair explosion. Beyond that, an expensive governmental aircraft serving the Russian president was destroyed in flight by a bomb created from the second missile warhead Yuri had retrieved in the waters off Cuba. Darien was arrested and brought to CIA headquarters for interrogation when Aaron explained his special role in the attack using the second bomb's core. Daniel had died in the midair blast. A young staffer inadvertently pulled the attaché containing the bomb from the pile of similar ones carted for loading onto the presidential plane. He took it with him onto the second of three Russian planes that came over for the Labor Day Sailing Summit. Daniel's plane blew up with a tremendous explosion, completely devastating the aircraft and its passengers in an instant. The powerful jet had just moved through 25,000 feet and was about ten miles behind the plane carrying Blinikov. Russian security personnel ordered Blinikov's plane turn around and go back to Washington for a complete check and security inspection before it resumed the flight to Moscow.

During the security check, President Conner called President Blinikov and told him the final chapter in the actions of Yuri Tarasov and Ivana Yenko. Blinikov appreciated knowing the details before the world press got a highly watered-down version which also explained in part the loss of a Russian presidential aircraft.

Wilson had spent the night preparing his final confidential field report on the events that began with the Sergey Kreftkova interview and concluded with the death of Yuri Tarasov and Ivana Yenko in the Caribbean. Dalton was scheduled to meet with the president, his press secretary, the Secretary of State, and Ed Kosko at 10:00 a.m. the day after his arrival home and go over the news conference President Conner had scheduled for prime-time. It was intended as highly edited factual summary which centered on the Russian aircraft loss. Portrayed as fuel ignition explosion from an unknown source, the plane and passengers were all sadly lost. This ruse kept Yuri's name out of the news so prosecutorial efforts could commence against the Tarasov empire.

The news conference caught the world by surprise. There was worldwide concern over the near deadly mid-air explosion which could have killed the Russian president and ended the exciting start to a new period of friendly relations with the United States. The worldwide outpouring of feelings of uncertainty further highlighted the two world leaders' remarks to move aggressively against terrorist organizations around the world. As promised, the president allowed Willy Boone to share the stage as the formal news briefing ended and opened him up to a few planted questions from the press to highlight his involvement in assisting in the president's plan to break ground on a new high-tech global command center to monitor terrorist activity. The project would be a joint Russian and United States financial effort. The president had a strong ally for the governor's remaining political career.

Dalton listened to the president and felt blessed to have survived, along with Carolyn, the unbelievable evil unleashed by Yuri Tarasov. In the end, Yuri had been taken down by his own greed and arrogance; and the world had the last true laugh.

ABOUT THE AUTHOR

Part adventurer, part businessman, part author, Richard Trevae is a chemical engineer with an MBA in Finance and Management. Trevae matured a startup design/construction/development firm into a publicly traded company that later merged with a parent corporation generating four billion dollars in annual revenues. His articles concerning business valuation, mergers, acquisitions, and management practices have been published in various trade associations and business newspapers. Writing "reality inspired fiction" has become his latest passion, commencing with, "THE FUSION BREAKTHROUGH," followed by the prequel, "THE TARASOV SOLUTION." His extensive world traveling has provided a rich backdrop for the exotic locales featured in his novels. Mr. Trevae lives with his wife along the picturesque shores of Lake Michigan where he is working on his next novel.

CPSIA information can be obtained at www.ICGtesting.com
Printed in the USA
BVOW031219310113

312074BV00001B/106/P